THE MATCHMAKER AND THE MARINE

LUCINDA RACE

XO
Lucinda

MC TWO PRESS

ACKNOWLEDGMENTS

When my muse knocks- I open the door and welcome her inside.

A special thanks to Suzanne

I couldn't write books and follow my dream without the support of many people:

Rick, Megan, Emily, Cheryl, Shirley and Pete

Your encouragement and support mean the world to me.

This book is a work of fiction. Names, characters, places, and incidents are the product of the author's imagination or are used fictitiously. Any resemblance to actual events, locales, or persons, living or dead, is coincidental.
Copyright © 2020 Lucinda Race

All rights reserved, including the right to reproduce, distribute, or transmit in any form or by any means. For information regarding subsidiary rights, please contact the Author Lucinda Race.
Edited by Mackenzie Walton

Cover design by Jade Webb www.meetcutecreative.com

Manufactured in the United States of America
First Edition May 2020

E-Book Edition ISBN 978-1-7331616-1-9

CHAPTER 1

Melinda flipped her planner shut after drawing a heart next to the two names on the page on the notepaper. Another success. The strains of the "Wedding March" played by a string quartet filled the small flower-filled chapel. Guests rose from their seats to watch the petite bride glide down the aisle toward her handsome groom.

Across the aisle in a pew, a tall, well-built man with blonde hair cropped military style and molten brown eyes locked on hers. He gave Melinda a half nod before his gaze followed the bride. The pastor's deep voice filled the room as he asked everyone to take their seats. He then turned to the couple to perform the ceremony.

After the newly married couple kissed, Melinda followed other guests in the receiving line to the bride and groom. She beamed. "Stacey and Will, it was a beautiful ceremony."

Stacey was radiant. Will's arm was curled around his new wife, holding her close to his side.

"Melinda, this day wouldn't have been possible without you." Stacey lovingly gazed at Will. "Thank you for introducing us."

Melinda kissed her cheek. "It was my pleasure."

Will lifted Stacey's hand to his lips, grazing her ring finger. "I will tell *all* my single friends if they're looking for love to give you a call." His eyes twinkled. "You certainly have a knack for matchmaking."

"You two made my job easy." She looked over her shoulder. "You have more guests to greet, but I'll see you during the reception."

She strolled down the brick walkway to her car, content to see the love between Stacey and Will. Just as it was meant to be.

After making the short drive to the country club, Melinda parked in the crowded lot. As she crossed the parking area to the reception hall she daydreamed of how nice it would be to take off her pumps and walk barefoot. She reached for the brass knob on the carved wood door. Before she could turn the knob, it burst open. She took a step back. Her heel caught a crack in the stone step. She began to fall backward when strong hands caught her and held on tight.

A deep voice next to her ear said, "It's okay, I've got you."

Melinda looked up into warm brown eyes. It was the man from the chapel.

"Um, thank you." She smoothed her hand over her simple navy-blue dress and then pushed a curl behind her ear. "I'm not sure what happened."

"It looks like your heel got caught."

She gave him a small smile. "It's a good thing you were there to catch me."

With a slight stiff bow, he said, "Adam Bell, at your service, ma'am."

His face held little emotion, almost formal, she thought. People strolled past them into the building, but Melinda couldn't help but notice he carried himself with a distinct military bearing. Unsure if he was being old-fashioned or teasing her, she said, "We should go inside."

He crooked his arm and said, "I'd be happy to escort you safely through the door."

With a small laugh Melinda placed her hand on his arm. In a soft southern drawl, she said, "Thank you, kind sir."

"So, tell me, are you a friend of Stacey or Will?" he asked.

"I guess you could say both." She looked at him. "I'm Melinda Phillips."

His eyes grew wide. "You're the matchmaker?"

"I am." As they stepped through the doorway, she withdrew her hand. They made their way to the table with the seating chart. Melinda found her card and saw she was at table six. Adam picked up his card.

"I'm at table eight." He glanced at her card. "It's too bad we're not seated at the same one. I don't know a lot of people. I haven't lived here long."

She looked around the room. "I've lived here for a few years and everyone is really nice."

"Good to know," Adam said with a smile. "Can I buy you a drink?"

"Thank you, and then I can introduce you to the gang." Melinda strolled toward the bar. Adam looked around and trailed after her. She understood his reticence. It was hard to get acquainted with a new group of people, especially when they seemed to be really tight knit. She still remembered what it had felt like when she moved to Chester. She fell in love with the small shore town and she had found the people in Connecticut weren't that much different from Pennsylvania where she lived previously. Heck, they were a lot like her friends back in Beaufort, South Carolina where she had spent most of her summers as a kid.

"Melinda!" One of the bridesmaids rushed over to hug her. "Wasn't it a beautiful wedding?"

With her glass of wine temporarily on hold, Melinda said, "Molly." She gave her a squeeze. "You look beautiful."

Molly stepped back and gave Adam the once over. She kissed him on the cheek. "Don't you look handsome today in your dark suit? And just look at that lavender tie, spiffy."

3

Adam grinned at her. "If I didn't try to match the wedding colors a little bit, Stacey would have my head."

Melinda watched as Adam and Molly shared a laugh. It seemed Adam already knew a few people.

~

*A*dam watched Melinda accept a glass of wine from the bartender and wandered toward the open French doors. She was dressed in a simple blue dress with polka-dotted heels that made her seem taller than her average height and showcased her legs to their best advantage. He appreciated that she looked fit, a nice hourglass shape. She had just the right amount of curves, at least in his opinion.

Molly had introduced him to every person within a twenty-foot radius. Now it was time to escape for a few minutes and maybe he could talk with, the aloof and beautiful, Melinda Phillips.

"I see you have a glass of wine." Adam said.

Melinda whirled around. Her lips formed a large O. "You startled me."

He half-turned. "I'm sorry to intrude. Would you like me to leave?"

With a slow shake of her head, she smiled. "No, gosh no. I was taking a breather." She looked toward the guests gathering inside the dining room. "Everyone seems to be in high spirits. Just as it should be at a wedding."

"Do I detect a note of melancholy?" He picked up a small plate and stabbed a square of cheese, then worked his way around the appetizer table.

"Not at all. I love weddings."

He handed her the plate. "Let me guess, its hard being the single girl in a room full of couples." She accepted the plate with a gracious smile. Adam continued, "I get it too, as the single guy. There is at least one well-meaning person out there who has already said she'd fix me up with someone's cousin." He tried to keep his voice light, but he knew it was bound to happen sooner or later.

Melinda laughed. It sounded musical to Adam, and he had to wonder why her left hand was without jewelry except for a simple thin band on her ring finger. But was she single?

Casually she asked, "And do you want to be set up?" She nibbled on a celery stick.

He couldn't help but notice her eyes were an interesting shade of green, almost like the waters of the Atlantic in midsummer, with hints of gold and blue. She tucked a stray copper colored curl behind her ear.

"Adam?" She raised a brow.

"Oh, sorry." He gulped down a drink of his beer. "I was wondering how you got into the matchmaking business."

Softly she said, her eyes holding his captive, "I love helping people find that special person who adds sparkle and a sense of completeness to their lives."

He teased, "Is that on your business card?"

"You got me." She laughed. "But it really can be that simple." She pointed to the banquet room. "The newly married couple has arrived. We should go back inside."

"I'll follow you." Adam and Melinda stepped into the hub of activity. The lead singer of the band was warming up the crowd by introducing the members of the bridal party.

Finally, he said, "It is my pleasure to introduce the brand-new Mr. and Mrs. Benson."

Whistles and applause filled the room as the couple sashayed their way to the center of the hardwood floor to have their first dance. As they twirled, Adam could see what Melinda had said —they both sparkled as they gazed into each other's eyes. With a stab of longing, Anita briefly crossed his mind, but he refused to think about her today. He leaned down to rub his knee, a lingering reminder of the past and the chance he was taking to start over.

As the song concluded, clinking glasses urged the couple to kiss. Adam found his way to table eight and waved to Melinda across the room. She waved back and turned to speak to another guest.

Molly slipped into the chair next to him. "Are you having a good time?"

He nodded and sipped his beer. "I am, and you?"

She gushed, "I love weddings, and since Melinda moved to town, I swear the number of happy events have skyrocketed." She pointed to a man in a tux talking to Will. "Tim and I were introduced by Melinda. We've been dating for almost six months."

"I didn't realize that's how you met Will's brother."

"Using Melinda was the best decision I"—she gazed lovingly in Tim's direction—"*we* ever made." Tim waved to Molly. "Looks like I'm needed. Toast time. Tim and I are at your table, so we'll be back shortly."

Adam half-stood when Molly hopped up. She certainly had a lot of energy as he watched her sail across the dance floor to Tim's side.

Tim tapped a knife against the stem of the wineglass. "Excuse me."

The chatter died down.

"On behalf of Will and my new sister, Stacey, I'd like to thank you for sharing this amazing day with our family and close friends."

He paused. "I'd like to propose a toast to Stacey and Will." He turned to look at the couple and in a loud, clear voice he said, "There was a time when I wondered if my older brother, and old being the operative word"—he grinned at Will—"would ever find a woman to stand by his side as he navigates through the ever-changing waters of life. Stacey is just that woman. Not only does she love sailing and spicy food as much as Will does, but she loves my brother with all her heart." He raised his glass a little higher and he said, "To Stacey and Will."

Echoes around the room said, "To Stacey and Will."

The newlyweds entwined arms and sipped pink champagne. After a few more toasts, the bandleader encouraged everyone to enjoy the buffet. Adam's eyes drifted to Melinda's table. Her chair was empty. Glancing around the room, he didn't see her anywhere. Had she snuck out while the toasts were happening? When Will and Stacey got back from their honeymoon, he'd get the low down on the matchmaker.

～

*M*elinda took one last glance over her shoulder. The reception was underway and it was the perfect opportunity to slip away, unnoticed. Swinging her small beaded handbag, she strolled to the car. Another happy couple would have the chance to spend their lives with their true love. Twisting the slim gold band on her ring finger, Melinda smiled; it was just like her life with John. She felt blessed to have been well loved, and Melinda had loved her husband with all her heart in return. She couldn't wait to get home and check her email to see who might be next on the road to happily ever after.

CHAPTER 2

It was hard to believe another week had come and gone. Time to enjoy the weekend. The sun was peeking from behind a white fluffy cloud in the bright blue sky. Dressed in a floral skort and pale pink tee, Melinda carried an oversized cooler and carefully picked her way down the well-worn wooden stairs to the sandy beach. The picnic was in full swing. Glancing around, she noticed the hostess Stacey hugging another late arrival.

With a big wave, Stacey hurried over to take one of the handles of the heavy cooler. "You should have left that up top. One of the guys would have brought it down for you." She grinned from ear to ear. The glow of a faint tan accentuated her light brown eyes and sun-streaked bob. Together they lugged it across the sand and set it under the blue easy-up tent well back from the rising tide.

"It was no trouble...well, until I stepped on the sand." Melinda kicked off the high-heeled wedge cork sandals. "They look cute, but these shoes were not the best idea for a beach party." She wiggled her toes in the sun-warmed sand.

Stacey drew her into a hug. "You look great as always."

"And you're always giving me compliments." Using her

hand, Melinda shaded her eyes and scanned the group. She laughed. "Did you invite the entire town?"

Stacey slipped an arm through Melinda's. "Come on. There are a bunch of people dying to meet you."

"Meet me? Why?"

Melinda saw the look of surprise flash across Stacey's face. "Everyone I know never thought I'd find anyone who could make me fall head over heels in love. So you did the impossible and now people are wondering if you can do the same for them."

"You've given me far too much credit. I just took some basic information, sent you a few profiles. You're the one who picked Will. After that, all that was left was for you two to sign the marriage license."

Stacey laughed. "You mean after you sent me more than a dozen matches. You make it sound like it was *so* easy."

"Love isn't complicated, people make it that way." Melinda smiled brightly. "So, give me the rundown on who is who."

In a conspiratorial whisper, Stacey said, "Okay. That tall, well-built man over there?" she pointed to the one person who left a lasting impression on Mel at the wedding. "That's Adam Bell. He and Will go way back to their Marine Corps days. They were deployed together and have been best friends since basic." She gave Melinda a wink. "He's single and Will is trying to get him to sign up with you. He could use a good woman. His ex-girlfriend dumped him after he came back from his last tour of duty."

Melinda bit back a sharp retort about the kind of woman who would do that to a man who served his country. She quickly reminded herself to not be judgmental. There could be a very good reason why his ex broke it off, but it did sound a bit heartless to do it right after he came back from deployment.

She inclined her head toward a pretty woman about their age. "Who's that?"

"The girl in the short shorts and crop top?"

Melinda gave a slow nod. "She seems to be a little out of place." Glancing around, she noticed most of the girls wore longer shorts or flowing skirts and tops that covered up their midsections.

"That's Mary, one of Will's other friends from work. I'm surprised you didn't notice her at the wedding. I saw a picture of her and whoa, I have no idea how she even danced in the dress she was wearing."

Melinda's eyebrow shot up. "She's very pretty."

Stacey grinned. "Someone said she's quite the party girl. Like she hasn't outgrown that stage of life yet."

Assessing the woman, Mel said, "I wonder if it's all a front. Maybe she dresses that way to get attention in certain situations but under it all, she's shy."

Stacey snorted. "You think so?"

Melinda nodded and continued, "I've met her type before and she really wants to belong, but she's just unsure where she fits in. Instead she goes for the shock value."

Stacey gave her a thoughtful look. "You're such a nice person."

Melinda had to chuckle. "You're still in the honeymoon glow. I can be a pain in the butt just like everyone else." She tugged Stacey toward the girl. "Introduce me."

"Sure, she did say she was interested to meet you." Stacey allowed herself to be led across the sand. "Mary, this is my friend I was telling you about, Melinda Phillips."

Mary cautiously reached out her hand, her deep blue eyes round as saucers. "Hello. It's nice to meet you."

Melinda was surprised her voice sounded soft, almost child-like. She shook Mary's hand. "Stacey tells me you work with Will."

"I sure do. I'm an accountant at the law firm."

"So, you deal with numbers all day, I'm impressed."

"It's not that big of a deal." Mary shrugged. "You just need to make sure everything balances at the end of the day."

Melinda smiled. "There are days I have trouble balancing my checkbook."

Mary's eyes lit up. "You can call me anytime, I'd be happy to help you."

Melinda thanked her. Stacey wandered toward a small group of people, leaving Melinda with Mary. "Stacey mentioned you wanted to meet me?"

With a quick look around, Mary said, "Did you really introduce Stacey and Will?"

Melinda smiled and said, "I did."

Mary played with a long blonde ringlet. "Do you think you could help me? I can't seem to find the right guy no matter what I do."

"Why don't you call my office?" Melinda withdrew a business card from her pocket. "We can talk about what you're looking for, and you'll need to understand my process to see if it works for you. If it does, you can fill out the questionnaire and we'll go from there."

Smiling, Mary said, "I'll call you, maybe on Monday, if that's not too soon."

"I'll look forward to it. Enjoy the picnic."

Melinda eased away from Mary and the crowd. She enjoyed parties but wondered why no one ever asked her what she was currently reading or if she liked to bike or hike. They always went right to her line of work. Walking along the water's edge with her head down, Melinda relished the brisk cool breeze as it caressed her face and tugged at her ponytail. She noticed a man approaching her from down the beach. Being social she held up a hand in acknowledgment and stooped over to pick up a wave-tossed piece of green glass.

"Hey, it's good to see you again." A deep male voice interrupted her quest for friendly glass on the beach.

"Hello. It's nice to see you too." She pushed up her sunglasses and said, "We met at the wedding, right?"

"We did. I'm Adam." He reached out his hand. "And you're Melinda."

"Guilty as charged." She grinned and scanned the water. "I love the ocean. It's one of the main reasons I chose to move to Chester. No matter the season, I love walking along the beach, looking for sea glass and drinking in the salty air."

Adam nodded. "There's nothing like it."

"Did you enjoy the wedding?"

He shot her a quizzical glance. "I did, and you?"

"It was lovely. Stacey and Will make a great couple."

"You didn't stay long," he stated with simplicity.

"No. I had work to do, and I also wanted to do some gardening."

"Flowers?"

"Well, some, but mostly vegetables." She examined the piece of glass she held in her hand and tossed it back into the ocean.

Adam frowned.

"It needs a bit more polishing before it's friendly enough for me to take home." Melinda blushed at her words and hoped Adam wouldn't think she had said something rude.

"Ah, I get it now." He bent over and picked up a piece, then handed it to her.

"Thanks." Melinda noticed he was wearing fishing pants. "Are you going fishing later?"

"Huh?"

She pointed at his pants. "All those pockets are good for storing supplies."

With a shake of his head, Adam said, "Nope, they're just comfortable."

She was mildly disappointed at his short responses. She surmised he wasn't much of a conversationalist. She looked toward the tents. The grills were smoking.

"Lunch must be almost ready." She turned inland. "Are you coming?"

"Yes."

The pair walked in silence with only the sound of the waves crashing on the shore behind them. Melinda wondered about Adam's story, but figured it was none of her business. Based on her past experience as a therapist, she guessed his brief answers might be a leftover of being in the military.

Blankets had been laid out over the sand as people filled their plates with burgers and salads. Melinda helped herself to a beer from her cooler. Adam was next to her. She held out a beer to him. "Would you like a cold one?"

"Thanks." He accepted the beer and popped the cap, carefully tossing it back into the cooler.

Unsure what else was left to say, she brought her plate to sit with Molly and Tim—they were never short on conversation.

"I'll see you around." Adam called after her.

She smiled over her shoulder. "Sure thing." Melinda plopped down next to Molly.

"Did I see you talking to Adam?" Molly asked.

"It was pretty one-sided. He doesn't say much." Melinda looked at Adam over her sunglasses.

"He's a super nice guy. But from what I've heard, he had a tough time after he came home from his deployment in Iraq. Got hurt pretty bad and had to retire. He planned to be career Marine. Only a few years short of full retirement."

Melinda set her bottle in the sand. "Sometimes it's hard to heal after a traumatic event. Hopefully time surrounded by good friends will help him."

Molly opened her mouth to say something else but closed it. Melinda was relieved. She wasn't looking to hear any speculation on Adam. Molly was right, he did seem like a nice man. Maybe a little lonely, but at least he wasn't alone. He was surrounded by an amazing group of people. After all, they had welcomed Melinda into the group, and rarely did she feel alone.

∼

Adam wasn't sure why he had been at a loss for words when he was walking on the beach with Melinda. He wanted to ask her if she'd work with him to find a date or two. It had been a couple of years since the breakup with Anita. It was time to get back in circulation. Will certainly had been pushing him hard enough to contact Melinda.

But what was it about the melancholy that hovered in her eyes? It was there when he met her at the wedding too. Adam was sure there was a story behind that and the slender ring on her finger. Where was her husband? Did he leave her, and matchmaking was her way of trying to heal a broken heart?

He kept an eye on her and watched as she laughed and chatted with Molly. There was something about her that he seemed to understand but couldn't quite put his finger on it. One thing was for sure, sometime in the next few weeks he was planning on dropping by her office and get things rolling. He was tired of being one of the only single guys in their group. And if he got really lucky, he'd be walking around grinning like his buddy Will.

Who knows, maybe he'd find someone who would want to have a kid or two, and his kids could grow up with Will and Stacey's. Wouldn't that be a kick in the pants?

CHAPTER 3

It had been a long week since the beach picnic. Melinda jerked open a side drawer in her office desk and the bottom fell onto the floor. Annoyed, she tossed the drawer frame onto the small sofa and knelt down to push the paperclips into a pile. Her office door opened. Work boots were in her line of sight. Her eyes slid from the toes to a face. A man leaned over her. He extended his hand.

"Hello, Melinda." An amused smile played over his face. "I didn't expect to find you on the floor."

She took his hand and stood up, tugging the hem of her purple print cotton dress and smoothing the skirt back down.

"Adam Bell." He paused. "We met at Will and Stacey's picnic a couple of weeks ago."

She could hear the teasing in his voice "You're being very formal." Paperclips forgotten, she said, "How've you been?"

"Ma'am, this isn't a social visit. I'm here on business, so I thought I'd do a formal introduction." He chuckled. "By the looks of things, better than you." He pointed to the square piece of wood on the floor and its companion piece on the sofa. "Having a little tussle with the desk?"

She shrugged. "We had a minor disagreement. The drawer won."

He bent over and picked up the wood. "I can fix this for you if you'd like."

"It's okay, I can call a handyman." Melinda took it from him and placed it on the side table.

When she looked back to Adam, he was holding out a business card. "It just so happens, I'm in the business of fixing things."

She grinned. "We can talk, but I'm sure you didn't just happen to stop by on the off chance I would need a handyman."

"Well actually I was curious about this whole"—he waved his hand through the air—"matchmaking process."

Melinda smiled. She knew that sometimes everyone needed a little help meeting someone. "Are you interested in finding a match?" She gestured to the sofa and took the drawer sides from him. "Please make yourself comfortable." She planted her feet on the floor as she sat in the chair across from him. "I'm happy to answer any questions you might have."

Adam leaned forward. "Tell me, how is it you got into the matchmaking business?"

Prepared to give her standard answer, she said, "I believe everyone should find their happily ever after and some say I have a knack for helping people find"—she did the air quote gesture—"the one."

"Will mentioned you moved to town and opened your office roughly three or four years ago." He looked around her sunlit office. "He didn't tell me your office was attached to your home."

Melinda smiled and shrugged. "I needed a change and I wanted a short commute. I always wanted to live close to the ocean. So, here I am." She shifted in her chair, anxious to turn the topic back to Adam, she said, "But we're not here to talk about me. Why don't you tell me a little about yourself?"

"It's a short and simple story. Later thirties, retired Marine.

Definitely single. When I got out of the service, I decided to hang my hat over my buddy's garage for a while and figure out what I wanted to do next."

Melinda nodded. She grabbed a pad and pen from the corner of her desk. "Do you mind if I take a few notes?"

With a slight nod of his head, he said, "Please." He leaned back and looked around her tidy office.

"Late thirties, a former Marine." She glanced up from the pad and looked him directly in the eye. "Thank you for your service."

He dipped his head and corrected her. "*Retired* Marine."

With the pen poised over the paper, she was surprised at the clipped tone in his voice. She knew he had gotten injured, but obviously it was not a topic he wanted to discuss further. Changing the subject, she asked, "Tell me about your interests and hobbies."

"I like kayaking, fishing, spending time with friends, movies, the typical stuff."

"Adam, there is no such thing as the typical stuff. Each person is unique." She thought for a minute. "Take me as an example. I love to garden, but you didn't mention that you do. Since I'm passionate about digging in the dirt and you might find that to be an absolute snooze fest, potentially we would not be a good match. Now that's a pretty simplistic example, but I'm sure you see what I'm saying, hypothetically speaking of course."

"I see what you mean." He tapped his fingers against the arm of the sofa. "So, I should give you a bit more about what I like to do?"

"The more you tell me, the easier it will be for me to give you high-quality matches."

"Well, for the record I do like to play in the dirt. I haven't had the opportunity since I lived at home with my parents. We used to have a huge garden, and fruit trees and berry bushes too. My sister and I liked the planting and harvesting the best." With a laugh, he said, "I'm not very patient waiting for it to grow and all."

"Ah, that's the part I love the best, nurturing the little shoots." She surprised herself by opening up. "So tell me more about yourself. What are your hobbies?"

Adam smiled. "I'm not much of a cook. Maybe someday I'll learn."

"That's good to know. A match might be someone who wants to take cooking classes." Melinda jotted that down. "Ultimately, do you want to get married and have a family?" She paused. "Those particular topics can be deal breakers."

He nodded. "Definitely. Maybe even a dog or two."

"No cats?" she teased.

"Cats are good too." He grinned.

"I have a few more questions and then we'll be done." Melinda ran through her checklist and Adam answered each question. She liked how he seemed to know exactly what he wasn't looking for, but not sure of what he was looking for. She loved a challenge.

She tapped her pen on the edge of the pad. "The next step will be for me to take your information and a headshot, put the details into a program I've created, and check for matches. I need to caution you, it's not a perfect science. As I send you matches, you can tell me if someone strikes your fancy or not before the woman is contacted."

He frowned. "You don't give my profile to any of your female clients?"

With a little laugh, she said, "Of course I do. But it is fairly anonymous. I don't give out personal information. This way you can read a bio and make a decision."

"That sounds pretty straightforward."

"I'd like to give you a piece of advice."

"Ma'am?"

His restrained grin was almost irresistible and Melinda was

confident she'd find him the perfect partner. "Keep an open mind as you go on each coffee date."

His brow wrinkled. "Meaning?"

Melinda leaned forward. In earnest, she said, "In my experience, some men look at a woman who isn't a size two and dismiss her without giving her a chance."

A momentary flash of anger showed in Adam's eyes, but she wasn't quite sure why, unless he was one of those kinds of men.

"I'm not shallow. We all have flaws, some are visible and some aren't. I've never been the type of man to judge any book by its cover."

She laid a hand on the arm of the sofa, very near his hand. She could have touched him, but that would be completely inappropriate. "Adam, I didn't mean to offend you, but…"

He held up his hand. "No offense. I have been around enough men to know exactly what you're talking about. Trust me, I'm not that kind of guy."

Melinda got up and turned away from him. She was relieved. He did seem like a wonderful man.

Adam stood and crossed the small office space. "Is there something I need to do now?" he asked.

She scanned the form on her clipboard. "I just need your email address and payment to get things rolling."

Adam pulled his wallet from his back pocket and handed her a credit card.

Giving him a broad smile, she said, "You should receive an email from me in a day or two. But if you have any questions before, feel free to give me a call." She handed him a card.

He slipped it into his wallet. "Thank you. This process was a lot less daunting than I anticipated. Will was right, you *are* easy to work with."

Melinda extended her hand. "I'm glad you came to see me. And I promise, this will be fun."

He shook her hand and glanced at her ring. "Maybe you've

had so much success because you have a wonderful relationship with your husband."

She felt the color drain from her face. She pulled her hand away and tucked it into her dress pocket. In a quiet voice, she said, "My husband died five years ago."

"Melinda, I'm sorry. I had no idea."

She refused to meet his gaze. "Not to worry." She walked him to the door, anxious to be alone. "I'll be in touch very soon."

~

*A*dam heard the door close firmly behind him. It was definitely to shut him out. He muttered to himself, "What kind of ass am I?"

He berated himself as he walked to his truck. "This is what I get for making a personal comment." He paused at the end of the walkway and turned to look back to the tidy house with colorful flowers flanking the stone steps. *At the wedding she said she was single. How was I to know she was a widow? She might have been wearing the ring to deter overly aggressive clients.* He walked the last few steps to his truck. *Chester is a good place to start over for all kinds of people.* He had to wonder… *Is Melinda running from her past, or has she made peace with it?* He pulled open the driver's door and got behind the wheel, rubbing his left knee. *You can never really run from the past.*

He put Melinda's number into his cell, and then eased the truck away from the sidewalk and drove back to the apartment. He was lucky to have friends who gave him a comfortable place to land.

His cell phone rang. He glanced at caller ID, surprised to see Melinda Phillips' name displayed. "Hello, Melinda. Did I forget something?"

"No, but I did."

"Oh?"

There was a pregnant pause. "I was wondering if you'd mind

coming back to the office. I tried to fix the drawer, but to be honest, I'm attached to my thumbs. I don't even own a hammer."

Chuckling, he glanced at the dashboard clock. "I have to meet a client about a new job. Can I swing by after lunch?"

"That would be perfect. Around two?"

"I'll see you then." Adam smiled into the phone. "I guess it's a good thing I dropped by this morning."

"Timing is everything. See you later."

Melinda disconnected the call and Adam thought, *Timing is everything.*

CHAPTER 4

*A*dam pulled into Melinda's driveway at two o'clock on the dot. After he parked the truck he wandered over to where she was working in the flower bed. "Hey, Mel."

She looked up and had to squint as the sun was directly behind Adam. "Hi. Sorry, I didn't realize I was running late."

He held out a cup. "Lemonade?"

Melinda scrambled to her feet and clapped her hands together. Even her nails had dirt under them, and she chuckled. "I just love digging in the dirt." She accepted the cup and pulled the paper off the straw. "You didn't need to bring me something to drink."

"It's a hot day and I stopped to get something for myself, so I thought I would get two."

Taking a sip, her face screwed up and her eyes popped. "Oh, it's got a bit of a pucker factor." She laughed. "Just the way I like it." She took another sip and noticed the logo. "Jules has the best lemonade in the county." She stepped in front of him and said, "Come on into the office."

Adam followed her up the walkway and opened the door ahead of her. Holding it, he said, "Ladies first."

"Thank you." She stepped into the room, which seemed dark

compared to the bright sun. She set her cup on the desk and handed the bottom piece of the broken drawer to Adam. "There's a groove on the sides. I think that's where the bottom is supposed to slide in. When I tried to fix it, it just fell out again."

Adam picked up the drawer sides and turned it over. "See here?" He pointed to the corners. "These are finger joints. I'd hazard a guess the glue is dried out and that's why it fell apart." He smiled. "It's an easy fix, but I'll need to take it to my shop." He took the wood bottom from her. "I can have it back to you in a couple of days."

"Will it be expensive to fix?" Melinda chewed the corner of her lip. Adam wondered if money was a concern.

"No," he said, "the first job is on the house." He laughed. "As long as the first job isn't to *build* a house."

She brightened. "That's a bargain." She sank on to the brown leather sofa across from her desk. "Have a seat. I don't often have a handyman here, and I'd like to talk to you about another project if you have some time."

Adam set the two pieces of the drawer near the door and took the chair opposite her. He was intrigued by what she might have to say to him. Looking around the office, everything seemed well put together and nothing in need of repair. But looks could be deceiving.

Teasing, he said, "So, tell me what do you have up your sleeve."

A mischievous look twinkled in her eye. "Well, I've been thinking..." She laughed. "Once you get to know me better that usually means trouble."

He rubbed his hands together and chuckled. "I'm all ears."

Melinda's gaze drifted to the window that overlooked the backyard. "I have this amazing space out there." She rose from the sofa and went to stand by the window. "It screams for something, like a dramatic focal point."

Adam eased out of the chair and went to stand beside her. "How about you show me what you have in mind?"

With a lopsided grin, she turned to look at him. "I thought you'd never ask. Let's go through the house." She opened a door for Adam to follow her through her home.

Stepping through the six-panel door, he could see the house was clean and comfortable, just like her office. The rooms were decorated in warm earth tones and there were colorful flowers everywhere he could see. He looked at the large commercial-grade stove and over-sized French door refrigerator. "You have a nice kitchen. Do you like to cook?"

Off-handed, she said, "I love to cook and do a lot of canning in the fall, so this setup works well for me." She opened a sliding glass door and stepped to a slate stone patio where pots of herbs and flowers lined the edges. She had a small round table and umbrella set up to one side.

Adam noticed the entire backyard was devoid of trees, except on lush maple, but instead was dotted with raised beds of various plants and sunflowers reaching toward the sky. "You have about a half-acre of land?"

"I sure do. And over the last few years I've built raised beds and hauled in soil and mulch to have the best possible gardens."

He didn't miss the pride in her voice. She wandered over to one bed to pluck a fat, round, deep purple radish from the loamy soil. She pointed to a bucket close by. "If you want, give that a rinse and taste it. I guarantee you've never tasted a better radish."

Adam took the vegetable and did as she suggested, breaking the leafy greens off and crunching down. He could feel his eyes begin to water. "That's hot. But really good."

"There's nothing like coming out here and getting salad right from the garden. Brings a whole new meaning to the phrase from garden to table."

Adam scanned the wide-open space. "I'm a little confused. What do you think this space needs?"

Melinda turned, her back to the beds and looked at the patio. "The back of the house gets a ton of sun in the afternoon, and it's unbearable to sit out here and enjoy dinner." She crossed her arms and after a thoughtful pause said, "I'm thinking about adding a pergola. I could plant some grapevines on one side for a bit of screening and keep the other three sides open." She shaded her eyes from the intense, early afternoon sun. "It would kill two birds with one stone. I could get grapes and shade, and as a bonus I think it would make the backyard look amazing."

Adam surveyed the back of her large Cape Cod-style home. "The patio is, what, sixteen by sixteen?"

"Good eye."

"What kind of a design are you thinking? Cedar or a manmade material?" He pulled a small notepad and pencil from the side pocket of his pants.

"Cedar, definitely. Have you ever seen a pergola where the grape clusters hang down through the beams, and the dark green leaves block just enough of the sun, giving it a dappled effect on the stones? That's what I'd like to have, and I'd like to use natural products that, with the proper care, will last for many years."

Adam liked how her eyes sparkled. He appreciated that she knew exactly what she wanted. "I can pull together some ideas and give you a quote."

"That's awesome. How soon can you start?" Her enthusiasm was contagious as it bubbled over.

With a chuckle, he said, "You should probably review the quote, check my references and then make a decision."

With a dismissive wave of her hand, Melinda said, "I'm sure you have glowing recommendations."

He hoped he didn't look cocky from her comment. "I'm going to run to my truck and get a tape measure for the estimate."

Melinda sighed. "How long will it take for you to pull it together for me?"

"Impatient, aren't you?" Adam teased.

"When I get something in my head, I like to get it done."

"How about we agree on this: I'll take measurements and drop off a drawing of what I have in mind, along with some pricing. If you agree, I can get started in, say, two weeks?"

She perked up. "That sounds great. And…"

He joked, "I know what your next question is going to be. How long will it take before it will be finished, am I right?"

She held up her palms toward the sky and shrugged. "I told you, when I make up my mind…"

With a chuckle he said, "I'm starting to see what you meant, and that's fine. Consider me forewarned."

～

Melinda watched Adam disappear around the side of the house. She did a little dance, a throwback to her childhood, with anticipation. Since the first time she saw the house four years ago, she'd known it cried out for something. Now she was going to get it.

She settled into one of the chairs on the patio stretched out her legs and closed her eyes. She could see the backyard clearly. Vines trailing up and over the beams with pots of flowers scattered around. In her mind, it was late summer and bunches of deep purple fruit were waiting to be plucked and enjoyed. She might try her hand at winemaking too.

"Mel?" Adam's deep voice interrupted her daydream.

She popped open her eyes and smiled. "I was just picturing what it was going to look like in a couple of years once my grapes get established." He extended the tape and Melinda got up to help him. "I was thinking I might try my hand at a little wine, but I'll make some jelly, too."

He jotted down a number and walked ninety degrees from her. "Is there anything you don't make?"

She thought for a minute. "I've always wanted to raise chickens. The manure would be beneficial to the gardens and I absolutely *love* fresh eggs."

"What's stopping you?"

She could feel Adam watching her as he moved around the perimeter of the patio. "In all honesty, the winter months. It doesn't seem like a long trek with a hose, but its daunting just thinking about hauling containers from the house so they have fresh water, then worrying about cold temperatures, I would hate for any chicken to freeze to death; the wind whips through the backyard like it's a tunnel." She glanced right and left. "I'm zoned for chickens and I don't think the neighbors would mind, especially if I was to share the bounty. But I think it's just too much to take on."

"Well, if you're serious, I could come up with a design, add some insulation and maybe some kind of heated area to alleviate those issues."

"Probably not, but thanks anyway." She held the tape while Adam went kitty-corner to her. As an afterthought, she said, "Well, I'll think about it. Who knows what the future will bring."

He tucked the pad and pencil into his pocket and clipped the tape to his belt. "Let me know if you change your mind, but there would be one stipulation."

She looked at him, unsure if he was serious or trying to be funny. "What might that be?"

"I'd want fresh eggs from time to time."

Melinda could see the corners of his mouth twitch and laughter filled his eyes. "I'll keep that in mind."

Adam retracted the tape and grinned. "I've got all I need for now."

"Let me know when the design is ready." Melinda tucked her hands into the front pockets of her shorts. She shifted from foot to foot. "I should get back to the flowers."

He nodded. "Yeah, I should be going too. I have a couple of other things I need to wrap up before the end of the day."

Melinda walked next to Adam, around the side of the house and stopped at his truck. "Thanks for coming over on such short notice."

"Not a problem. It looks like it will be a fun project and, more importantly, a nice addition to your backyard." He opened the truck door to get in and said, "I'll give you a call later."

"Oh, wait. You forgot the drawer." Before he could get out of the truck, Melinda ran lightly up the front steps and through her office door. She returned moments later with the broken pieces. She handed them to Adam through the open window.

"Thank you. I'll have the drawer ready for you in a couple of days and the quote even sooner."

"And I should have a potential match for you by tomorrow. I'll email you her contact information." She felt an odd twinge of envy when she thought of the potential match, but dismissed it as quickly as it came.

"Okay, great. And all I'll need to do is give her a call?"

"Or you can send an email and get acquainted first. It might be easier to break the ice, so to speak."

"Good idea, coach." With a laugh he started up the truck and dropped it into reverse. "We'll talk soon."

Melinda watched as he drove off down the road. She mused, "I really hope I can find him the perfect match. He's a great guy and some girl is going to be very lucky."

CHAPTER 5

*A*dam spread the plans for Melinda's pergola over his drafting desk. As he reviewed the details, his mind drifted to the time he spent with Mel. She was an intriguing woman. A widow and a matchmaker, with a passion for gardening.

He slid the pergola design aside and added a few details to the next page. His idea for a chicken coop looked more like a cottage for a child's playhouse, except with an easy access panel to clean out the mess the chickens would make. He smiled as he added a couple of birds into the drawing. When she was ready to talk chickens, he would be prepared.

His email pinged. He opened a message from Mel. He scanned the contents, clicked on the attachment. A picture of an attractive lady with a nice smile and pretty eyes filled his screen. Using the mouse, he minimized it to half the screen, then carefully read the information Melinda sent him.

Hi Adam,

Meet Susan. She lives in Newton, which is about twenty minutes from here. She enjoys the outdoors, movies and reading. You should contact her and arrange a coffee date. I've listed her email address below. But of course, the choice is yours.

If you decide to pass, please let me know and I'll send you another match. We'll do this one at a time. If you do meet her and don't feel any sparks, drop me an email and I'll let her know.

Above all I want to encourage you to have fun with the process. Meeting potential matches is like shopping for a new car. Sometimes it can take several test drives before you find one that is a good fit.

Melinda

Adam looked at Susan's picture again. She was pretty, with nice brown eyes. He started a new email. In the subject line he typed: *Matched by It's Just Coffee.*

Hello Susan. I received your information from Melinda Phillips, It's Just Coffee. I was wondering if you've read my profile and if you have any interest in meeting. The location is lady's choice. I look forward to hearing from you.

Adam Bell

Before he could change his mind, he hit *Send*. He leaned back in his chair, wondering how long it would take for a reply as he waited for his computer to shut down he texted Melinda.

Got your email about the match. I've emailed Susan. Drawings are ready—when can I stop over?

He got a speedy reply. *Anytime!*

On my way. He rolled up the plans. Before he got up, he massaged his knee. It was aching. Rain must be coming.

~

Melinda took the printed pages lying on her desk and put the stacks in color-coded folders. Business had been surprisingly brisk over the last year as even more people contracted for her services.

She pushed away from her desk, stretched her arms overhead and walked through the side door into her sun-filled kitchen. After pouring a glass of iced tea, she leaned against the counter and took a sip. Her thoughts drifted back to her client list. Was she doing the right thing, working with so many people? What would happen if she started to rush and matched the wrong couples? Her intuition was strong and she was seldom wrong about a match. Still, she worried. But it was always up to the people if they wanted to see someone after the first date.

Tires crunched in the driveway. She set her glass down and hurried to the front door and she saw Adam through the side window poised to knock. She pulled it open and smiled.

With a chuckle, he said, "Hello there."

"Come in. I just poured some iced tea; would you like a glass?"

"I am a little parched." He grinned and held up a hard, plastic tube. "I brought your plans."

"Well then, what are you doing still standing in the doorway?" she teased. "Come in. I can't wait to see them."

Adam followed her through the living room and into her kitchen. "Something smells good."

"Oh, I baked cookies earlier. Oatmeal. Would you like one?"

He gave her a lopsided grin. "Homemade cookies? Absolutely."

Melinda stifled a laugh. "You haven't tasted them yet."

He set the tube on the island and joked, "Did you add something weird to them?"

"Just raisins." She set an empty glass and the cookie jar on the counter. Opening the refrigerator, she took the pitcher of tea out. It slipped from her hands. She watched, as if in slow motion, as the glass hit the tile floor and shattered, spraying bits of glass and a half-gallon of iced tea in front of her feet.

"Wait!" Adam's hand shot out to stop her. "You'll step on glass. You've got bare feet." He frowned and glanced around the room. "Where are your shoes?"

She pointed to the back door. "Rubber boots."

Instead of getting the boots for her, Adam scooped her up and set her on the counter. "What do you have to clean this up?"

She was surprised at his commanding tone. "I can get it. Would you hand me my boots?"

"I've got this." He pointed to her feet. "Stay there. I don't want you to cut your feet."

She did as Adam asked and watched as he opened the broom closet and pulled out a mop and bucket, along with the broom and a dustpan.

Adam handed her the boots and began to sweep the broken glass into the pan. After slipping into the boots, Melinda hopped off the counter and began to fill a bucket with water and vinegar.

Adam said, "I'll sop up the tea if you want to use the mop. Together we'll get this done in no time."

"Adam, I really appreciate your help."

"Think of it as payment for the enormous number of cookies I'm about to eat."

Softly she said, "Thank you." She wasn't accustomed to having help around the house.

He dipped his head to the side. "You're welcome." He held up the bottle of white vinegar. "Now about your cleansers..."

With a small laugh, she said, "Trust me. That's all you need, best natural cleaner on earth."

His eyebrow arched. "Really?"

Melinda started the kettle and Adam tossed the wet paper towels in the garbage can. He put everything away and sat down on a stool. She could feel Adam watching her while she poured hot water over the tea bags.

"I didn't realize people still made iced tea the old-fashioned way," he said, "When I was a kid, my grandmother used to."

Melinda smiled. "Mine made it from a bottle of dried tea, like instant coffee." She wrinkled up her nose. "It was awful."

She set out several cookies on a plate and slid it over the countertop. "While the tea finishes steeping, why don't you show me your ideas for the patio?"

Adam popped open the tube and looked at the countertop. "Let's unroll this outside and I can walk you through the ideas."

Melinda felt herself grin. "Like you can paint me a visual with the drawings and actual description." She started to walk toward the back door and turned to see Adam was still sitting at the counter. "Are you coming?"

He had a pained expression on his face. "Sorry, I got a muscle cramp."

"We can stay inside if that would help." She stood in the open doorway.

With a shake of his head, Adam slowly stood up. He half limped down the short hallway, stiff-legged. "Not to worry, it'll be fine."

∼

*I*t wasn't a cramp. It was a quick, searing pain that spread downward. But he couldn't tell her the truth. The last thing he wanted was sympathy, or worse, pity.

He couldn't stand to have her feel sorry for him. This was not what he wanted the afternoon to be like. "After you." Melinda stepped out the door. In the distance, thunder rumbled. "We should probably hurry." He wanted to massage his knee again, but that would draw too much attention to something he wanted to avoid at all cost.

Adam ignored the pain and strode over to the table. With a flick of his hand, the plans rolled out. "Mel..."

Melinda pointed to the drawing. "So, tell me, how is this going to look?" She glanced around the patio and back to the paper.

Adam leaned in and ran his hand over the plans. He tapped a couple of circles. "Right here we're going to have columns where your grapevines can climb. As you asked, all the wood is going to be cedar."

She pointed to a rectangle on the drawing. "What's right here?"

"I added a bench so you can sit and relax."

"Could it be a swing instead?" She looked into his eyes. Adam couldn't help but notice her eyes, framed by long lashes.

They still had flecks of gold, but today they were more green than blue. He liked how they seemed to change, like the Atlantic Ocean. They reminded him of that friendly glass she had been looking for when they walked on the beach the day of the picnic.

"Sure, that's easy enough to do." With a sweeping motion of his arm, he gestured to where each column would stand. "The overall height would be nine feet."

"I can see it." She half closed her eyes and smiled at him. "It's going to be just perfect."

Something inside him stirred. Adam really wanted to make this a special place for her. He handed her a smaller piece of paper. "This is the total damage." He grinned. "But with the cedar wood, it will last for many years to come."

She glanced at the price. If she was shocked, she didn't let it show. "When can you start?"

He cocked his head. "You're okay with the estimate?"

"If anything, I'm surprised it wasn't more." She gave him a bright smile. "So?"

He ran a hand over his chin. "I can start the week after next."

Her face fell. "Okay."

"Is something wrong, Mel?"

She tilted her head and wrinkled her nose. "Why do you call me Mel?"

"I'm sorry. It seems to suit you, but if it bothers you I won't do it again."

With a shake of her head, she said, "It's just that my husband used to call me Mel."

Adam could feel his heart constrict. "I'm sorry, again. I didn't mean to dredge up a painful memory."

Melinda laid a hand on his arm. "It's okay, really. You can call me Mel, but when it's just the two of us. I like to use Melinda in business; I think it gives me a professional edge."

He stuck out a hand. "Care to shake on it?" Her hand fit into his perfectly. He held on to it and said, "I promise to call you Melinda. But don't get ticked off if I slip up."

She gave him a sad little smile. "Thank you for understanding."

Fat drops of rain cut short his next comment as she pulled her hand free and dashed towards the back door. "Are you coming?"

Adam rolled up the plans and hurried after her, ignoring the twinge he felt in his knee. He couldn't tell what was stronger—the jab to his leg or the jolt to his heart.

CHAPTER 6

Nervous, Adam wiped the palms of his hands on his jeans. Sitting in a coffee shop was not his idea of fun on a Sunday morning. Even if it was to meet his first date in years. In fact, that made it much worse. Dating sucked no matter how old you were.

He had to wonder what had possessed him to sign up with Mel anyway. He should have just waited to meet a nice girl the old-fashioned way, by chance or fate. Or were they one and the same?

He snorted and a woman with two small children looked his way. He held up his hand and smiled. He gave a quick nod, and then his gaze slid to the window, which overlooked the sidewalk and parking lot. A tall, blonde bombshell-type was walking his way. Could that be Susan? If it was, she sure hadn't looked like she wore that much makeup in her profile picture. He preferred a more natural look. Like Melinda. Now why did that thought pop into his head?

As the woman approached his table, he stood up. She made a beeline in his direction.

"Adam?" She stuck out her hand and shook his with an overly firm grip. "Susan."

"Pleased to meet you, Susan."

"I hope you haven't been waiting too long. I couldn't decide what to wear for a first meeting." She leaned forward and, with a conspiratorial wink, said, "I hate first dates. Don't you?"

Adam was surprised that such a high-pitched voice could come out of such a tall woman. He'd expected something sultrier. "I have to admit I haven't gone on a first date in years. Not since before I enlisted in the Marines." He thought he detected a slight frown. But he had no idea what he might have said to cause it.

"You look just like the profile picture I got from Melinda." Resting her elbows on the table, Susan leaned forward. "Would you like to order soon?" Susan glanced toward the waitress and waved her fingertips, calling her over to the table. "I detest coffee."

Unsure what to say next, Adam waited.

The waitress stopped at their table. "Would you like to order something?"

Susan half-rolled her eyes. "That's why I called you over."

She patted Adam's hand, which was resting on the tabletop. He couldn't help but notice hers was like ice.

"I'd like to order two large hot chocolates and a couple of chocolate croissants." She smiled at Adam.

"Actually, make mine a large black coffee and a banana nut muffin."

"Oh, well, you can pack the second croissant in a bag and I'll take it with me." She looked at Adam. "That is, if you don't mind."

"Of course not." He smiled at the waitress. "Thank you."

Without acknowledging Susan, she said, "I'll be right back with your order."

Adam had a sinking feeling about Susan, but he was determined to give her the benefit of the doubt.

She moistened her lips. "I have to confess, I'm a bundle of

nerves. Dating a Marine." She picked up a napkin and unfolded it on her lap. "My ex was in the Army."

"I retired as a major."

Her eyes grew wide. "Wow, that's impressive, and it explains your haircut." She rearranged the condiment containers on the table. "But whatever made you want to go into such a dangerous"— she waved her hands around— "occupation?"

"My father and grandfather were both Marines. It was an honor to serve."

"So it was kind of expected of you?"

He kept an eye out for the waitress anxious for her to return. He wasn't comfortable with where Susan's line of questions seemed to be headed. "Not at all. I went to college first and then decided to enlist."

"Oh, you went to college. For what?" Susan's eyes were roaming around the coffee shop while asking Adam questions. He couldn't help but wonder what seemed to be distracting her.

"I went to engineering school." Out of the corner of his eye he saw their waitress approaching with what he hoped was their order.

She set down Susan's selections first, then placed the muffin and coffee in front of Adam. "Can I get you anything else?"

Adam looked at Susan. She was already sipping her cocoa. "No thank you."

Setting her mug aside, Susan smiled. A bit of whipped cream graced her upper lip. "This is delicious. Are you sure you don't want to try it?"

He held up his coffee and said, "I'm all set, thanks." He broke the muffin in half and asked, "Your profile said you're an entrepreneur?"

Susan stirred her cocoa. "Yes, I'm currently between jobs. I'm trying to figure out what I want to do next. I've been a secretary, worked in retail, worked for a doctor's office and a bunch of other things." She nibbled on her croissant. "I'm thinking about opening an antique shop next."

"Oh, I don't remember seeing that in your profile, that you were passionate about antiques."

With a shrug she said, "I don't know much about them. I just think it would be fun."

Adam was surprised at her lack of preparedness for such an investment but changed the subject. "I did read you enjoy the outdoors. What is your favorite pastime, hiking, biking, and maybe kayaking?"

"I hike for exercise. I love climbing the most difficult peaks as they usually offer the best view from the top."

This wasn't good. There is no way he would be able to climb rugged terrain. Now he was really running out of questions to ask. He definitely needed to talk to Melinda about this date.

"Do you really do all those things you listed on your profile? Like fishing?" She wrinkled her nose. "I thought people just made up stuff to fill up their bio." Using her moistened fingertip, she popped the crumbs from the plate and licked her finger clean.

"I do enjoy them." He signaled for the check. "I hope you don't mind, but I have a business appointment." He glanced at his watch, "I didn't realize how late it was."

"Not at all." She beamed. "This was so much fun. I hope we can get together soon."

Adam took a few bills out of his wallet and handed them to the waitress after he glanced at the check. Anxious to leave, he said, "Keep the change."

Susan looked across the room at a group of ladies. "I see some friends over there, so I won't walk out with you."

Adam stood up and shook her hand. "It was nice to meet you, Susan."

"Likewise." She gave it one last vigorous shake and kissed his cheek. "I'll look forward to your call."

"Enjoy the rest of your day." Adam kept his gait steady as he hurried through the parking lot. Fighting the disappointment, he had to admit his first date was a complete bust.

He shot a text to Will. *Fishing?*

An emoji of a thumbs-up came back. Adam got into his truck. Before driving to meet his buddy, he sent Melinda a short text. He spoke as he typed, "Zero chemistry. We'll talk Monday." Without waiting for an answer, he started the truck and headed toward the marina.

~

Melinda checked her cell and saw that Adam had sent her a text earlier. She was surprised to read that the date with Susan hadn't gone well. Curious as to what might have gone wrong, she wandered into her office. She snapped on the overhead light and then powered up her computer. She pulled up Susan's and Adam's profiles and compared them. Per the questionnaire they had filled out, they were a suitable match at eighty-eight percent.

She clicked on a few additional profiles for several more candidates. She flagged Debbie, Laura and Beth. They ranged from eighty-two percent to ninety. She skimmed Beth's: ninety percent. She had a hunch about Laura, who was eight-nine percent, so she attached her profile to an email to Adam. Then added a note saying they could talk about Susan when she saw him on Monday.

She shut down her computer and clicked off the light. Closing the door tight, she went back into the kitchen. The house seemed very empty tonight. It wasn't often Melinda felt at loose ends, at least not since moving to Chester. It had been heart wrenching when she lived in Philadelphia. After John died, every time she turned a corner in their house she expected to see him, or have him walk through the front door, sweep her into his arms with a kiss and a bear hug. The only solution had been to pack up the memories and move. She had often told her therapy clients they would know when it was time to start over.

Slowly, she shook her head. What had taken her down

melancholy lane tonight? After setting the teakettle on the stove, she selected her favorite herbal blend. From experience she knew tonight was going to be one of those sleepless nights that seemed to go on without end. If she did happen to fall asleep, she'd relive the worst moment in her life and wake with her pillow drenched in tears. Would it ever get easier? The teakettle sang and she poured the boiling water over the teabag.

The phone rang, breaking the oppressive silence. "Hello?"

"Hi Melinda, it's Stacey."

"Hey, Stacey, what's going on?"

"I was wondering what you're doing Saturday. Will went fishing today and caught some nice bass. We thought we'd host an impromptu cookout."

"That sounds like fun. What should I bring?"

"Just yourself, we've got everything covered."

Melinda could hear the smile in Stacey's voice. "What time?"

"Around six. It's just the regular gang."

Stacey said goodbye, and before Melinda heard the phone disconnect, she heard Will ask, "She's coming, right?"

That made her smile. To be welcomed into the established group all because she helped Will and Stacey find each other. She wished every match was as successful, which turned her thoughts back to Adam and Susan.

"What did I miss?"

CHAPTER 7

Melinda picked up her office phone on the second ring, not bothering to look at caller ID.

"Hello, this is Melinda Phillips."

"Hi Mel, it's Adam."

Melinda put down her pen and sat back in the chair. Smiling she said, "Hi there. How are you since your date with Susan?"

"I'm fine." She could hear the grin in his voice. "Hey I was just sitting here thinking. It's a nice day and since we're still waiting on the building permit for your place would you like to have lunch with me today?"

At a loss for words she wasn't sure how to respond. She should say no, but she was surprised to realize she wanted to say yes, but was he asking as a reaction to his lackluster date with Susan? She hadn't gone out to lunch in ages with anyone.

"Adam, that's really nice of you to offer, but I'm up to my eyeballs in work."

"Oh, come on. It's sunny and warm and there's a seafood place, the Salty Dog, that I've been dying to try, only about thirty minutes down the coast." Before she could say no, he plunged ahead. "It's no fun to go to a cool new place by yourself."

She bit her bottom lip. Making a snap decision she said,

"Sounds like fun. But," she chuckled, "if I get in trouble with the boss for goofing off, I'm blaming you."

"Not a problem. Besides, I think she likes me, so I'm sure she'd encourage you to take off for a while."

Mel was shocked when she heard herself actually laugh with a snort.

"What time will you swing by or do you want me to meet you there?" She pushed back from the desk and stretched one arm overhead.

"Look out your window."

Melinda pushed the curtain away from the side-lites next to the front door. She grinned. "Adam, I gotta let you go. There is some guy waving at me from the driveway."

She hit the disconnect button on the phone and swung the door open. She couldn't keep the smile from her face. Leaning against the doorjamb, she smirked. "You were pretty sure I'd say yes."

Adam sauntered up the walkway. "Let's just say I was cautiously optimistic. With the lure of fresh seafood and my sparkling conversation, well, I think the combination speaks for itself. Besides, if all else failed I was going to beg you to take pity on a new friend."

"I need to grab my keys and lock up." She deliberately tossed a teasing look over her shoulder. "We'll take my car."

He protested, "I can drive, my truck is gassed up and ready to roll."

She ignored him and closed the front door firmly after her, and within minutes the garage door slid open on its tracks. He stepped to one side as she backed the car out. Melinda grinned when he hopped into the passenger seat.

"Buckle up." She flashed him a wide smile. She pushed a button and the trunk lifted up, and then the hard top disconnected and folded into the trunk space. When the trunk went back down, she grinned.

His smile widened and he plopped his ball cap on his head,

forgoing sunglasses as the brim shaded his eyes. "I had no idea this was a convertible."

"Leave it to the Swedes to make a Volvo sedan not just luxurious but also with flair." She secured a scarf around her hair and pushed her sunglasses into place "If we're going on an adventure in this kind of weather, the only way to do it properly is with the top down."

She backed out and cruised down the street, driving through downtown Chester. She could see Adam out of the corner of her eye. He looked relaxed and happy, just like she felt.

After she got through the town, he gave her directions to the restaurant. They were going to pretty much follow the coast until the road veered east, driving until they ran out of black top. Adam had taken his ball cap off and held it in his hand. With his short blonde hair, he didn't have to worry about the wind whipping it into his face, but Melinda had to do a one-handed twist to get her hair out of her eyes. The sun was glorious on her bare arms. *When was the last time I left work before the end of the day?* she wondered.

"Do you often take off on a whim?" She had to speak louder than normal with the wind carrying her words away.

"No, but it's a nice treat, don't you think?"

Keeping her eyes on the road she nodded. "I'm glad you stopped over. It is too nice to be stuck inside all day."

"Stick with me, Mel, and we can have all kinds of impromptu adventures."

His comment was curious—was it in the context of friends or was he implying something more? A flush of color rose in his cheeks, giving his complexion a handsome ruddy look.

"So tell me, Adam, how do you like living in Chester? Do you find it a touch dull from other places you've lived?"

"I have been lucky to live in a lot of places." He paused. "You know, every place has its own kind of beauty. Even when I was deployed. War is hell, but there were moments when I could appreciate the landscape and the people who lived there. But if you're talking the United States, Camp Pendleton in San Diego, that was probably my favorite. I lived off base and the weather is spectacular."

"I remember reading about Pendleton. I seem to recall it was supposed to be a temporary facility in the '40s, but then it was turned into a permanent base."

He nodded. "You are spot on." He gave her a warm look. "After all the places I've lived, I've come to appreciate small-town life."

Her breath caught. Was he implying he might have found his home in Chester? Why did she suddenly seem to want him to stay?

Mel said, "When I moved from Philadelphia to Chester, it was a bit of a culture shock for me. I lived in a development with a lot of neighbors, and here, not so much. There is more land per house here. I've been able to really expand my gardens and I like the fact there is a nice breeze from the ocean most of the time."

Joking, he asked, "Even in the winter months?"

She did a one-shoulder shrug. "I'll admit it gets cold here, but not any different than Philly."

"I haven't gotten through a winter here yet."

"A hat, gloves and a down jacket will get you through the worst of it." She laughed. "And book all inside jobs."

He wagged his finger at her and chuckled. "Now that is a brilliant idea."

Glimpses of the ocean on the right popped up from time to time as they drove in companionable silence. Adam pointed to a road sign. "Looks like our turn is just ahead."

"That's a good thing, I'm starving. I just realized I never ate breakfast."

He gave her a sharp look. "Not good, Mel. You should eat a little something."

She was surprised to see he was very serious—her breakfast habits were none of his concern. She couldn't help keeping the defensive tone from her voice. "Normally I do, but today I jumped right into the pile of emails I had."

He gave her a sheepish smile. "Sorry about that. Sometimes I get a little pushy and overstep boundaries."

She got the feeling he let the rest of his thought hang. "No big deal." She slowed the car and turned on her blinker, taking a sharp right. Stones kicked up from the edge of the pavement. The posted speed limit kept her puttering down the narrow two-lane road.

"Do you know anyone who's eaten here?"

Adam's fingers tapped on the door. The look on his face was absolutely without a care in the world. "A couple of clients and I saw"—he pointed to a small weathered sign painted in bright blue letters— "that sign last week and just decided we needed to come."

She saw the entrance to the dock and turned into the parking lot. Boats were tied along rows of wood and metal docks. The sound of a bell chimed in time with the rise and fall of the vessels.

"Hopefully it was a good day for fishing." She turned the car off, leaving the top down. "Ready?"

Adam got out of the car and waited for her to do the same. As they crossed the asphalt, she ducked quickly to avoid a seagull diving out of the sky. She stumbled. Adam reached out a steadying hand. He held her tight in his arms for a moment, and she could smell his musky aftershave. Looking up she was shocked to see a spark of interest lingering there.

"Um," she stammered. She lowered her lashes and then looked up again. The expression was gone. Her heart skipped in her chest. "Thanks."

His voice was soft, but he hadn't let go of her. Not yet. "Are you okay? You didn't twist an ankle or something?"

"No." She held her breath. Waiting for what, she wasn't sure, but it did feel good to be held. It had been a long time.

Adam ran his hands down her arms slowly before letting her

go. He cleared his throat. Glancing towards the end of the pier, he said in an off-handed way, "There's the Salty Dog."

After taking a step back, her breath returned to normal. Her reaction was from the fear of falling. Nothing more than that, she told herself.

His hand skimmed over hers. As if he was going to hold it as they walked the rest of the way. She slowed, putting more space between them.

"Best watch out for the birds. They're like vultures when they think there's a chance for an easy meal." He pointed to the sky. "It's like someone rang the dinner bell."

She gave a strained laugh. At least that was how it sounded to her ears. "They must equate people with food." Determined to put their conversation back on easy street, she said, "It must take a lot of hard work to be a commercial fisherman. Always putting your faith and wallet on the hopes it'll be a good day at sea."

"Sometimes faith can go a long way to giving you what you need or want most." He gave her a guarded look. "You must believe in fate. After all, isn't the matchmaking business more than hoping you've found someone a good match? People have to have faith in your abilities."

She gave him a sidelong look. "I guess you're right. Most people do trust me to find them their happily ever after."

They reached the door. The smell of fish and the chatter of people talking inside permeated the air. Holding his hand on the doorknob, he didn't open it.

His eyes captivated her. They were unreadable. "I trust you with my heart."

Humbled didn't describe how she felt in that instant. She placed her hand on his arm. Her heart constricted. "I promise she's out there."

Adam gave a half nod and pulled the door open. "After you."

CHAPTER 8

Adam squinted against the bright sun as he checked off each item on the delivery slip. Wood was on one side of the yard and other supplies were stacked in neat piles on the side next to Mel's garage.

Out of the corner of his eye he saw Melinda appear from around the house, wearing a floral sundress and bright green flip-flops to match. Beaming and carrying a mug of what he guessed would be coffee. "Good morning," she called.

"Hey. You look terrific." He thought he saw a faint hint of color rise in her cheeks.

"I'm a morning person. There's nothing better than having my feet hit the ground at a dead run." She held out the mug to him. "Coffee?"

"You're an angel in flip-flops." He grinned.

"Caffeine is a major food group for me and I suspect it is for you too. After all, don't a lot of military people, and for that matter a large portion of the population, survive on the brewed ambrosia?" She laughed. "Well, at least that's my definition of it."

"I couldn't agree more." He took the cup. "This sure does smell good."

An almost imperceptible shake of his head had her responding, "Do you need cream?" She half turned. "I have some inside."

"Not at all. Most people I run into don't make it strong enough to suit my taste."

"Then you should love mine." She took the slip of paper from his hand. "Was everything delivered?" She glanced down. "I see you're methodical too." She pointed to the check marks next to each item.

"I would hate to get started and be missing something critical." He took the slip back.

Melinda frowned and walked around the piles. "Just look at those ruts in the grass. Are they from the delivery truck?"

"Yes, but it's to be expected."

She put her hands on her hips. "Why didn't they just put it all in the driveway?" She chewed on her thumb nail.

Adam stated, "It's much easier for me to get things as I need them rather than to cart everything in from the front of the house." He certainly couldn't tell her why he needed the wood closer to the back. Heck, if he could, he would have had the material delivered next to where he would be working. As it was, hauling each load was going to give his leg grief.

Melinda glanced at the slim gold watch on her wrist. "I have to get into the office, but if you need something, let me know and help yourself to more coffee or water in the refrigerator. The back door is open."

"Mel, you don't need to keep me hydrated." He said, "I've worked on jobsites and always bring a good-size cooler with plenty of supplies."

She flipped her curls and drawled, "My momma always said, 'Make sure to keep anyone who's working at your house happy.'"

He chuckled. "So we don't make mistakes?"

Mel clapped her hands together and grinned. Nodding she said, "Something like that." With a quick wave she dashed up

49

the front steps. Before she closed the screen door, she called over her shoulder, "I was serious about you helping yourself. There are even fresh-baked cookies in the jar." Then she disappeared.

Adam couldn't help but chuckle to himself. *This is going to be a fun project.*

∽

Melinda got up from the computer and rolled her head from side to side. She had a wicked kink in her neck. She was stiff from sitting in one position too long.

The shrill hum of a saw caught her attention. She wandered to the back window and looked out. Walking barefoot out of her office, she stepped into flip-flops and scuffed her way to the back door, pausing to grab a glass of water on her way. Stopping in her tracks, she was dismayed to discover her backyard looked like a bomb had gone off. Short pieces of wood were in one pile and what looked to Melinda like a huge puzzle was arranged on the ground.

Thump. Pause. Thump.

Melinda gingerly stepped around pieces of lumber. "Adam."

He didn't look up.

"Adam!"

Thump. Another short piece of wood was tossed into a pile.

She waved her arms in the air and got his attention.

Pushing his sunglasses to sit on the top of his head, exposing his deep brown eyes, he pulled headphones from his ears. "Sorry, Mel. I didn't hear you."

Hoping to hide her dismay, she said, "You've got quite the…" She hesitated to use the word *mess*, so she opted to say, "…project going on here."

Adam leaned against a sawhorse. Sweeping his arm in a circle, he said, "It's controlled chaos. But I'm sure to you it looks like a huge mess."

Rueful, she shrugged. "I'm not gonna lie, I didn't expect my yard to look like this."

"Until things start to take shape, it always looks awful." He pointed to six round short tubes. "I need to get those sunk in the ground, mix some concrete, and they'll support the overall structure. Then I can set the posts in place."

She rolled her shoulders and told herself to relax. It was going to be fine. "I'm going to trust you on this one." With a laugh she said, "How are you going to get those posts up? They're like nine feet long, aren't they?"

He tapped the top of his head. "I've got that all figured out. Will owes me a favor and I've already talked to him. He's going to stop over on Wednesday or Thursday depending on my progress. Between the two of us, we'll get them anchored in place."

Adam took a step toward Melinda and seemed to stagger a little bit. She reached out a hand to steady him and was surprised to see an annoyed look flash across his face. Ignoring it, she asked, "Are you all right?"

"Yeah. I'm fine."

"I'm going to get you a glass of something cold to drink. You've been out here for hours."

"Really, I'm fine. You don't need to wait on me."

Melinda wondered why he seemed irritated with her. "I was being nice."

He gave her a whole-hearted smile. "You're right. I'm sorry. I'd love something, as long as you'll sit with me for a few minutes."

"That I can do. If for no other reason than to make sure you take a break." She walked into the house and didn't look back at Adam.

What was his problem? It wasn't like I was offering to hold the glass while he sipped something through a straw. Sometimes he gets so prickly. She took a pitcher of lemonade from the refrigerator and filled her glass and one for Adam with ice cubes, filling them almost to the rim with the pale, yellow liquid and then for an extra touch added a twist of sliced lemon. She put everything back in the fridge. Before going outside, she thought, *I guess I was a little prickly too. I've spent too much time at home alone. Having someone around more forces me to talk to a human being. Maybe this project is good for me, making me connect with more people than just clients.*

Picking up the glasses, she walked through the door backwards pushing it open with her foot and turned to hold it open with her hip. She took a step back and she couldn't feel the door. She tossed a look over her shoulder to discover Adam holding it for her.

"Thank you." Despite the heat, she could feel the pink rise in her cheeks. Hoping he wouldn't notice, she dipped her head. "Lemonade."

"What," he teased, "no cookies?"

She handed him the glasses and grinned. "You take these and I'll bring out the jar." She couldn't help but laugh. "Are you like a Cookie Monster or something?"

Adam stood in the back door and called after her, "I heard you, ya know."

"I wasn't trying to whisper." She carried the clear cookie jar to the door and then handed it to him, noticing the glasses were on a box. She teased, "Making yourself useful?"

Giving her a mock bow, he said, "At your service, miss."

Melinda followed Adam outside. It had been a long time since she had bantered like this with anyone. It felt good to be able to have a conversation with a real friend that was lighthearted and easy.

In the few minutes she was inside, Adam had put two lawn chairs under a lush maple tree. Then he set a small cardboard box, turned upside down, as a table where their glasses sat glistening with sweat from the afternoon humidity. Melinda sat, facing the back of the house. "So tell me, how did you really come by handyman work after being in the military?"

THE MATCHMAKER AND THE MARINE

Adam grabbed a cookie and ate it in two short bites, seeming to stall for time.

"Earth to Adam," she prodded.

He picked up his glass and took a long drink. "This is good stuff; did you squeeze the lemons yourself?"

She had a stab of suspicion. "If you don't want to talk about it, just say so. No need to dance around the question."

The grin he wore seemed to fade. "I don't really like to talk about my past. But if you don't mind, I'd rather talk about my date with Susan."

Melinda turned her attention to look at him. "I'm glad you brought it up. I was really surprised you weren't a good match."

Adam took another cookie. He said, "She wasn't at all what I expected from her profile. In her picture she looked more like the girl next door, wholesome and outdoorsy. In person she wore a lot of makeup, I tend to think less is more. She was late and I value punctuality. And then she orders for both of us. Like she's in charge or something. Hot chocolate and chocolate croissants." He shrugged a shoulder. "I would prefer someone a little less controlling."

"Are you sure it wasn't just nerves on her part?"

He replied, "She said she was a little nervous, but wait, it gets better."

Melinda had a sinking feeling in the pit of her stomach that this woman had misrepresented herself. "I'm not sure if I want to hear what comes next."

"Trust me, you do. If for no other reason than you'll be able to update her profile in your system."

"Okay..." She dragged out the word. "I'm listening."

In a rush he said, "She hikes only for exercise and because she likes the view from the peaks. Otherwise she's not a fan of outdoor activities. As she's telling me this she's cleaning the plate with her finger by licking it and plucking up the crumbs. I wanted to ask her if her momma taught her any manners."

Melinda bit back a laugh. This really was starting to sound

comical—if it hadn't been one of her clients, that is. "So how did you leave things?"

"Well, for one, I couldn't get out of there fast enough. In being totally honest with you, I made up a story about having to leave. Then she said she'd be waiting for my call." Adam's tone became tinged with sarcasm. "Um, like that is going to happen."

Melinda leaned forward and patted his arm. "I'm sorry, Adam." She could tell he hadn't been on a first date in a long time. His reaction was a bit over the top.

"Wait, there's more."

Melinda had to smile again. "You keep telling me to wait, there's more. How much more could there be? The date didn't last that long,"

He snorted. "The best part of this entire conversation, she said she thought people made things up on their profiles and even thought I did too." He leaned back in the chair, seemingly not the least bit annoyed. After talking, he actually seemed to find the humor in the situation.

"Oh, Adam. I want to reassure you that is not how I run my business, or what I ask clients to do."

"Mel, don't worry. I've already got you pegged. You're a kind-hearted lady who really does want the best for everyone. I have faith in you, and I have a feeling you're going to find everything I'm looking for in a woman." He grinned. "Or as you might say, my HEA. And, yes, I do know that stands for happily ever after."

Melinda pretended to swoon and fan herself. She batted her eyelashes and grinned. "Well, thank heavens you know the lingo."

CHAPTER 9

Melinda carried a woven basket with a strawberry rhubarb pie tucked inside as she climbed the steps to Stacey's front door. This was her first fish fry and she wasn't sure what exactly to expect. Was it like a normal cookout? She raised her hand to knock when it swung opened.

"Hey Stacey," Melinda greeted her warmly. She held up the basket. "I brought pie."

Stacey took the basket from her. "Come in. We're all out back."

Melinda glanced at the number of cars parked on the street in front of their house. "I hope I brought a big enough pie." She chuckled. "I didn't realize this was going to be a party."

Stacey glanced back over her shoulder. "Once Will starts inviting people, things tend to grow. But it's everyone you already know." She set the basket down on the only open space on the counter. "Adam is out there. I think he's keeping an eye on the grill."

Looking around the kitchen, Melinda noticed there were several plates of cookies, a cake and a big bowl of cut-up fruit. Relieved there were more dessert choices, she said, "Is there anything I can help you with?"

"Not at all. Everything is done." She gave Melinda a smile. "Will said Adam has been working hard at your place."

"I'm excited to see how it will look when he's done. I heard on the news there's a storm blowing in late tomorrow, so hopefully that won't put him behind schedule too badly."

While Melinda was talking, Stacey poured two glasses of white wine and handed one to her.

After accepting the glass, Melinda stepped through the open sliding door and onto the deck. She noticed Molly and Tim grinning and gesturing for her to join them.

Melinda crossed the grass to where they were standing. Happy to see them she said, "Hi, you two."

Molly gave her a quick hug. She gushed, "I'm so glad you're here." She glanced at the group of people, and Melinda looked around to see what Molly was looking at, or for who.

"Is everything all right?" Melinda couldn't help but notice Molly's eyes were bright and she almost seemed to be bouncing in place.

Molly took Tim's hand. "We're going to make an announcement tonight, but we wanted you to be the first of our friends to know." She kissed Tim on the lips lightly.

Melinda could guess what they were about to say.

Tim said, "Well, since you seemed to have piqued her interest, you'd better tell Melinda before you bust."

Struggling to keep her voice low, Molly held up their joined hands. A flash of brilliance was caught by the sun. "We're engaged!"

Melinda felt tears prick her eyes. She blinked them away and said, "Congratulations to you both." First, she kissed Molly's cheek and then Tim's. "I'm sure you'll both be very happy."

"If it weren't for you, there wouldn't be an us," Molly said.

"You're giving me far too much credit. All I did was make it possible for you to meet." Melinda clasped their entwined hands. "You did the hard work of discovering the wonderfulness about each other."

Tim wrapped an arm around Molly's waist. "We expect to see you at the wedding."

"Wild horses couldn't keep me away. Have you set a date?"

Molly's head bobbed. "The last Sunday in July."

"Of this year?" Melinda asked as she mentally counted the weeks until the end of July.

Beaming, Tim said, "Yes, and the theme will be Christmas in July." He kissed Molly's cheek. "She wants all the colors of Christmas, and we don't want to wait and have to worry about snow and the cold, so it's the best of both seasons."

"Sounds perfect." Out of the corner of her eye, Mel noticed Adam walking toward them. "You can tell me more after you make the big announcement to the group."

"What announcement?" Adam asked as he stopped beside Melinda.

"We're getting married!" Molly screeched.

Silence fell over the backyard and Stacey came rushing over. "Did you say what I think you did?"

Molly nodded her head up and down. It made Melinda dizzy watching at the speed it moved. "We are!"

Melinda and Adam stepped aside as their friends rushed over to shake Tim's hand and hug Molly. Adam steered Melinda toward the grill. "Care to help me burn," he chuckled, "I mean, grill the fish?"

"Sure, but do you know what you're doing or should I take over?" She couldn't help poking fun at him. "You said you don't cook."

"You're looking at a grill master." He picked up a baseball hat sitting on a table. "See, the hat even has it on the front."

Melinda took the hat from his hands and laughed. "Wearing this won't help us have a tasty dinner if you aren't equipped with the proper skills."

Adam tapped the center of his chest with his fingers. "Not to worry. All I need to do is oil the fish and add some seasoning.

Slap it on the grill for a couple minutes, flip it over for a few more and *shazam*, dinner."

Melinda hip-checked him and said, "Move over. Let me show you how it's really done."

Adam handed her the hat. "If you're going to cook, you have to wear this."

She wrinkled her nose. "You're kidding, right?"

He slowly shook his head and grinned. "Nope. If you want to run with a grill master, ya gotta wear the right hat."

Reluctantly she accepted the well-worn baseball cap and perched it on top of her head. "Be prepared to weep over the most delicious fish you've ever eaten." Melinda smirked over her shoulder and turned down the grill. "They need a medium heat. I don't fancy sushi today."

"So far you haven't done anything I wasn't going to do." Adam crossed his arms across his chest and attempted to look stern. "But I am impressed."

"The magic is in the flipping." She laughed, surprised at how much fun she was having.

"Again, Mel, I know how to cook fish." She could hear the teasing in his voice but noticed he was very attentive to everything she was doing.

Looking over her shoulder, she smiled as she watched Molly and Tim bask in the group of well-wishers. "Do you think they'll tie the knot in July?"

"Nah. Molly is going to want a very specific kind of wedding and I don't think there is enough time." Adam leaned close to Melinda and said, "You do seem to have the magic touch. For matchmaking."

She turned her head to look at him, taken aback by how close he was. She didn't want to pull away and seem rude, so instead she said, "I'm very fortunate to be able to find people that seem to mesh." She relaxed and grinned. "And you're next."

Adam frowned. "I hope the next one won't have treated the profile process like a joke."

"That isn't typical of the people I work with." Quietly she said, "I talked to Susan and she was very nervous to meet you. Sometimes anxiety can take over and highlight a person's flaws."

He adjusted the cap on her head. "I know I was hard on her but I am taking this process very serious. I had high expectations."

For the first time, Melinda really noticed they were almost the same height; she could look into his eyes. "You know, you're pretty easygoing for a Marine. At least with me."

He snorted. "How many Marines have you met?"

She tapped her fingertip to her chin, pretending to think really hard. "Just one. Well, two. Will and you."

"That just goes to show you, stereotyping can lead to a completely wrong conclusion."

Adam held out an oversized platter and Melinda slid the fish from the grill to it. "Whenever I've seen pictures of the Marines, or a commercial on television, the men and women look so serious. Like they lack an obvious sense of humor. Is it a requirement for the Corps?"

"Ah, that's all for show. You'd be surprised how many of us are jokesters."

Without looking up, she said, "John was a police officer."

"I had no idea."

Melinda was surprised at the gentle tone in his voice.

"A lot of his buddies used to hang out at our place and they were always laughing and joking around."

She was interrupted when Molly came over. "Hey you two, is dinner ready? I can corral the troops."

Adam held up the platter. "We are."

Molly turned around, put her fingers in her lips and whistled. "DINNER!" She grinned. "That should get them moving."

For a moment Melinda felt a stab of emptiness. She closed the lid on the grill after running a wire brush over the grates, thoroughly cleaning the remnants of fish off. She wished John could be here to meet these wonderful people who had become her good friends.

When she looked up, she saw Will was watching her. He said, "Thanks for cooking. If Adam had, who knows how much char we'd be eating instead of this delicious-looking fish."

Melinda smiled, happy to be distracted from the melancholy moment. "I'm sure you're exaggerating." She looked across the yard to where Adam was peering into the drink cooler. He held up a bottle of beer in her direction and she nodded. "He seemed to have it under control."

Will's gaze followed the direction Melinda nodded in. "You know I'm really glad you and Adam have become friends." He took a step toward her, closing the gap between them. "When he arrived, he was at loose ends, and frankly I was worried about him. Meeting you seems to have brought him out of his shell."

"I'm sure it must have been an adjustment retiring from the military and moving to a new town, but he had you, Stacey and all your friends for support."

Will slowly nodded. "Don't let his happy go lucky demeanor fool you. There's a lot going on behind his grin and teasing facade."

"Will, I think what you and Stacey did, renting him your garage apartment, was the best thing for him. He had friends, who are more like family, as neighbors from day one."

Will folded his arms over his chest. "Was it hard moving here by yourself?"

"Not really. I was ready. Leaving Philly was the only decision I could have made. It was time." She didn't want to relive the memory of packing each box with John's personal belongings after the house had been sold. Reminding herself this was a party and not the time to take a sad stroll down memory lane, she forced a sunny smile. It didn't matter—Will didn't know it was fake.

"Mel?" Adam touched her arm. "I brought you a beer."

She accepted the frosty bottle and kept the smile plastered to her face. Her voice strained, she said, "Thank you."

"Hey, you look a little pale. Do you want me to drive you home?"

"No, I'm fine." She grinned and took a sip of her beer. "Just parched." She teased, "Doing *your* job was thirsty work."

Adam let out a big laugh and clinked bottles with her. "And you did it admirably. I can't wait to eat."

Melinda swallowed the lump in her throat. "Let's find a place to sit and for giggles, I'll let you fix me a plate."

"By all means, chef, it would be an honor."

He gave her a quick salute and Melinda felt the stranglehold around her heart loosen just a bit. Losing John was horrible, but being around good people, and Adam, made it just a little more bearable.

She looked at Molly and Tim. After all, today was a happy day.

CHAPTER 10

Adam checked his email. He had one from Mel. With a sinking heart he saw a new match. Did he really want to do this again?

When clicking on the attachment, he saw a picture of a woman, Laura, who looked a lot like Anita. His first reaction was hell no. His second reaction was to read the bio.

He scanned the contents, but his eyes kept drifting back to the picture. Nope, there was no way he could date this woman. It was like looking at his ex's long-lost twin.

He quickly composed an email to Mel and then deleted it. He'd tell her in person when he went back to work at her place. It would give him a good reason to talk to her again. Maybe he should ask her out for ice cream or something else equally innocuous.

Checking his cell, he saw Will and Tim had texted saying they'd meet him at his place. It wasn't often he had to ask for help, but his buddies knew setting the posts would be challenging without the extra hands.

He got up from his desk and, hopping on his right leg, made his way to the sofa. He sat down and picked up a gel-padded liner. Starting just under what was left of his kneecap, he rolled it up his thigh and into place. He then took the soft cotton sock from the coffee table and slipped it over the liner. Finally, he positioned the prosthesis and stood up. Bearing down, he waited for the series of clicks, confirming it was secured in place. He rolled his pant leg over the hard plastic and titanium.

Adam had come to terms with his prosthesis, but it wasn't something he wanted to broadcast to the world. He was one of the lucky ones: he'd survived only to have lost people under his command. But only in the privacy of his apartment did he wear shorts, no matter how hot it was.

After picking up his lunch bag, baseball cap and keys, it was time to head out. It felt good to be physically tired at the end of a productive day. In another week he'd be done at Mel's and moving on to his next project. Maybe he'd talk to her again about the fancy chicken coop she dreamed about so he could have an excuse to see her again.

The sound of slamming doors drifted through the open window. He could hear Tim talking to Will. The sound of boots thumped on his stairs, and he opened the door. Will was halfway up. "Hey, slowpoke, Tim's here and we're ready to roll."

Adam held up his lunch bag and jingled his keys. "I've been waiting for your slow butt to show up."

Will backed down the stairs. "Tim, I'll ride with you?"

"Morning, Adam," Tim called out.

"There's the groom-to-be." Adam stepped off the bottom step and gave his buddy a playful slug to his arm.

Tim chuckled. "Yeah, Molly is like a whirlwind planning our wedding. She wants to get married on the island at her parents' place. I keep telling her we don't have enough time, but well, you know my girl. Once she gets something in her mind, off she goes."

Adam opened the passenger door on his truck. Stowing his stuff, he asked, "Why the rush to get married this year?"

Tim casually leaned against his SUV. "Molly wants a Christmas-themed wedding and wants to get married near the ocean, and that doesn't work for December at her parents' place. And something about it being an even-numbered year is good luck. But I'm concerned the place will be booked being we're so late to plan."

"You are a man in love," Adam stated. "And it will all work out."

"You'll find out when you meet that special someone too." Will chuckled. "Look at me and Stacey. I'd do anything to put a smile on her face."

Tim nodded. "I know exactly what you mean. I want Molly and me to have the wedding of her dreams."

Adam clapped him on the back. "Well, since you two make finding a great girl so attractive, it's a good thing I'm working with Melinda. If she can help the two of you find the perfect girls, I'm a slam dunk with my good looks and charm." He climbed into the truck and slammed the door. "Guys, we're going to be late, so let's get going. Time is money."

"Yes, Major." Will gave him a stiff salute.

With a hearty laugh, Tim said, "And in case you forgot, we're working for free. On a Saturday too."

Adam hung his arm out the window. He set his mouth in a firm line. "We've been over this. I'm paying you and you're going to take it."

"Not necessary. Besides, I'd rather have you keep your money and help me renovate the basement. Stacey has an idea about a craft room and I'm sure a few other ideas will pop up."

Adam felt his insides relax. Will wasn't looking at this job as pity help. It was more of a barter situation. With an easy smile, he said, "That I can do."

Tim said, "Hey, can I get in on this action, like when we buy a house you could help us out?"

"Sure, Tim." He tapped the truck door with his hand. "Let's get going before Melinda thinks we've taken the day off." He started the truck and watched in his rearview mirror as his buddies got in Tim's SUV and backed out into the street.

Adam followed them on the short ten-minute drive to Mel's. He parked in front of her house as Tim pulled into her driveway.

All looked quiet. He wondered where Mel was—maybe she wasn't home. Not that it mattered, he reminded himself. He was here to work on her house.

Tim and Will grabbed the toolbox and ladder. Adam strapped on his tool belt. They were ready. As an after-thought, he grabbed an ancient-looking portable radio. He thought he'd put the ball game on while they worked.

Following the guys around the back, he saw Mel was up to her elbows, happily digging in her garden. He called out hello, but no answer. He crossed the yard as quickly as he could, making sure his gait was smooth, just in case she looked up. He tapped her shoulder.

She jumped up and pulled ear buds out. "Adam, hey." She glanced toward Will and Tim. "I didn't realize it was so late." She gave him a sheepish grin. "I tend to lose track of time when I'm puttering in the dirt."

"It's no problem. I just didn't want to scare you." He reached out and brushed a smudge of dirt from her cheek. "You really dig it." He smirked. "Sorry about the pun. I couldn't help myself." He wondered if the gesture would bother her. It felt natural to him to wipe the dirt from her face.

She pulled her wide-brimmed hat from her head and laughed. "If it's only one streak of dirt, it's a record for me."

He shifted from one foot to the other. "I need to get to work."

Melinda dropped her tools in her garden cart and grabbed it by the handle. Adam reached out and took it from her. "Allow me." They walked toward the guys, who were busy setting up sawhorses and extension cords.

"Hi, Melinda," Will said, while Tim focused on testing the ladder.

Melinda looked down at Adam's legs. Concern filled her eyes. "Are you limping?"

"No. Just a minor muscle cramp. I'll walk it off." His stomach clenched. Did she have to pay such close attention?

"If you say so." Melinda took the cart from him and stowed it near the garage door. "I have to get into the office, but I'll pop out later to check on you guys." She opened the back door and paused. "Remember, there are water and snacks in the kitchen. Help yourselves."

"Thanks, Mel." Adam waved his hand in acknowledgement.

The door closed behind her and Adam discovered the guys watching him watch her. "What?"

Will asked, "Since when did you get so relaxed around her *and* start calling her Mel?"

With a shrug he said, "It just sort of happened."

"Interesting." Tim winked at Will. "Nicknames now…"

"She's working as my matchmaker. It's only natural we've become friends."

Will crossed his arms across his chest. "If you say so."

"But do me a favor, don't call her Mel." Adam turned his back on his buddies. Briskly, he said, "Let's get to work."

~

Melinda combed out her damp hair and twisted it into a knot at the base of her neck. Wearing capris and a lightweight top, she padded into the kitchen for a cup of coffee. She needed to get into the office since she had two appointments after lunch with potential new clients. Maybe she'd get lucky and one of the ladies would be a good match for Adam.

She could hear the deep murmur of male voices drifting through the open window as the guys worked. Last week Adam had set the cement pads. He said it wouldn't be long now and her patio would be complete.

Leaning against the counter, sipping her coffee, she watched as the first column was positioned into place. Adam was using a level to make sure it was straight and Will was knocking the post with a hammer near the ground. Tim seemed to be hanging on to the other side of the post. She hoped it was safe for all of them.

It started to move. Her heart flipped. *Adam.*

Shaking off the worry, she heard him grumble, "Hold on to it, Tim."

She breathed easier when it stopped moving. Turning away from the window, she picked up her phone and hit a few buttons. She listened as it rang several times until a female voice said, "Hello."

"Hi Stacey. It's Melinda."

"Hey, girl. What's going on?"

"Did you know your husband, Adam and Tim are working extra hard at my house?"

With a laugh Stacey said, "I'm sure you're getting anxious to get things back in shape."

Melinda grinned into the phone. "You know me so well, but that got me thinking."

"Do tell."

Melinda knew she'd piqued Stacey's curiosity. "What if I host a small shower for the engaged couple?"

"That sounds like a great idea, but only if you let me help."

Melinda said, "I'd like that."

Stacey asked. "Do you want to get together soon and we can pick a date, make up a guest list and food options?"

"Yeah, since the wedding is right around the corner, we shouldn't waste any time." Melinda walked over to the wall calendar. "We've got less than two months until the big day, so maybe we could target four weeks from now?"

"I'll send Molly's mom a text and see which weekend she thinks is best. Then we can make definite plans."

Melinda asked, "Do you want to meet at my place or yours?"'

"After I talk to Molly's mom, I'll give you a call, and if you want to swing by the house we can get Will to weigh in on the plans."

After agreeing, Melinda said goodbye and hung up. A sharp knock on the back door caught her attention. "Come in," she called out.

Adam popped his head in the door. "Mel, we're putting the next column up. Would you like to watch?"

She looked at the clock and then at Adam. "I do. My boss can spare me for a few more minutes." He held the door open for her and she stepped out. "Hi, guys," She was pleased to see it was coming together. "I see you're making steady progress."

Tim grinned. "Adam is a slave driver. He wants to have all the columns up before the end of the day."

Will nodded in agreement. "Yeah, that's right. He is."

Adam leaned toward Melinda. His voice warmed her cheek. "Don't listen to them." He joked, "We'll have them done by dinner or I'm bringing in flood lights for us to finish."

Melinda looked from Tim to Will and then Adam. "I think you three will spend too much time razzing each other to finish today."

Adam arched an eyebrow. "Is that a challenge?"

Melinda laughed. "We all have to work today. I need to get into the office and you all"—she pointed to each one — "need to be careful."

Adam grinned. "Ma'am, yes, ma'am." His buddies were in position to hoist the next post upright. "You heard the lady, now we work."

She felt her cheeks grow warm and his laughter followed her into the house. She traced the smile on her lips. This almost felt the same as when John's friends used to hang out at their house. Almost.

CHAPTER 11

Melinda sat on the back step soaking up the late afternoon sun. She sipped a glass of wine as she admired the seven towering columns, which were the supports for the pergola. Once the first column went up, the rest had quickly followed. Adam and the guys wrapped up a short time ago with a promise to be back in the morning to add the crossbeams. She didn't want them to work on Sunday, but both Tim and Will said they didn't mind. The pergola was going to be quite a statement. It was taking shape and would complement the backyard better than she had hoped.

She opened the folder in her hands and scanned the pages and then studied a woman's picture. She had a new match for Adam. She held the phone in her hand. She usually just emailed her clients, but something about this man was special. She really wanted to find the perfect woman for him.

He answered on the third ring. "Hi, Adam, it's Melinda."

"Mel, this is a nice surprise." He sounded genuinely happy to hear her voice.

She set the folder on the step. "What did you think of the last match I sent over?"

LUCINDA RACE

"I hate to say it, but I'd rather pass. Her facial features remind me too much of my ex."

"Well, in that case, I have good news. I found a new match for you and I wondered if you'd like to stop over and we can talk about it."

"Do you give each of your clients this personal service?" His voice held a hint of laughter.

"I don't think my clients have any complaints with my commitment to working with them." She joked, "If they did I think my referrals would go way down."

She heard him chuckle. "I just got out of the shower, so I can swing by in about fifteen minutes."

"I was going to throw a burger on the grill if you'd like to join me?" With a shake of her head, she had to wonder why that popped out of her mouth.

"I haven't eaten yet. Do you want me to bring something?"

"Sure, that'd be nice. Maybe some ice cream?"

"I'll see you in a while." He disconnected the call.

Melinda took another sip of wine as she watched two birds splashing in the birdbath at the edge of the patio. John had given it to her on their first wedding anniversary. It seemed like another lifetime. She remembered that John had told her love birds would follow her always.

She stood and leaned back, stretching her upper body, humming as she set her glass aside to uncover the grill. She pulled her bistro table and two chairs back onto the patio and then went into the kitchen to toss a salad and make burgers.

A knock on the front door caught her attention. She crossed the hall and found Adam on the step. The moment he saw her, he held a brown bag up for her to see. "I hope you like coffee."

"How did you know, it's my favorite." Melinda took the bag from his outstretched hand. "Come on in. I was just finishing up in the kitchen."

Adam followed her. "I'm curious. Did you design the kitchen

or was it like this when you bought the house?" He ran his hand over the breakfast bar. "I really like the layout."

"Thanks, I had it redone before I moved in. I'm really pleased with the way it came out. Beer or wine?" she asked.

"Beer's good."

She handed him a bottle after she twisted off the cap. She glanced around the room and smiled. "I took the smaller dining room and the original kitchen and did a complete gut." She picked up the plate of burgers and set it on a tray with the salad, plates, forks and condiments. "Will you hold the door?"

Adam set his beer on the tray. "How about I take the tray and you get the door?"

She gave him a smile. "Thank you." Melinda held open the screen and let Adam go out first. "You can set it on the table." She watched him. Other than John, she had never had dinner with a man in her home before. Melinda was surprised how natural this felt.

She opened the grill and hit the igniter button. With a soft whoosh, it came to life. "How do you like your burger?"

"Rare." He pulled out a chair and patted the back. "Have a seat. I'll cook tonight just to show you I can handle a grill."

She laughed. "Making up for the fish?"

His smile warmed his eyes. "Yes."

"While you're doing that, I can fill you in on the details of your next date." She crossed the patio and retrieved the folder under her wine glass. "Are you ready?"

Adam slipped the burgers on the hot grate. "Lay it on me."

As the burgers sizzled, Melinda sat at the table and scanned the first page again to not miss any details. "Beth is a nurse at the medical center. She likes running and does a few 5ks every year. It says she also loves playing tennis and enjoys the outdoors when she can." She looked at Adam. "How does that sound?"

He laughed. "I wonder if I can keep up with her."

With appreciation Melinda ran her eyes down his physique.

"You obviously work out, so I think the fitness component is a good match."

Adam turned his attention to the grill and flipped the burgers. "What else does she like to do?"

"Movies, primarily comedies, nothing horror or westerns."

"Well, that might be a deal killer. There's nothing like a good cowboy movie." He pushed a burger around on the grill. "Anything else?"

Melinda hesitated. She could hear a distinct undertone in Adam's voice. Unsure what it meant, she had to wonder if Beth was a good fit after all. Then she was surprised at second guessing herself again. This match felt like it had potential. "She likes to cook and prefers vacationing in Puerto Rico every winter."

"Well, the cooking thing is good, and I do like the beach, but I'm really up to going anywhere and don't like to go to the same spot twice."

Melinda handed Adam Beth's picture and waited for his reaction.

"She's pretty," he said.

"Do you want her number?"

He handed the page back to her. "Mel, I'm sorry, but I'm not sure."

Was Adam losing faith in her ability? She asked, "What do you have to lose? You have coffee. If there is a spark, ask her to lunch, and then maybe dinner."

Slowly he said, "You're right. She does sound interesting." He held out his hand. "I'll call her."

Melinda passed him a piece of paper. "Here are her details. And for what it's worth, in my opinion you need to go out with someone three times before you really know."

"Does that mean you think I need to take Susan out again?"

Melinda had to laugh when she saw a frown appear on Adam's face. "Obviously she's going to be the exception to this rule."

Adam pretended to wipe sweat from his brow. His smile crinkled his eyes. "Whew. I wouldn't want to have to suffer through that twice." He opened the cover on the grill. "How do you want your burger?"

Melinda gave him a sidelong glance. "Remember rare."

She watched as he moved the buns over the flame to give them a quick toast. She laid out the plates, silverware and tossed the salad. "Adam?"

He seemed distracted as he carefully stacked the burgers on the buns and didn't look up. "Hm?"

"Is there something you're not telling me? Something I need to know to help you find the right woman?"

His back went rigid. "What do you mean?"

"I'm not sure. It's just that, well, I'm surprised you're not more excited about meeting Beth." Melinda glanced at her pale pink nail polish. "Do you think that I can't help you meet someone?"

He turned and took a step toward her, setting the plate of burgers on the table. He ran his finger lightly down her arm. She looked up at him as a long dormant sensation slipped over her. It reminded her of how good it felt to be touched.

He said, "Absolutely not. Susan was a fluke. Some people don't take this as seriously as they should. How can you weed out all the bad apples? You're not a mind reader."

"It is my specialty to be able to cut through the BS."

Adam guided Melinda to a chair and sat down opposite from her. He moved the folder to one side. "How about we enjoy dinner?"

Melinda felt herself relax. She picked up the ketchup bottle and covered her burger. She grinned. "While we do, will you tell me what it's like to be a Marine?" She took a bite and juice ran down her chin.

With a slow shake of his head, he said, "If you don't mind, can we talk about something else?" He jabbed a forkful of salad. "It's not that interesting."

Melinda wiped her face with a napkin. "Does that mean you don't want to talk about your time in the service?"

Adam gave a shrug and, looking resigned, said, "I enlisted after I graduated from college, went in as an officer with a degree in civil engineering. My father and grandfather had both served before me." He took a sip of his beer and said, "I guess it was a part of my DNA."

"I had no idea you were an engineer." She toyed with her salad. "So why are you a handyman?"

"While on my third tour, I was on a routine mission. There was an incident. I was hospitalized. During my recovery I had a lot of time to think about what I wanted to do with the rest of my life. Building roads, tunnels and bridges just didn't hold any appeal. I wanted to be on my schedule, not someone else's."

He attacked the burger with gusto while Melinda mulled over what he said. Something didn't add up. "I thought you were a career Marine. Couldn't you go back to a different job?"

"No. They retired me."

Melinda was surprised at his matter-of-fact answer. She sensed there was a lot of emotion simmering under the surface. There was more to this story, she was sure of it. But for tonight she was going to put it aside. "So tell me, how did you meet Will?"

Adam's face visibly relaxed. "In boot camp. I'm not sure what made him decide to join, but we became fast friends. We were lucky to follow each other around for the next eight years. After our first tour he didn't re-up. He moved home. By that time we had become like brothers."

They finished their dinner over stories of Will and Adam's escapades.

Melinda laughed. "I'm surprised you two didn't get kicked out of the Marines."

With a sneaky grin, Adam said, "Nothing can happen if you don't get caught."

"So how did you end up in Chester? You could have gone anywhere after you retired."

With a shrug he said, "I don't have much family left except for Will, and now Stacey. When he heard I was getting out, he suggested I hang my hat here, permanently or until I figured out what I wanted to do next." He held up his beer. "So here I am."

Melinda took a sip of her wine. "And I'm glad you did." She looked around her backyard. "If you hadn't, I probably would never have taken the plunge with the pergola."

"I'm sure you would have, once you found the right contractor."

"No, I don't think so. I had talked to other companies, but there was something about the way you knew exactly what I had in mind."

Adam smiled. "Great minds think alike."

Melinda leaned back in her chair and smiled back. "You might be right."

CHAPTER 12

*A*dam was driving home when he realized he had forgotten the paper with Beth's phone number and email at Melinda's. He slowed and clicked on his blinker, and pulled a U-turn in the road. *Should I call Mel to let her know I'm coming back? It'll be quicker just to drop by.*

A few minutes later he parked on the street in front of her house. He was walking up the sidewalk when he heard a soft mewling sound. Taking a look around, he noticed a cardboard box next to Mel's garbage can. He waited. He heard the faint sound again. If it hadn't been quiet, he would have missed it altogether.

Moving closer, he knelt down and pulled back the flaps of the box. Sitting inside was a very tiny gray-striped kitten. By the size of it, it couldn't have been more than a few weeks old. His little eyes looked up and locked on Adam. He was shivering and cried again.

Adam reached inside and brought the kitten to his chest. "Hey buddy," he crooned, "what are you doing out here?"

The tiny bundle of fur shook in his hands. He tucked the little guy inside his shirt to warm him up. He glanced around. Was anyone lurking who might have left the box? Not seeing a soul, he walked up Mel's front steps and knocked.

The front door swung open. She greeted him with an easy smile. "Hey there. I thought you left."

Mewl. Mewl. The kitten continued to cry as he poked its head up under Adam's chin.

Adam pointed to the kitten. "I came back to get Beth's information and I found this little guy."

Taking his arm, Melinda pulled Adam into the house. "Where on earth did you find him?"

He jerked his head toward the curb. "In that box next to the garbage can."

In a carefully controlled voice, she said, "This sweet baby was left for the garbage man?"

"Yeah. He wouldn't have survived long; it's going to get cold tonight."

"I don't know anyone in the neighborhood whose cat had a litter. Someone just dumped him, like trash," Melinda said. "Go into the kitchen, I'll get a towel for you to wrap him in."

Adam did as she asked, all the while talking to the kitten, reassuring him that he was safe. Inside his blood boiled. He had zero tolerance for anyone who abandoned an animal, let alone one this vulnerable. It would have surely died if left undiscovered.

Melinda came around the corner and handed him a small towel. "Here you go."

Adam extracted the kitten from the front of his shirt. It cried as he wrapped it in the towel. "Ouch, little guy, your nails are like razors."

She chuckled. "You might as well give it up, he's attached to you now."

Adam looked at the little face and melted. "In more ways than one." He looked up. "Do you want to keep him?"

Melinda shook her head. "No. I'm not much for pets." Adam

saw a funny look cross over her face. He wondered if that was the real reason.

"Have you had pets before?"

Melinda walked behind the counter and folded a dishtowel and then set it aside. "I grew up with a cat and a dog." She smiled slightly. "But they got older and passed away. It was heartbreaking."

"It is hard. But don't you think having a pet would be nice?"

Melinda avoided the question and said, "It's obvious you've been adopted, so what are you going to call him or her?"

Adam stroked the top of the kitten's head. "I'm not sure I'm going to keep him. I've never been much of a cat person, although I do like them. I'm more of a big dog kind of guy."

Melinda grinned. "Yeah, right." She reached out and scratched under the kitty's chin. A soft purr was the response. "He's keeping you."

"I wonder when he ate last. He's too young to be away from his momma." He looked at Melinda. "Any idea what to feed him?"

"No. I'll grab my laptop and we can look it up." Melinda walked to her office. Adam settled down on a barstool and stroked the tiny puffball.

"Here we go." Melinda came back into the room, her laptop open and the screen glowing. She placed it on the counter and clicked a few keys opening an internet search window. "Okay, it says here the kitten needs to see a veterinarian. Since that isn't practical at the moment, he needs to be fed every two to three hours."

"I'll warm up some milk and get an appointment tomorrow."

Melinda held up a hand. "Not so fast. According to what it says here, cow's milk can make him sick. We need to mix up a kitten formula." She scanned the page and turned it around for Adam. "I have the ingredients for the last one."

She moved around the kitchen with ease. Once she had the

ingredients on the counter, she shook everything together and popped a cup of milky kitten formula in the microwave.

Confused, Adam asked, "What's that for? Are you making a cup of coffee?"

"Do you think I'd stop to make myself something when there is a tiny baby in need of our help?" she teased.

"Well, no."

She frowned.

"What's wrong?"

"I don't have an eyedropper."

Adam looked around her kitchen. "Do you have a tiny spoon? I can use that to dribble the liquid into his mouth." He gently detached the kitten from his shirt and set him on the towel on the counter.

She dug into a drawer and held up a measuring spoon.

"That will work." He dipped the spoon into the mixture and held it up to the kitten, who cried. Adam tried to insert the spoon into his mouth, but the liquid dribbled down his fur and onto the towel. He then dipped his finger in. Time after time he continued to encourage the kitten to eat. His patience was rewarded when he saw the tiny pink tongue poke out and lick the droplets of Mel's mixture.

His eyes grew wide. "Look, he's eating." He set the kitten down in front of the saucer and he eyed it. Adam dabbed his finger in and held it out for the kitten. "We did it."

Her smile grew as the kitten began to lap up his special 'milk' from the saucer.

Adam's grin filled his face. "I'm going to let him drink all he wants."

The kitten stopped lapping at the milk and picked his way across the towel. Adam set him on the floor. "Look at that, a little bit of food and he's ready to roll." He couldn't begin to explain the feelings he had watching the fur ball totter around Melinda's kitchen.

"You still haven't said what his name will be."

"That depends on if he's a boy or girl." He glanced at Mel. "Any idea how you can tell?"

She snickered. "Turn him upside down and look."

Adam gently picked up the kitten and turned him stomach side up. Out of the corner of his eye he could see Mel was shaking with suppressed laughter.

He turned him over and set him down again. "I've got no clue, but I'm calling him Skye."

"I knew it. You're keeping him." Melinda's eyebrow arched.

Adam grinned. "Yes, I guess I am."

"Why Skye?"

"He makes me smile and all I can think of is an old song my grandmother used to sing."

Melinda touched his arm. "I haven't seen you smile like you are right now."

Adam turned his head away from her. It wasn't something he could explain. For the first time in a long time, Adam had a purpose. Another living being was depending on him.

He cleared his throat. "I think we're going to head home so you can have your evening back."

"This was fun." She scooped Skye up. "You know, I was just thinking...you're going to need supplies. If you want, leave Skye with me and you can run to the grocery store. You should be able to get everything you'll need until you can get him checked out."

"You wouldn't mind?" Adam hesitated. It would make it easier than tucking the kitten in his shirt. "That'd be great. Thanks Mel." He dropped a kiss on his head and said, "You be good for Mel. I'll be back very soon, and then we'll go home."

Mel chuckled. "Go, he'll be fine." She pushed him to the door.

"You're sure?" He looked over his shoulder. "Maybe I should just take him now."

"Trust me it will be easier for both of you. Stop worrying."

Melinda's laughter followed him down the path as he hurried toward his truck.

On the drive he thought about how he and Mel made a good team taking care of Skye. He wondered why she didn't want to keep him, she was good with him and somehow that didn't jive with not being a pet person. Skye would have been good company for her too.

Adam made the trip in record time, getting everything he could think the kitten might need in addition to a few toys and treats too. He parked the truck in Melinda's driveway and hurried up the walk. He pushed open the front door. "Mel?"

"In the living room."

He discovered Melinda cuddling the sleeping kitten in her lap. She looked up through her lashes and said, "Someone was exhausted after all that exploring and conked out."

Adam smiled. From the looks of things, Mel was a cat person after all. He sat on the cushioned footrest and stroked Skye's little paws. "Thanks for taking care of him."

"Did you get everything you needed?"

He nodded. "And then some."

"Just what I expected." She picked Skye up and passed him to Adam's waiting hands. "Here you go."

Adam held the kitten close. Skye started to purr as they walked toward the door. Melinda opened it for him and handed him a jar. "Here's the leftover kitten formula. Store it in the fridge and shake before giving it to him."

He looked at her and said, "Thanks for your help tonight." Something was different about Mel, he just couldn't put his finger on it. "All right, see you tomorrow."

Adam was halfway to his truck when Melinda called after him, "Adam, aren't you forgetting something?"

He stopped and thought for a moment. "Oh, right. Beth's information." He held up Skye. "I got sidetracked."

"Hold on, I'll get it for you."

Adam waited in the driveway while she ran back into the house and skipped down the steps. She handed him a slip of paper. "Here you go. Email and phone number."

He tucked the paper in his pants pocket. "I'll call you tomorrow after I get back from the vet's."

"You'd better," she teased. "He's my first official rescue."

Keeping his eyes on her face, he said, "We made one helluva team tonight."

Her smile warmed his heart. "We sure did."

He got into the truck and made sure Skye was safely tucked into his jacket on the passenger seat. He looked out the windshield and gave Mel a wave.

It was too bad it wasn't her name on the paper in his pocket. She sure was a great lady. Adam dropped the truck in reverse and slowly drove home.

CHAPTER 13

*A*dam woke to the sound of purring and the sting of tiny pinpricks on his chest. He opened his eyes to see Skye perched on him, kneading his T-shirt. The little kitten's eyes were mere slits and he wore the look of pure kitty contentment.

"Hey, buddy. How did you climb up here?" Adam absentmindedly stroked Skye's head. "Last I saw you were a tight ball in your bed."

He swung his legs over the edge of the bed and went through the process of attaching his prosthetic leg. "Are you ready for some breakfast?" Upon standing, he set Skye on the wood floor and watched as the kitten skittered out of the bedroom and into the living room. With a chuckle, he said, "Good to see you've got energy to burn."

He picked up his phone to check messages and saw a text from Melinda and smiled. *How was Skye's night?*

He typed in *All's well here,* and hit send.

He started a pot of coffee and pulled up the internet looking for a veterinarian and then stopped. He could ask Will. They had cats and dogs running around their house. He hit speed dial and waited, grinning as Skye pounced the rays of sun on the floor.

Will answered, "Hey, bud, what's up?"

"Morning. I was wondering if you'd give me the name of your vet."

"Sure, are you thinking of adopting?"

With a low chuckle Adam said, "It seems a kitten has adopted me." He went on to explain about his evening and how it was his only choice to bring the kitten home.

"That is great news!"

Adam was a bit taken aback by his friend's enthusiasm. "That is not the reaction I expected."

Will laughed. "I didn't mean anything other than it'll be good for both of you, the fluff ball for being rescued and you to have company."

"I guess this means you don't care I have a pet in the apartment?" Adam dangled a ball on a string for Skye. He was surprised at how light his heart was as he watched the little guy get tuckered out from his gymnastics routine.

"Not at all. I'll text you the number. Hopefully you can get in today and get him checked out."

"Sounds good. Let Stacey know about Skye and tell her to stop over tonight. He's mighty cute."

"Will do. See ya." Will disconnected and Adam set the phone aside.

"Time for breakfast, buddy." He scooped up the kitten and carried him into the kitchen.

~

Melinda smiled as she read the text from Adam, thrilled that all was going well. Checking her schedule, she saw she had four new clients today. The first would arrive in ten minutes and she needed to be in her office ready and waiting.

The doorbell rang and Melinda rose to answer it. Her heart caught in her throat as she opened the door. She put her hand on the casing to steady herself. For a brief second, the man standing before her seemed to be the spitting image of her John. He had the same dark olive complexion, ebony hair and deep brown eyes that were almost black. But they lacked the familiar warmth John had when he'd look at her.

"Ms. Phillips, are you all right? You look like you've seen a ghost."

Melinda blinked again to discover his nose was a tad longer, his face more angular with higher cheekbones and his eyes had flecks of amber in them.

"I'm sorry. Come in. For a moment you looked like someone I used to know."

He held out his hand to her. "I'm Nicholas Taylor. We have an appointment at nine. Would you prefer to reschedule?"

Melinda moved to the side and said, "Not at all. Please come in."

The moment he stepped into her office he filled the room with his presence. Memories of John washed over her. She gestured to the sofa. "Would you like a cup of coffee or water?"

"Coffee—black would be nice. Thank you. I just got off work and the caffeine would do me good."

Melinda crossed to the side table where she had a coffeemaker. She busied herself with pouring him a mug, willing her hands to be steady. "Just black, you said?" Her voice cracked.

"Ms. Phillips, are you sure you're feeling okay? We can postpone if you'd like."

With a shake of her head she said, "I'm fine, really." She gave him a weak smile and silently admonished herself to get it together. She was a professional. She handed him the mug and sat in her chair across from him. She took out a pad and pen. "Now then, Dr. Taylor."

"Please call me Nick. After all, I'm about to share my heart's desire for a partner. I think being on a first name basis is friendlier." He shifted the coffee cup to his left hand and smiled. "So how do we do this? Do I just tell you everything I'm looking for in a woman and you ask questions in case I've missed something?"

She leaned back in her chair and took a deep, calming breath. "Nothing that rigid." She forced a smile. "Did you bring a copy of the questionnaire I sent to you?

He reached into his sport coat pocket and withdrew a folded paper. He handed it to Melinda.

"Thank you." She scanned the contents and continued, "I have a few follow-up questions and then the balance of our time will be more conversational." She smiled, regaining her composure. "I find it best if you say the first thing that pops into your head. From there I'll get a good picture of who you are, and then we'll move forward."

Nick leaned back against the sofa cushion and crossed one long, lean leg over his knee, showing off perfectly shined shoes.

Melinda glanced down at her printed paper. "I saw from your email that you're a doctor and have lived in the area for about two years." She looked up and he nodded over his coffee mug.

"That's right. In fact, I work in the ER. I just got off before I came here." He yawned. "It was a busy night."

"So tell me, what brings you to a matchmaking service such as It's Just Coffee?"

"To be honest, I've tried a few online dating services with little success. I'm tired of meeting the wrong kind of women. I want to find someone who shares some of my interests and will be open to new adventures we can discover together, but while still respecting that we are individuals." He smiled. "You know, a healthy balance."

Melinda jotted down a few notes. "Are you looking for someone in the medical profession?"

"Actually no. I'd like to leave work at work as much as I can, but someone who takes their career seriously would be a plus.

Someday I'd like to have a family." He smiled broadly. "I love kids."

Melinda relaxed. She could think of several women already who would meet that criteria. She asked, "What are some of your hobbies?"

"I enjoy travel both in the US and internationally."

Melinda glanced down and then at Nick. "A particular destination in mind? The beach, mountains?"

He grinned. "I have a huge bucket list of places I'd like to visit: Europe, a safari or maybe even an exotic beach or two. I like to enjoy life and I have the financial means to do so." He clasped his hands. "I hope that doesn't sound arrogant. I'm just stating facts."

She shook her head. "I didn't take it that way." She gave Nick her best professional smile. "The more facts I have, the easier it will be to match you with the right woman." Internally she choked a bit on what she had just said. It did sound like Nick was trying to impress her, not that gobs of money ever did. "Tell me a bit more. Do you enjoy hiking, biking and the theatre?"

"Concerts are fun, and I enjoy sailing. And I love old movies —classic screwball comedy and westerns."

Melinda could feel Nick watching her as she glanced at the papers in her hands. Casually he asked, "So, what do you do in your spare time?"

She laughed as she nervously clicked the cap on her pen. It was a habit she did when she was uncomfortable, and thankful no one knew that about her. "Nick, we should stay focused on you." She laid the papers in her lap. "I see you don't have any objections to dating someone with children."

"I'm open to it. It will be more about my connection with the lady, and I truly feel the rest will just fall into place." He leaned forward his arms resting on his legs. "Do you have children?"

"Um, no. I don't." She stood up quickly, the papers sliding to the floor. "I think I have all I need for the moment. I'll enter your information in the database and email you with my results. I'll be sending your information to select women too. You may hear directly from a match."

Nick picked up the papers and handed them back to her. He took Melinda's hand in his and shook it, holding it for a moment longer than necessary before releasing it. "I'll look forward to hearing from you." He opened the door and paused on the threshold. "It was a pleasure meeting you."

He closed the door firmly behind him. Melinda waited until she figured he was in his car before sagging into her office chair. *Well, that was interesting. If I had passed him on the street I would have mistaken him for John.* A familiar ache flooded her heart. Would the hurt ever really fade?

She got up and refilled her coffee, then printed off the paperwork for the next three clients. After checking the time, she had a few minutes to enter Nick's information in the computer. She ran a search on her database and let the computer do the work for her. Then she could review the results and add her special touch.

As she waited, her thoughts drifted back to John. It was wonderful to have someone to plan a vacation with or even talk about the potential for a family. She blinked hard. How could meeting Nick get her thinking about things that were a part of her past? A family and partner were ripped away when John died.

Her thoughts slid to Adam. There was a great guy. If only…

A sharp knock on the door interrupted her train of thought. She opened the door. Her next client was standing on the step. "Gretchen. Come in."

A tall, attractive redhead entered, impeccably dressed. The edges of her lips curved into a slow smile. "Hello, Melinda. I'm pleased you agreed to take me on as a client. Your reputation precedes you." Her words came out in a soft rush, revealing the smattering of nerves she must be feeling.

Melinda gestured towards the sofa. "Let's get started."

With a musical laugh she said, "Well, it just so happens,

while I was waiting in my car I saw a very handsome man leave your office. Is he a client?"

Without answering her question directly, Melinda smiled. "Let's begin and see what we can do about finding a match for you."

CHAPTER 14

Melinda looked up from her computer as she heard a car door slam. She didn't have any more appointments today. Her front bell rang and she closed down her computer, calling, "Coming," as she hurried from her office to the front hallway.

She was pleasantly surprised to discover Adam standing on her step, looking almost the same as he did last night, cradling the kitten to his chest.

She pushed back her bangs and opened the door. "Hey, stranger. I wasn't expecting to see you today."

Adam stepped into the foyer and held up Skye. "I thought you might like to hear how we made out at our first doctor visit."

Melinda wondered briefly if it was an excuse for Adam to stop by. If it was, she was glad for the visit. "Come on in. I was just going to make a fresh pot of coffee. Would you care for a cup?"

"Yes, please."

Melinda glanced at Skye. "You can put him down."

Adam wrinkled his nose. "I don't want him to have an accident in your house."

"I have paper towels and cleanser." She smiled. "I'm also going to set out a bowl of water for the fur ball." True to her word, Melinda took a shallow dish from the cupboard, filled it with water and set it on the floor. She clinked the side of the dish to draw Skye's attention to it.

Skye did a sideways hop and raced to the dish. His antics made Melinda and Adam chuckle.

"Don't keep me in suspense," she prodded, "what did the vet say about him?"

"Well, the first thing, Skye is a girl."

Her lips twitched. "Good thing the name fits a girl or boy."

Adam nodded. "I know. And we guessed pretty close on her age—she's around five weeks. Overall, considering everything, she's healthy." Adam took the coffee mug Melinda handed him.

"Does this mean regular food instead of the stuff we whipped up last night?"

Adam blew on his coffee. "It does."

Melinda cocked her head and studied him. "You're still going to keep her, right?"

"Absolutely. This morning when I told Will, he said the company would be good for me."

Melinda smiled. "He's right. We all have a basic desire to feel needed."

Looking at her over the rim of the mug, he asked, "Even you?"

Adam's simple question struck a chord with Melinda. "Of course. That is one of the main reasons why I love matchmaking. The people I work with find love. It makes me happy to help others find it."

Quietly, he asked, "Don't you want love too?"

Melinda contemplated how she should answer his question, evade or be honest and talk about John.

Adam reached out and lightly touched her arm. "I'm sorry if I am getting too personal. I feel like we have more than just a business relationship."

"No. It's okay. You're right." She laid her hand on his. "We are friends."

"If you don't want to talk about your personal life, you don't have to."

She sat on the stool next to Adam and measured her words carefully. "I had a great love. My husband, John."

"You don't like to talk about him?"

Thoughtfully, she said, "I don't mind sharing my past with you. But please"—her voice quivered—"keep whatever I say between us. I don't want anyone to feel sorry for me."

Adam gave her a knowing look. "I understand. You have my word."

She leaned back on the stool and watched Skye flop to the floor, rolling around playing with her tail. "I met John when we were in high school. It was love at first sight for him. He was some superstar jock and I was a nerdy girl who loved books. But he was persistent. He wanted us to be friends and then we ended up at the same college." She smiled. "That was when we started dating, junior year. He went to a state university to be with me. He had other options. We were together through undergrad. Once we became a couple I knew we'd end up married to each other. I couldn't ever see myself with anyone else."

She swallowed the lump rising in her throat. "We weren't in a rush to get married, we had all the time in the world. After college he went to the police academy and I got my doctorate in psychology. He always wanted to be in law enforcement." She looked at Adam. "I get the feeling you felt about the Marines like he felt about police work."

"He sounds like a good man."

"He was." She got up, grabbed the cookie jar, handed it to Adam and then sat down. "We got married and had three wonderful years together. We talked about having kids, but again, we felt there was plenty of time." A lone tear clung to her bottom lashes. "Turns out we were wrong."

THE MATCHMAKER AND THE MARINE

Gently Adam asked, "What happened?"

"He was on patrol. There was a car broken down on the side of the highway and he stopped to provide assistance." She looked away. Her voice broke. "John never knew what happened. He was struck by a drunk driver."

Adam stretched his hand and took hers. Giving it a squeeze, he said, "Melinda, I am truly sorry."

She pulled her hand away and wiped away the tear as it slid down her cheek. "That was four years ago."

"It still feels like it just happened, doesn't it?" Adam stated.

With a small nod, Melinda said, "I miss him every day, but we shared a lifetime of love in twelve short years." She looked up, her heart full of memories, and smiled through the tears that slid down her cheeks, her eyes bright. "I wouldn't trade what we had for anything."

He wiped away her tears from her cheeks with his fingers.

"To cry in my soup would be to tarnish the memories. John wouldn't want me to continue to grieve."

Adam arched a brow. "Then I don't understand." He looked at the gold band on her hand.

She knew what he was asking without saying a word. "The stars aligned when I met John. I couldn't settle for less than what we had and what if I lost him too. I couldn't live through that again, I just couldn't bear it. Instead, I can help others find it. It seems to be the greatest gift John left me. Each couple that finds their happily ever after is like a part of me and John live on."

She didn't know why she let so much spill out, but Adam was easy to talk to. "I'm sure that makes zero sense to you."

"I understand what you mean. You have tucked yourself away so you wouldn't have to open yourself up to losing someone you love again." He grazed her hand with his. "You're short changing yourself and some guy who would be lucky enough to have you in his life."

Melinda blinked away what was left of her tears. Was he

insinuating she was hiding as part of some self-preservation thing?

Before she could speak, Adam shrugged. "Trust me, I know what it's like to do things out of self-preservation."

It was as if he was reading her mind. She studied him. "What are *you* hiding, Adam?"

Color flushed his neck and face.

"I can tell you're protecting a part of yourself."

Adam stood up. His eyes were filled with something Melinda thought was a mix of anger, sorrow and regret. "For now, let's just say we both carry scars from our past." He scooped up Skye and turned toward the door. "I need to get Skye home. She's had a busy day. See you later, Mel."

"Adam, wait!" she cried. "Don't leave angry."

He paused mid-step. "I'm not." He gave her a half smile. "Really."

Melinda watched as Adam walked out without a backward look. She leaned against the closed door. Suddenly the house felt empty and she was alone. Adam was right about one thing. Her decision to remain the single matchmaker really was an excuse to protect herself from any further pain. How on earth did he penetrate her carefully crafted shell?

∼

Adam took his time driving home. His heart was heavy. Mel had endured so much loss at a young age. Losing the person you love couldn't be easy. They had both suffered a significant loss due to a horrific, random act. He'd lost a physical part of himself, and Mel's heart had been shattered.

He pulled up behind the garage and turned off the truck. His cell phone pinged. He looked at the screen. It was a text message from Beth, his most recent match. He dropped the phone in his shirt pocket and picked up Skye. He would contact her later. Right now, he needed to call Mel. He should have told her when he was at her place that he'd be back to work on the pergola tomorrow, weather permitting of course. The last thing he wanted to do was have her think he was walking off the job after leaving her place in a black mood.

After climbing the stairs and feeding Skye, he pulled out his phone. Should he text or call? "A coward would send a text."

He dialed the phone and it seemed like forever until he heard her say, "Hello."

"Hi, Mel."

"Hi." He could hear the surprise in her voice.

"I wanted to let you know I'll be over tomorrow, as long as it doesn't rain."

"Adam..." She hesitated. "I'm sorry I upset you."

He sighed. "No, it's not you. I've got a few things that I've been dealing with. I apologize, Mel."

He heard her say softly, "I guess we're both a bit tender from things. Still friends?"

"Absolutely."

"That's good, because I really don't have a lot of friends in town."

He kept the shock from his voice. "What are you talking about? Everyone loves you."

She laughed. "If you say so." Changing the subject, she asked, "Did you contact Beth yet?"

"No, but she sent me a text. I'll touch base with her later." He smiled into the phone. "Don't worry, I'll give you the four-one-one tomorrow."

"Sounds like a plan. Have a good night and see you in the morning." Melinda disconnected, and Adam wondered what had just happened. Did Mel admit that she really did feel isolated in a town where people respected and genuinely liked her?

Before he could overthink anything, he called Beth. She answered on the first ring.

"Hello, Beth. This is Adam Bell."

"Hello, Adam." He liked the sound of her voice. Warm and friendly, a nice combination.

"I was wondering if you'd like to meet for coffee on Saturday or Sunday?"

"That would be nice. I was impressed with the information Melinda Phillips sent me. You are a Marine? Thank you for your service."

He was pleasantly surprised she used the present tense. Always humbled when someone said that, he said, "It was my honor."

"I could meet you on Sunday. Say two?"

Adam didn't hesitate. "Two is fine. Do you want to meet at the coffee shop downtown?"

"I have a better idea. I'll bring a thermos of coffee and we could meet at the beach. Weather permitting, of course." She continued, "The forecast doesn't look that promising for the balance of the week, and if we don't get a break I'll call you to make a different plan."

"Let's meet on the bench at the end of Shore Line Drive. Do you know where that is?"

Beth said, "I do. I'm looking forward to it."

Adam said goodbye and disconnected. He had just made a coffee date with one woman, but a very pretty matchmaker dominated his thoughts instead. Before he could change his mind, he dialed.

"Hey, Mel, I know I just left your place but do you want to grab ice cream? I was thinking maybe you could coach me on first date conversation." Inwardly he groaned—now that was lame, and he hadn't even let her say hi.

A soft chuckle answered him. "Hello to you too."

"Sorry, I just got off the phone with Beth. We have a date Sunday and I'd like to make a good impression so I thought maybe we could go out and have ice cream. Sort of a practice run."

"That sounds like fun. Give me twenty minutes and I'll meet you at the diner?"

"No, I'll swing by and pick you up. No reason to take two cars."

"See you soon." The phone softly clicked. He was shocked at his own impulsiveness. He was taking Mel for ice cream. He grinned and scooped up Skye.

"You be good and I'll be back soon." He gently set her on the back of the sofa and picked up his keys from the coffee table. He'd stop in and chatted with Will and Stacey before heading over to Mel's place.

~

Melinda ran a brush through her long waves. She leaned toward the mirror and checked to make sure her mascara wasn't smudged. She brushed her teeth, swished some mouthwash. What had possessed her to agree to go with Adam? Well, it didn't really matter now because he would be here in a few minutes. This was the second time he had asked her to do something with him on the spur of the moment.

Her nerves jumped when she heard the doorbell chime. On her way down the hall, she grabbed a light cardigan sweater and her brown leather bag from the living room chair.

She grinned as she opened the door. "Hello there."

Adam met her eyes and smiled back. "Hi yourself."

"This is a great idea. I can't remember the last time I did this."

His smile brightened. "Did what?"

"Got picked up for ice cream." She stopped short of saying the word *date*.

"Then it's long overdue." After a grand sweep of his arm, he walked with her to his truck. "Shall we?"

She stepped onto the running board of the silver Ford pickup and slid across the leather seat. This felt like a date. How could she make it clear why she had said yes?

She waited for Adam to buckle up and start the truck. Deciding to jump right in, she said, "I was surprised when you said you wanted to have a dry run for your date with Beth."

He drove carefully as the night went from dusk to deeper shadows. "I've been thinking about my date with Susan, and maybe I played a part in the date falling flat. I didn't want to repeat the same mistake, especially when you're trying so hard to find a good match for me."

Surprised she felt a tinge of jealousy, Mel said, "So give me your opening line."

He tipped his head from side to side. "I'll say it's nice to meet her."

"And then?"

He laughed, "I have no idea." He slowed the truck as they approached a roadside ice cream stand. "Do you like soft serve?"

"It's like you read my mind. I think there is a place just up the road."

The truck picked up speed as he drove past. "Good. That place serves hard ice cream."

"The Dairy Barn has soft serve and the chocolate dip too."

"Tell me, vanilla, chocolate or twist?"

She relaxed and leaned back into the seat and said, "Mmm, twist, dipped. There is nothing like it. Heaven on earth."

He shook his head. "Vanilla dipped in cherry."

She said, "Nope. If you're going with a vanilla cone, the coating has to be chocolate."

He held up a hand in mock surrender. "I give! I'll try it your way." He flashed her a wide smile. "We'll be twinning it."

He slowed the truck and flicked on the blinker. Coming to a stop in the busy parking lot away from a bunch of small kids playing tag. They strolled through toward the takeout window in the cool evening breeze. Melinda pulled her cardigan closed.

Waiting in line to order, she watched as a mother smoothly

steered her children, who were balancing small cones, around other patrons. A stab of longing washed over her. Wistfully she thought, *If only John and I had had more time.*

Adam touched her elbow. "Mel, ready to order?"

She gave the girl on the other side of the window her order and handed her a ten. "I'll pay for his too." She flipped her head toward Adam standing right behind her. "He'll have the same."

Taking the change Mel dropped the coins and a bill in the tip jar and then handed the first cone to Adam. "Here you go."

He looked a little confused when she turned with another cone in her hand. "You didn't need to pay for mine."

She gave a one-shoulder shrug. "You drove, so we're even."

Licking the first drip that landed on her hand, she wished she had asked for a bowl to lay them in. Glancing at the long line of patrons, she knew that ship had sailed.

He pointed to a bench on the edge of the parking lot. "Let's sit over there."

They crossed the pavement as a man approached them from the opposite side off the lot. He held up a hand in greeting to Adam as he walked purposefully toward them.

"Hey, Adam. I'm not sure if you remember me, but we talked a couple weeks back at the hardware store."

"Hi, Scott, how's it going?" He half-turned to Melinda. "This is my friend Melinda."

Scott smiled and reached out his hand to her. "Nice to meet you."

"Hi, Scott."

Adam said, "So what's going on?"

"Remember the gazebo we were talking about? Well, I hate to interrupt your evening, but could you take a quick look at the overall measurements and let me know if you think I've gone too big. I've got the plans in my van."

Mel noticed a van lettered with *ELECTRICIAN* in bold letters.

Adam hesitated. "Mel, do you mind?"

She stood up. "Do you mind if I take a look too?"

"Not at all," Scott said.

After they walked across the parking lot, Scott pulled the plans from his passenger seat. He handed them to Adam, who looked at Mel and asked, "Would you hold my cone?"

"Yeah, sure." She made sure to have an extra napkin ready when Adam passed it over.

He studied the plans, pointing out a couple of areas for change that would make the roof have a better pitch for snow in the winter.

Melinda felt the cool drip of his ice cream on her hand. And then another. Adam was totally absorbed in his conversation.

Should she let it just drip all over or... after giving it a thought, she brought the cone to her mouth. She licked the melting ice cream. She looked up through her lashes to see Adam's eyes open wide. With a sheepish grin, she said, "Sorry." She gingerly held out the cone to him.

He handed Scott the plans and without hesitation took a big bite out of his cone. "Good stuff, right, Mel?"

She gave him a shy smile. "Right down to the last drip."

CHAPTER 15

The next day Melinda was at her desk chuckling over the impromptu ice cream get together with Adam. He had been so comical, practicing his opening line with her. She kept reminding him to relax and be himself. That was all he needed to do. He was a fun guy to hang out with; she could see how a girl would be smitten with him, if he would just be Adam.

She checked her email and was pleased to see she'd received a message from Beth. Scanning the contents, Beth had said the plan was to meet Adam for coffee at the ocean overlook on Sunday. Melinda made a note in her calendar to follow up with Beth on Monday. She had been very careful this time and re-interviewed Beth. She certainly didn't want Adam to go through another lackluster first date.

She picked up a paperclip and toyed with it. She had to wonder what would Beth think when she met Adam in person. He was very handsome, a touch formal until he got to know you, and then he was utterly charming. At least that is how she saw him. Hopefully Beth would as well.

The sound of the electric saw distracted her. She glanced out a small office window. Adam was whistling as he worked. She returned to her chair and leaned back. It struck her as odd; why was she so invested in getting it just right for Adam? Yes, he was a client, but it was more than that. They had spent quite a bit of time together and had become good friends. This was the first time a personal friend was using her service.

She set the paperclip aside. That was all it was, they had become friends. She didn't need to overanalyze everything.

Satisfied they were on the right track, she turned her attention to Nick and Gretchen. She was disappointed to see that other than a match based on physical attributes and the desire to discover new things, they didn't have much in common. But Melinda had a hunch they might find discovering new things to do together would be a strong motivator.

She drafted an email to Nick, since he was the most particular of the pair.

Nick,

Enclosed please find a bio and contact information for Gretchen. I feel there is a strong potential for a connection. Please take a look and let me know what you think. If you'd like to pass, I have a couple of other matches to send to you.

All the best,

Melinda Phillips

It's Just Coffee

She read it over and clicked send. She made the decision to not contact Gretchen. Melinda knew that she'd flock to Nick like a bee to honeysuckle.

The steady sounds of carpentry drifted in through the open window. Curious what was going on, Melinda pushed her chair back and went to look. Adam was loading small pieces of wood in a wheelbarrow. She could hear him singing a Motley Crue song, *Home Sweet Home,* loud and clear. He had a remarkably good voice.

She called out, "Can I interest you in something cold to drink?"

Adam flushed a very attractive shade of red. "How long have you been standing there?"

She could hear the teasing in his voice. She laughed, "Long enough to know you have a great set of pipes."

Ignoring the compliment, he said, "Lemonade would be great, if you've got some made. Plain water has gotten boring."

She smirked. "Your wish will be granted, oh master of carpentry."

She sauntered into the kitchen and stirred up a fresh pitcher of lemon juice, ice and water. She poured two large glasses filled with lemon slices and a sprig of mint.

Adam appeared as she kicked the door open with her foot. Holding the screen for her he asked, "Did you just whip that up?" His smile warmed his eyes.

Melinda was pleased to see they still had that easy banter between them. "I had everything ready, so I just needed to give it a stir." She handed him a glass as they crossed the grass to a couple of Adirondack chairs. She was admiring his handiwork. "The pergola looks amazing."

Adam's eyes followed her gaze. "We should add something to the back corner, maybe lattice. You'll have no privacy in the fall when the leaves come down."

Melinda's smile dipped. "I really don't like the look of lattice. I prefer climbing vines. Remember, I want to plant grapes."

"I do, but they will take a few years to get established." He paused.

She was surprised that she knew that look on his face: his wheels were turning.

"What if I drew something up to illustrate what I have in mind? If you don't like it, no harm. If you do, I can get it done in a couple of days."

"Well, I don't know…"

Casually, he tossed out, "I've got time."

"Adam, I'm sure you have other clients and I don't want to hold you up." She wouldn't admit she looked forward to seeing his smiling face every day.

He held up his hand. "Mel, I was just"—his voice trailed off, he did a rewind motion, which made her grin. "Let's try this again."

She exhaled and smiled.

He touched her shoulder to draw her attention to the back of the yard. "So, we might be able to do something, besides lattice, in the back corner. Would you like for me to draw up a rough draft?"

"Absolutely." She took a long drink of lemonade and smacked her lips. "Wow, that is tart! I forgot the sugar!"

Adam's glass was half empty.

"How could you drink it?" she asked, laughing.

"Are you kidding? It's perfect." He grinned. "Tart, just like you."

She could feel a flush rise in her cheeks. Eager to change the subject from this mild flirtation she said, "Well, since I'm the nosy one"— she grinned — "tell me about Sunday?"

"So you heard." He shifted uncomfortably in the chair.

"I did, and it is good news."

He shrugged. "When I called Beth and asked her for coffee, I suggested the diner and she suggested the beach." He drained his glass and set it on the small table between them. "That's about it."

"Are you still looking forward to meeting her?"

Slowly, he nodded. "Sure I am." He turned abruptly. "I'm just about done here for now, so I'm going to head home and get those drawings for you.

Melinda was enjoying the way the filtered sun danced over the patio and the company. "You're rushing off already?" *What are you doing? It sounds like you're asking him to stay.*

"I'm going to check on Skye; it's her first day alone. I want to make sure she's not getting into too much trouble."

"You're a real softie, aren't you?"

"Only when it comes to animals, kids and nice people." He picked up Mel's glass. "I'll set these in the kitchen on my way out and be back after lunch."

Masking her disappointment, she said, "I'll be here." Melinda leaned back in her chair. "I'm going to sit right here, soak up the sun and enjoy my new pergola."

Adam tugged a stray lock of her hair. She glanced up and her eyes met his. A long-forgotten sensation drifted through her.

He mumbled something that sounded like goodbye, and hurried into the house. Moments later, Melinda heard his truck roar down the street. She wondered what the heck that was all about, and why did she get a flock of butterflies dancing inside when his fingers grazed her hair?

~

*D*uring the short drive back to his place, Adam's thoughts raced. What had he been thinking, letting his fingers have a mind of their own just to satisfy his curiosity? Her hair was as silky soft as it looked.

Melinda was his friend. But he was slowly recognizing his feelings for her were more complex. There was a connection that seemed to be growing stronger each time he was with her. He pulled into his driveway and sat. What was he going to do about it?

Stacey's car pulled in next to him. She got out and waved. "Hey, Adam."

He looked at her. "Hi, Stace." He pushed open the truck door. "Any chance you have a couple of minutes?"

She closed her car door. "For you? Of course. Let's sit out back."

He followed her around the side of the garage. Stacey dropped her bag on the table and pulled a couple of deck chairs into the sun. Sitting down, she stretched her legs out, closed her eyes and tilted her face toward the sun. "Pure heaven."

"Busy day at the office?" he asked.

"Our other dental hygienist is on vacation this week, so I'm booked solid. I was on the run from the minute I got there this morning. Thank heavens it was only a half day today." Without looking at Adam, she asked, "What's on your mind?"

Adam perched on the edge of the chair. "What do you know about Melinda?"

"She's a great matchmaker and a very nice person." Stacey opened one eye and looked at Adam. "Why?"

He clasped his hands together. Making a quick decision, he said, "My first match turned out to be a bust."

"Did you expect lightening to strike the first time?" Stacey asked lightly.

He thought for a moment. That was what it had felt like when he met Melinda. Electric. "No. I guess not." He leaned back in the chair. "I have another coffee date on Sunday and I was wondering if you and Will could drive by. What if she turns out to be as bad as the last one, I could use a wingman or two. We're meeting at the overlook at the end of Shore Line Drive."

"Why did you agree to meet there instead of someplace with more people?"

"She suggested it, and in the spur of the moment it didn't seem like a bad idea, but now I'm having second thoughts. It'd be better to have an out." He looked at Stacey. "I know planning for it to be a flop isn't the best way to start things."

She gave him a warm smile. "I did the same when Will and I met for the first time. We were at the luncheonette and I had Molly stop in on the ruse of picking up a takeout order."

"Will never told me that."

Stacey laughed. "I think he had a back-up plan too. I saw him wave to Mike, who had walked in for a to-go order." She grinned. "I think that's when I knew he was the guy for me."

"That's all it took?"

"We thought alike. We still do."

"He never told me about Mike."

Stacey gave Adam a sly smile. "I'm sure Will doesn't realize how I know what he's thinking pretty much all the time. Or if he does, it's not something he'll admit."

He stood up. "Thanks, Stacey. I'll let you know after I confirm with Beth. It's tentatively at two."

"Hey, give the process a chance and let Melinda work her magic. She really is one in a million."

The image of her face made him smile inside. "Yes, she is."

"Is there something you're not telling me?"

"Why do you ask?"

"It's just that when you talk about Melinda, you seem to smile a lot more. Is there something going on between the two of you?" Stacey sat up in her chair.

"We're just friends." Adam felt like he was a kid fibbing about a girl at school he had a crush on. Oh jeez, did he have a crush on Mel? "I need to go upstairs and check on Skye."

"Be careful, Adam. I wouldn't want you to get hurt."

"Not to worry." Adam gave her a smile while his heart gave a quick thud in his chest. "Catch you later."

~

Mel continued to enjoy sitting on her patio. She closed her eyes and let her mind wander to Adam. Spending time with him made her think and feel things that she had considered long dormant. Images in her mind invariably turned to John. Loving and living with him for all those years were a gift. He had been her best friend, confidante and biggest cheerleader. When she'd struggled with her dissertation, he had made pots of coffee and read every page. When she had received her doctorate, he took her to the swankiest restaurant in Philadelphia and they spent the night at the Ritz. She remembered he had been so proud of her. He told everyone who would listen from the waiter to the front desk clerk to other guests what they were celebrating.

"Melinda?"

Her eyes flew up and she sat straight up. Her heart pounded in her chest. "Stacey, hi."

"I'm sorry I didn't mean to startle you. I hope you don't mind me just dropping by." She held up a bottle of wine and two paper cups. "I was looking for some girl time."

"Sure, join me." Stacey handed her a cup and Mel looked her in the eye. "Seriously, if we're drinking wine at lunch, we can't drink out of paper. I'll be right back."

Melinda hurried into the house, her steps light with relief. It seemed like perfect timing as she was starting to drift down memory lane and that always ended with tears.

She took two clear wine glasses from the shelf and returned to where Stacey was sitting. She seemed to be taking in every detail of the pergola. "Adam is doing an amazing job."

Mel beamed. "It's coming out perfect. From the first time I looked at this house I thought it cried out for something exactly like this." She held out the glasses for Stacey to pour the wine. "It's as if Adam saw my vision, and then created it."

Stacey nodded, accepting a glass. "That's what I think Will does a lot too. It's like we communicate without words."

Melinda took her seat again and sipped the cool white wine. Over the rim of the glass she studied Stacey. "This is good."

"It's from a winery in Rhode Island. We got a case as a wedding present." She held up her glass and took a sip. "At first I thought, who'd give wine as a gift? But after the first taste I was like, this is a great idea."

Melinda went straight to the point. "Stacey, what's on your mind?"

She feigned innocence. "What do you mean?" Her shoulders moved up and down as she held back a laugh. "All right, you got me. I've been thinking about this for a long time and I'm wondering why you don't date."

It was a good thing Melinda was sitting down as that was not what she expected Stacey to blurt out. What could she say to explain her decision? She looked off toward the hummingbird feeder hanging from the maple tree.

Her voice was soft. "John was the love of my life. He was

generous, quick-tempered but the kind to get over it. He was a man you could count on. We were together for more than a decade. We were best friends as well as lovers. There hasn't been a day that's gone by that I didn't feel lucky to have ben his wife."

Stacey swirled the wine in her glass. "Do you think he would want you to be alone?"

Mel slowly shook her head. "Probably not. We never talked about the what ifs of life. You know, like the danger of his job. I've told myself you only get one great love in a lifetime. But lately I've been wondering am I really just protecting myself from getting hurt."

"What's made you change your mind?"

Melinda drank a little more wine. She needed time before she answered Stacey.

She shrugged as an image of Adam popped into her brain.

Stacey set her glass on the round, glass-topped table. "Have you considered plunging into the dating pool again?"

With a small laugh she said, "Jeez, you are blunt, aren't you?"

"Why pussyfoot around? If you want an answer, why not just be direct?" Stacey's eyes were bright. "If I lost Will, I would want you to help me find love again. When the time was right."

"Have you guys talked about it? What you would do if one of you found yourself alone?"

Stacey leaned forward. "We have and we agree. If something were to happen, we both would want the other to find someone to share the rest of their life with. Humans aren't meant to be closed off from others." She grasped Mel's hand. "Even friendships need the opportunity to blossom."

Melinda was surprised tears didn't well up in her eyes. Stacey was really and truly her friend. She squeezed Stacey's hand. "You've given me a lot to think about."

Stacey got up from the chair. "I need to run, but I'm glad I dropped in."

Melinda stood up. Stacey pulled her in for a hug. "My door is always open. It's time to let yourself be surrounded with love."

She pulled back and winked. "Who knows maybe your super matchmaker skills will point you in the direction for a new relationship."

Melinda watched as Stacey walked back to her car with the promise of getting together soon. She sank to the chair—she had a lot to think about.

CHAPTER 16

Adam ran a hand over his closely cropped hair and straightened the collar on his dark green polo shirt. He checked the mirror and then his watch. He was meeting Beth in a half hour.

Skye pounced on a shadow on the bedroom floor and tumbled over. He scooped up the kitten and looked at her little face. "Are you having fun today?"

Skye purred. He chuckled and carried her into the living room. "You're getting quite a belly on you." He scratched the kitten under her chin and Skye reached up to gently tap his cheek with her paw. "Now you be a good girl and I'll see you later." He set her on the back of the chair as his cell phone rang.

"Hey," Will said, "just wanted to let you know Stacey and I are going for a drive along the shore."

Adam gave a snort with a half laugh. "And should I feel the need for an escape, I'll pretend I'm surprised to see you."

"Yup, and I'll say that we're sorry to interrupt but I need your help."

Adam dropped his head, irritated with himself for being a pessimist. "You know what, don't worry about anything. If it doesn't go well, I can just suck it up and be nice until it's time to go our separate ways."

"Are you sure?" Will asked. "Because we're still planning on going for a drive."

"Yeah, I'm sure." He checked his watch. "I need to run. I'm going to stop and look at a job before I meet Beth."

"All right. Stop down for dinner when you get back. I'll burn some burgers on the grill and you can tell us all about it."

Adam shifted and took the pressure off his leg. It was aching today. "Maybe. I've got a busy week coming up."

Will said, "No worries. Come by, if you want."

He hesitated and then said, "Sure. Sounds good."

After disconnecting, he picked up his keys. He had just enough time to run by Mel's before meeting Beth. He wanted to see if she had made up her mind about the new design. She had still been on the fence the other day when he had explained his idea.

When he got to her house, the garage door was open along with the back door. He crossed through the darkened garage and exited into the backyard, which was a riot of colorful flowers and sunny areas dotting the landscape. Melinda appeared to be completely engrossed in digging a deep hole. An open bag of mulch and peat moss were next to her.

She looked up as he approached. Her eyes were protected by dark, oversized sunglasses and her hair was secured in a knot on top of her head. A large streak of dirt covered one cheek. She held up a gloved hand and smiled. "Hey you."

Without thinking he wiped the dirt from her cheek as if it was the most natural thing to do. "I was on my way to the beach and thought I'd drop by to see if you'd decided about the screen." He looked around and saw the new plantings Mel was working on.

She pulled off the gloves as she jumped up. Taking a step back she swept her arm around the expanse of the yard. "I noticed you surveyed my progress with that eagle eye of yours." She pulled out a paper from her back pocket and held it up. "Yes, I'm following your design." Making a goofy face, she said, "So you know what direction we're going in before I even tell you."

He grinned. "I'll be over first thing tomorrow and get to work." He pointed to the exposed back corner. "I'll use cedar and it will weather to a pale gray just as the beams will. You'll get a small potting table and the privacy you need. Not to worry, it will blend in nicely."

She pushed her sunglasses to the top of her head. "If you have another job, I can wait."

"No." He shook his head. "You're at the top of my priority list."

She looked him over. "You're looking handsome today." Softly she continued, "Green is your color."

He tugged at the collar on his shirt. "Thanks, I guess." He pointed to a bag of soil. "I can stop back around later and give you a hand."

"You've done enough and I have my handy-dandy cart." She pulled a glove back on. "I should get back at it." She smiled and said, "But I'll see you tomorrow."

He held up a hand and waved. "See you in the morning."

He started up the truck feeling less than enthused about meeting Beth when what he really wanted to do was stay and dig in the dirt with Mel.

∼

He drove slowly down Shore Line Drive and pulled into the small parking area. There was a vintage cherry red Mustang with a white ragtop parked near the bench. A woman was sitting inside. She got out and held up her hand in greeting. He parked and got out of the truck, took a deep breath and walked across the parking area.

"Hello, Adam." She extended her hand. "I recognize you from your picture."

He grasped hers and was surprised at the gesture. "Beth, it's nice to meet you."

She looked just like her picture. Her dark brown hair was short and stylishly arranged. She wasn't as tall as Mel, but looked healthy and fit. He guessed it was from the active lifestyle she described in her bio. Why had he compared Beth to Mel?

Beth held up a thermos and two metal mugs. "As promised, I brought the coffee."

"I'll be right back." He walked to his truck and reached into the open window. He pulled out a brown paper bag and held it up. "I picked up muffins."

Beth gave him a friendly smile. "Shall we sit and get to know each other?"

She was certainly direct, which he thought was refreshing, and gestured toward the bench. "After you."

"Isn't it the perfect day?" she asked. "Puffy white clouds lazily floating through the deep blue sky."

He nodded. "We've been pretty lucky this year. We've had the right mix of rain and sun. It's made the gardens really grow."

"Do you garden?"

"No, but my friends have a big vegetable garden and I've been fortunate to have them share the fruits of their labor with me."

"I'm not so much a fan of planting and weeding. I don't like all that work, but I love farm stands." She opened the thermos, poured a mug and passed it to Adam. "Here you go."

Accepting it, he said, "Thank you." He set it aside, turned back the top edge of the paper bag and set it between them. "Help yourself."

"I will, thank you." She peeked inside. "What kind are they?"

"Cinnamon swirl. I wasn't sure where you stood on fruit." He smiled. So far, so good.

Her eyes grew big. "They're huge." She broke one in half and then in half again. Taking a bite, she said, "They're still warm."

Adam nodded and chuckled. "They are." He took a sip of the piping hot coffee. "So, have you gone on many first dates?" He felt heat flush his face. "Does that sound rude?"

She laughed. It was light and carefree. "I've had a couple, but I haven't had a lot in common with them. Which is why I thought I'd give *Its Just Coffee* a try." Her eyes drifted to the ocean. "They've all been really nice. Just nothing has clicked, if you know what I mean." She gave him a quizzical look. "What about you?"

"I've had one, but she wasn't honest in her interview with Ms. Phillips. Therefore, it wasn't a good match."

"That stinks. If you're going to spend good money on something like this, you really should do all you can to be completely honest. It's your best chance of a strong match."

He nodded in agreement. "I can assure you I was completely honest with her and"—with a wave from his head to toes — "what you see is what you get."

Inwardly, he cringed. He had left out one very important detail.

"Good to know." Beth took a sip of her coffee. "I'll go first and fill you in on some details. I was in a long-term relationship. I wanted to have kids but he didn't, so we decided to go our own ways. I've lived in the area my entire life and can't imagine not being near the ocean. I have two siblings. My parents are alive and in good health, and I love horror movies, all things suspense and mystery related. Last but not least, my favorite holiday is Halloween."

He teased, "You forgot your sign, favorite meal and color."

She laughed. "Taurus, lasagna and green." Her eyes danced. "Like your shirt."

"Good to know."

She gave him a broad smile. "And I'm unflinchingly honest."

"That's a trait I admire."

"I would expect that. I remember you served in the Corps."

Slowly he said, "Correct."

"Tell me all about it." She nibbled on a piece of muffin.

"Not much to tell. I served and then retired, relocated here to be with my friends and now I'm in business as a carpenter." He drained his coffee cup and said, "I recently adopted a kitten, Skye."

Beth wrinkled her nose. "I'm not a huge fan of cats. I prefer dogs."

Inwardly he groaned again. "I found her in a box next to a garbage can. She was just about five weeks old and I wasn't going to drop her at a shelter."

"I understand totally. It shows you have a kind heart."

He shrugged. "It's not that big of a deal." Moving away from the subject of Skye, he asked, "So what do you do for work?"

"I'm a cardiac nurse." She looked down when her cell phone buzzed. She gave it a cursory look and put it back in her pocket.

Adam took notice and decided to be direct. "I take it you think our first date is going well?"

A look of surprise flitted across her face. "What makes you say…" Her voice drifted off and patted her pocket. "Yeah, my back-up plan. If I answered, they'd know to drive by, see the 'stang and pull in and say I was needed at work or something."

Adam gave a snort. "Well, I had set the same thing up with my friends, but I decided to fly without my wingman today."

"Honesty." She laughed again.

He shook his head and grinned. "I think I'm free to hang out for a while longer."

"So," she teased, "you still haven't told me what your sign is, favorite meal and color." She poked him in the arm. "Fair is fair."

He relaxed. He was having a good time. "Aquarius, seafood and blue."

Beth asked, "Do you like to fish?"

"I do, actually. Do you?"

"I have gear in my car if you want to go drop a line off the pier." She tilted her head. "It might be fun."

Adam weighed the pros and cons of going fishing without his gear. "How about we make that one of our future adventures? And if we catch something, I'll cook it for us."

"That sounds like we have another date."

"It does." Adam watched as her smile brightened.

"That sounds like fun." Beth tightened the top on the thermos and flattened the now empty paper bag. "I'll look forward to seeing you again." She held out her hand. "It's been a pleasure having coffee with you."

Adam gave her a firm shake. "It's been nice." He walked her to her car and held the door for her. "We'll talk soon."

CHAPTER 17

Adam was setting up sawhorses when Mel wandered out the back door. She was wearing jean shorts that hit mid-thigh, a faded novelty T-shirt, and well-worn canvas sneakers. Her copper-colored hair was pulled off her face in a long, wavy ponytail. She wore a mischievous grin that made her amazing, color-changing eyes sparkle.

"Morning," she said, coming over to stand next to him. "I've been dying to talk to you."

He chuckled, folded his arms over his chest and sat on a sawhorse, careful not to expose his artificial limb. "I'm surprised you didn't call," he teased.

"I didn't want to appear too pushy." She rubbed her hands together and grinned. "But how did everything go?"

Deciding to keep her in suspense another minute or two, Adam hid his smile. "What are you talking about? I'm just getting started on the bench."

She bumped his shoulder. "That's not what I'm referring to and you know it."

"Do you do this with all your clients?" He turned away so she couldn't see his grin.

She kicked a pile of mulch with her toe and said, "Well, no. But our relationship isn't exactly the norm for me."

He could hear her voice drop. He reached out and lightly touched her arm. "I was just having a little fun with you."

Her smile brightened. "So are you going to tell me how it went with Beth?"

"She was nice. She's smart, quick-witted and seems like a genuine person."

"When are you going to see her again?"

"We have tentative plans to go fishing and have dinner."

Melinda beamed. "That is fantastic news."

"We'll see where it goes after that, but I'm feeling optimistic."

"I'm relieved. After your first match, I was concerned I had lost my touch." She turned to go inside. "Do you want some coffee? I need to get to work, but I can bring a mug out to you."

"No, I'm good." He pointed to his bag. "I brought water. It's going to be hot today."

She paused on the bottom step. "Did you hear about Molly and Tim's wedding?"

He looked up as he nodded. "I did. It's out on the island. A weekend event, by the looks of it."

"Are you going?"

"I am, are you?" His heart rate increased while waiting for her answer.

"Of course I wouldn't miss it."

He asked, "Do you want to hangout together for the weekend?"

"That sounds like it would be fun. You know, take the pressure off from being the single person. It's not so bad when it's just an afternoon, but we need to arrive Friday and the wedding is Saturday. Then there is a brunch on Sunday before we can catch the ferry home." Melinda was rambling on. Adam smiled at her.

"Sounds like you've given this a great deal of thought."

Her face flushed a cute shade of pink. "Well, I'm a planner."

"I'll make reservations tonight," he said.

"I can make them and book the ferry tickets."

Adam dug in his back pocket and pulled out his wallet. "Are you sure you don't mind? I'll drive us to the ferry and be your chauffeur for the weekend."

She took his credit card and said, "Sounds like a plan." The door banged shut behind her as she disappeared inside.

Adam sat there looking at the closed door for what seemed like hours. Under other circumstances, he would think they had just agreed to a date for the weekend.

~

Melinda tapped the computer keys to finalize the hotel reservations for the wedding. She was glad to have someone to spend the weekend with. All of their friends would be paired off, and being with Adam was fun. She printed the ferry schedule and then sent the hotel and ferry information to Adam in an email.

Her office phone rang. "Hello, Melinda Phillips."

"Melinda, hi. This is Nick."

"This is a surprise. Did we have a phone conference scheduled?" She flipped through her appointment book on her desk and didn't see anything with his name listed for a call.

"No. But I enjoyed meeting you and wanted to see if you were free for a drink this evening."

She hesitated. *Shoot. I didn't want this to happen.*

Taking a deep breath, she said, "Nick, thank you for the invitation, but I don't date clients." Her thoughts slid to Adam. He wasn't her date for the wedding, going for ice cream wasn't a date. They were two friends sharing a ride and spending time together while they attend an event for mutual friends.

"Couldn't you make an exception with me?" he drawled.

She sighed and then hoped he didn't hear it. "Nick, I have a wonderful match for you. Gretchen. Have you contacted her yet?"

"No." He sounded disappointed.

"Why don't you give her a call? I think you'll be pleased."

"Well, you do have an excellent reputation, but do me one favor?"

"If I can." Melinda had a hunch she knew what he was going to say next.

"If you ever change your mind, let me know."

With a nervous laugh Melinda said, "Thank you. I'm sure you understand I'm doing the job you hired me to do."

"Is it wrong for me to hope you'll change your mind? What would one little glass of wine hurt?"

"Now, Nick..." Her voice was firm. "You should give Gretchen a chance."

"I will." After he said goodbye, she set the phone back on the base and laughed.

"He certainly is persistent." At that moment she heard a string of colorful language coming from her backyard. She moved to the window and pulled up the sash. "Hey, what's going on out there?"

Adam held up his hand. She saw the blood dripping from his arm. Steeling herself, she said, "I'll be right out." Melinda stepped from view and put a hand over her roiling stomach. She had never been good at dealing with blood. "I can do this."

She grabbed a roll of paper towels as she raced through the kitchen, regretting that she didn't have a first aid kit on hand. Taking the back steps two at a time, she ran to him. Melinda kept her eyes focused on him searching for signs of him passing out.

Her stomach got that queasy feeling again as she unrolled an arm's length of paper and then held it out to him. "What happened?"

"I was using the saw and the guard slipped. It was stupid. I caught my finger. I'm not sure, but I might have lopped it off."

She took a quick look around as the blood was turning the

paper towel bright red. She swallowed hard and deliberately tried to slow down her fast breathing.

"Mel, are you okay?"

Adam's voice seemed very far away. She chided herself to get a grip. "I'm not a fan of blood." She started to wrap more towels around his hand. "I won't hurt you."

"I'm okay." He took a step and paled.

She grabbed his arm. "I've got you." "We need to go to the emergency room and have someone take a look at that. At a minimum you're going to need stitches." She finished securing the paper towels and pushed on his elbow. "Keep your hand above your heart and let's go."

She steered him toward the kitchen door. Adam stopped in his tracks. "I can't go in there. I'll get blood on the floor."

"I need my handbag and keys."

"We're not taking your car—you've got cream interior. We'll take the truck."

Melinda kept her temper in check. He was being exasperating. "Fine, but I still need to lock the house and get my keys."

"I'll meet you out front." Adam held tight to the makeshift paper towel bandage. "Hey, Mel?" She turned toward him. "Any chance you have an old towel I can use? This isn't going to cut it." He gestured to his arm.

"I'll grab something." The door banged behind her and she flipped the lock. On her way to the linen closet she slung her handbag over her shoulder and shook it to make sure she heard her keys inside. She grabbed a clean white towel and ran to the front door. She hopped down the front steps just as Adam got to the truck.

She rushed to open the passenger door for him and handed him the towel. "Put your seatbelt on." After she climbed into the driver's seat, she looked between her legs and on the side of the seat. "Where can I adjust this darn thing?" Muttering to herself, she said, "I never considered myself vertically challenged until now."

Adam's face was pale, He chuckled in spite of the pain he must be feeling. "I have long legs."

She flashed him a look. "Stop laughing."

"It's not electric, the lever is between your legs."

She jerked the seat forward and then back, finding the spot that worked best for her. She turned the key and the engine roared to life. "Okay, we're off."

He frowned when he looked at the towel. "You had to get a white one?"

She flashed him a quick look. "What? Oh, all I have is white. I like to use bleach."

He mumbled, "I doubt bleach will take care of this mess."

She drove quickly but with confidence, stealing looks at him from time to time. "How's the pain?"

"Not too bad. I've been through worse than this."

She was curious about those details, but now was not the time to pepper him with questions. "We'll be there in about five minutes."

"I'm glad you live close to the hospital." The truck hit a pothole and he grimaced.

Melinda cringed. "I'm so sorry."

The sign for the hospital was up ahead. She slowed the truck and turned into the entrance. "I'll drop you off at the door and park."

"No! I'll stay with you." He looked at her. "In case of dizziness."

She could feel her face drain of color. "Do you think you've lost a lot of blood?"

"Not me. You." He gave her a weak grin.

"You never pass up the opportunity to tease me, do you?" She pulled into a parking lot that said EMERGENCY.

"Why would I? It's fun. Besides, right now I could use the distraction."

He popped his seatbelt with his good hand, and she could see the towel was going to have to be thrown in the trash. That blood was never coming out. Maybe she should have taken a couple of minutes to look around. What if he *had* cut off his finger?

He caught her staring at his hand. "I'm going to buy you a new towel."

She pushed open her door. "What makes you think that's not an old towel?" She hurried around and opened Adam's door.

"Mel, relax. I can get out by myself." His laughter was strained as they crossed the pavement. "I'll bet you don't have old, holey socks either."

The emergency room door silently whooshed open. They stepped inside. Cold air washed over them. Melinda pointed to the check-in desk. "You need to go over there and I'll wait for you here."

He gave her a quick look.

She said, "Never mind, I'm coming with you."

He dropped his voice. "Are you worried what they're going to find when they unwrap your paper towel masterpiece?"

"No." She took his elbow. "I've got nothing better to do until you're stitched up, so why not keep you company?"

He looked relieved. "Thanks, Mel."

CHAPTER 18

Melinda held back her emotions as she sat in the exam room with Adam. He was waiting patiently to be seen by the emergency room doctor. She had always hated hospitals. Inwardly she groaned. Well, that was a lie, it was only in recent years that she'd begun to hate them. The building, the antiseptic smells and the sounds. The page system was enough to drive anyone crazy.

Adam was perched on the edge of the exam table and Mel was in the chair next to him. He bent toward her. "How are you doing?"

Her hands were clammy. She prayed her face wasn't completely devoid of color. "Oh, fine," she said with false bravado.

If only she could halt the flood of memories. That would help. Instead she said, "How is your pain?" Carefully enunciating each word to give her something to focus on.

"I'm not going to kid you, it hurts like a son of a…"

She raised an eyebrow.

He flashed a small, apologetic smile at her. "Sorry. It isn't the worse pain I've had, but still…"

She cut him off to get his mind off the injury and joked, "It's not like you're giving birth or dealing with a kidney stone."

"One I'll never experience and the other I hope never to."

The curtain was drawn back and a tall, older man entered the cubicle holding a chart in his hand. "Mr. Bell? I'm the on-call doctor." He was all business as he reviewed the details in Adam's chart.

"Yes. Excuse me for not shaking your hand." Adam's attempt at a joke fell on deaf ears.

The doctor glanced at Melinda. "Are you Mrs. Bell?"

Out of the corner of her eye, Melinda saw Adam's eyes open wide in surprise. "No, I'm his friend." Seeing the doctor holding the chart made her flash back to the last time she was in an ER.

The doctor began to unwrap the towel. Melinda felt as if a band was tightening around her chest and her head began to spin. She stood up from the stool and glanced at Adam. "I'm going to wait outside." She thought she heard Adam call her name before the darkness claimed her.

The irritating smell of ammonia wafted into her senses and someone was helping her sit up.

"Ms. Phillips, can you hear me? I'm Wayne, a nurse. Let me help you up."

She coughed and pushed herself to a full sitting position. "What happened?"

Adam chuckled. "You took one look at my hand and it was good night Irene for you."

She struggled to stand, embarrassed she had caused such a fuss. Wayne held her arm. "Go slowly. If you start to feel faint again, let me know."

She felt shaky and lightheaded. "All right."

The nurse helped her to a chair next to the exam table and Melinda looked at Adam. "I'm sorry." She grimaced.

"Don't we make a great pair?" He winced as the doctor turned his hand over and examined it.

"How long was I out?" she asked.

"For only a few seconds. Around here they seem to take exception to people passing out." Adam gave her a cock-eyed grin. She knew he was trying to make her feel better.

"Here, have a sip, slowly." Wayne handed Melinda a small plastic cup filled to the rim with what she hoped was cool water.

She took a tentative drink and looked into the kindly face of a very young-looking nurse. "Thank you." She took another sip and was beginning to feel a bit better. "I'm sure you don't often need to scoop women up from the floor."

He gave her a friendly smile. "It's more common than you think." She finished the water and handed him the cup. "Would you like to stay here? Or I can escort you to the waiting room if you're feeling better."

"Adam?"

"I'm good if you want to wait outside." He kept his eyes locked on hers.

Melinda had to wonder, did he need her, or did she need him? She pulled up a chair next to the gurney. Letting him believe it was the blood that caused her to faint, she said, "As long as I don't have to watch, I'll stay." She wrinkled her nose. "Your hand looks nasty."

"Hey," Adam joked, "that's my hand you're talking about."

The doctor held a syringe poised over his hand and said, "This might sting a bit, but then it'll feel better."

Adam's face turned to stone. Melinda situated herself so she could see him but not have the injured limb in her direct line of sight. It wasn't easy. Her eyes were drawn to his hand, but she forced herself to keep her eyes locked on Adam.

"Mr. Bell, you're pretty lucky. The finger seems to be intact. We'll be able to stitch it up and it should be good as new once it heals. But I'd like for you to have an X-ray first just to make sure the bone isn't broken. After that you'll be released."

"Thanks, Doc."

The doctor hurried away with another nurse keeping pace with him. Wayne, who had helped Melinda, brought a wheelchair for Adam. "I'm going to take you down for some films and Ms. Phillips can wait for you here." He glanced at Melinda. "We won't be long."

She felt her stomach flip. She couldn't stay in this room alone.

Adam said, "Mel, why don't you hang out in the waiting room while I'm gone?"

She stood up, grateful he seemed to just know what she was feeling. "I hadn't thought of that." She touched his arm. "When you're back, maybe one of the nurses can find me."

Wayne stood behind the wheelchair and said, "I'll be happy to."

Should she volunteer to keep him company on the way to X-ray? He would be fine. She swallowed the lump in her throat and gave Adam a thumbs-up. "Be nice to the technician."

"Will do." Adam gave her a half-hearted smile.

He slid off the gurney and stood next to the wheelchair. "She can come with you," Wayne said.

"Thanks, but I'll be in the waiting room." She hurriedly escaped the brightly lit exam room and leaned against the cool cement wall. She waited as the nurse pushed Adam past her. His hand had been wrapped and he was holding it in the air as he disappeared down the endless corridor.

Melinda had found an empty chair away from the main entrance. She glanced at the door again. How long before she could leave the hospital and the antiseptic smell behind? She gave an involuntary shudder. The last time she had been in an emergency room was with John.

She twirled the slim gold ring on her finger. She had held his hand as he hovered at death's door, and then in an instant he was gone. She never had the chance to say goodbye before he succumbed to his injuries.

Wayne came through the door. She saw he scanned the waiting room and then headed her way. "Ms. Phillips?"

Melinda jumped up. She struggled to keep the panic from her

voice. "Is something wrong with Adam?" She felt a band tighten like a vise around her chest.

"He's fine. He asked me to let you know he is out of X-ray."

"Did he send you out here to check on me?" She gave him a tentative smile. "You can be honest."

"How about I say both statements are true?" He gestured for her to sit down and he laid his fingertips across the underside of her wrist. He checked his watch. "Any more wooziness?"

With a slow shake of her head, Melinda said, "No, I'm fine. I've never been a fan of hospitals, but I never dreamt I would faint." She felt the white lie was best rather than confess what her real issue was.

He cocked his head and looked at her. "Happens to the best of us. My mom still can't believe I chose the medical profession. At the mere thought of someone bleeding, her head is between her knees."

Melinda said, "You're very kind."

The nurse slowly stood up. "I'm going to check on Adam. He'll get cleaned up and then he'll be ready to go."

"Thank you." She gave him a weak smile.

"You bet." He sauntered down a different hallway. Melinda watched him disappear and thought how sweet Adam was to be concerned about her when he was the one injured.

She closed her eyes and leaned her head against the concrete wall behind her. Her thoughts drifted back to the knock on her door that changed everything.

John's partner, Rob, was standing on the bottom step. His face was ashen. "Mel, there's been an accident. John's being rushed to the hospital. He's been hit by a drunk driver."

Her feet felt like lead as she rushed into the bustling emergency room. She wasn't aware of anything or anyone around her except that Rob was by her side. She stepped around the corner and saw John lying motionless on the gurney. His face was the color of the stark white sheets.

She picked up his cold, limp hand and rubbed it. She asked for more blankets. The doctor was trying to tell her something, but her focus was on John. Rob took her arm and led her out of the room. She leaned down and whispered in his ear, "I'll be right back."

It never crossed her mind these might be the last moments she'd spend with him. Rob reassured her they'd come back. As she sat down in the waiting room, she heard the speaker blare CODE BLUE.

She shuddered. Tears coursed down her cheeks.

"Melinda." A deep voice penetrated the pain that constricted her heart, threatening to cut off her very breath.

Her eyes fluttered open. "Adam," she breathed.

With his good hand, he wiped the tears from her face and rubbed her hands until she could feel them getting warmer. "Mel, what's going on? Are you sick?"

She tried to stand up and felt her head swim. He said, "Whoa. You're as white as a ghost."

"I'm okay, really." She could hear her voice crack.

Gently, he said, "Talk to me."

She looked around, hoping she hadn't made a spectacle of herself. "Not here," she begged. "Later."

Gently he said, "I'm going to hold you to that."

She noticed he had some papers in his lap. "Can you leave now?"

He held them up. "I've been given my walking papers." She could see the concern in his face. He took her hand and said, "Are you okay to drive?"

Melinda took a deep calming breath and slowly exhaled. She gave him a tiny smile. "Let's go home."

CHAPTER 19

Melinda turned the truck down Adam's street after stopping at the pharmacy for his prescriptions and an impulse toy for Skye. "I'll drop you at your place and then walk home."

"Are you kidding?" Adam asked. "It's a couple of miles."

She wouldn't look at him. "The fresh air will do me good."

Melinda could feel Adam staring at her. "Mel. You're not going anywhere until you talk to me."

The timber of his voice almost brought her to tears. "Adam, please." She slowed and turned on the blinker. After parking, she held up the key ring and asked, "Which one is for the apartment?"

"It's not locked." He pushed the door open with his good hand and a foot. "Are you coming up at least?"

Curious to see how he lived propelled her forward. "I'm going to get you settled and make sure you're comfortable." She led the way up the outside staircase. "This must be fun in the winter."

"It wasn't too bad, just start at the top and push the snow over the side of the stairs."

Melinda noticed he took the stairs very slowly. Worried about him, she asked, "Adam, do you need help?"

Curtly he said, "No. I'm fine."

She turned the doorknob and pushed it opened. A little fur ball rushed toward them. Melinda scooped her up and gave her a kiss on top of her head. "Your daddy got hurt today, so you need to be very gentle with him."

She glanced around the spacious and tidy room. "Nice place." This certainly didn't look like the typical bachelor pad. It was simply furnished with a dash of color here and there. It even had curtains.

"It's comfortable." He slumped into the recliner.

"Can I help you get your work boots off?" She started to bend over.

"NO!"

Stunned by Adam shouting the single word, she stumbled backward. "I'm sorry."

"Mel, *I'm* sorry." He dropped his chin towards his chest. "It's been a rough day and for now I just want to chill." He pointed to the sofa. "Would you grab me a pillow so I can elevate my hand?"

"Here you go." She handed him two slender pillows. "Are you comfortable? Should I adjust the AC?"

"I'm good." He looked at her. "Please sit down, you don't need to fuss over me."

She picked up Skye and perched on the edge of the sofa. "Can I get you something to drink, water?"

"You can tell me what was going on when I found you crying in the waiting room."

Mel concentrated on petting Skye. She wouldn't look at him in the eye. "It was nothing, really."

"Bull."

She lifted her face. Her eyes locked on his. "Do you really want to know?"

"Yes." That one-word answer was almost her undoing.

She took a deep breath and blinked away the tears that threatened to spill down her cheeks. "The last time I was in an emergency room was the day John died."

"Mel," he exhaled, "I had no idea."

She looked away. Struggling to keep her voice steady, she continued, "I told you he was hit by a drunk driver." She clenched her hands, her nails biting into the palms of her hands. "The jerk came flying down the road, swerved to supposedly miss a squirrel, and he hit John." She wiped away the tears that she could no longer control. "He never regained consciousness."

She pushed to tell Adam the rest of the story. "His partner picked me up from our house. When I got there, I knew it was bad, really bad, but I never dreamt he wouldn't make it. I saw him for a brief moment, I was holding his hand until the doctor asked me to wait outside the room. While he was examining John, he coded. They did everything they could, but his internal injuries were just too severe."

Tears flowed down her cheeks unchecked. She choked out the words, "I never got to tell him I loved him or kiss him goodbye."

Adam held open his arm and beckoned her to him. In two quick steps she rushed to the warmth of his embrace. He held her in his lap while she cried. After her tears had run dry, she put a hand on his chest. She could feel the flush rise in her cheeks.

"Adam, I am *so* sorry." She tried to get up, but he held her close.

He kissed her temple as if to soothe away the agonizing memory. "Thank you for telling me."

Humbled by the sincerity of his statement, she said, "I haven't talked about that day to anyone, other than Will and Rob, John's partner, right after the funeral."

"You told Will?"

She sighed. "Yeah. He was easy to talk to."

"You've had that bottled up inside of you all this time?" He brushed her damp cheeks with his thumb.

"It's not something I want to remember."

"I believe that sharing your pain with a friend helps to lessen the burden of carrying it alone." He took her hand. "I'm here if you ever want to talk about anything. Your secrets are safe with me."

She slipped from his lap. "Thank you." Unsure what else to say, she changed the subject. "I'll get you some water, maybe a snack? Those pain pills can do a number on your stomach."

He nodded. "There are some cookies in the cabinet next to the sink."

She was happy to escape his intense gaze. What was she thinking, blubbering all over him *and* telling him about John's death?

Skye came mewling into the kitchen and walked in between and around Melinda's ankles. "Hey, sweetie pie, what do you need?"

The kitten gazed up at her. *Mew, mew,* she squeaked.

Melinda wanted to laugh, but she didn't have the heart. Instead she found some kitten treats on the counter and shook out a couple into the palm of her hand. "Here you go. Snack time for you and your dad."

∼

Adam was dumbfounded. He had no idea what really had happened to Mel's husband until now. His injury was nothing compared to her heartbreak. He'd lost a partial limb, she'd lost the love of her life. He wondered, did she have family to support her, either hers or his?

"Mel?" he called out.

She poked her head out of the kitchen. "Can I bring you something else?"

"Do you have any plans? Maybe you'd like to stay for dinner. I don't feel like being alone."

She seemed to debate for a half a second before giving him a tentative smile. "Sure, I can pick up a pizza or something." She frowned. "Shoot. I need my car."

"Stacey will be home soon, or you can take my truck." He grimaced as he tried to use the lever to raise the footrest on the recliner.

"Here, I can help with that." Melinda walked toward him.

He was concerned there was a slight chance she might see his foot so he thought fast. "You know, I'm thinking sitting upright would be best. Keep my hand straight and all." He held his hand up and Mel helped him reposition the pillows. He relaxed and gave her a tight smile. At least that's how it felt to him. "Any idea when I can take another pain pill?"

"Two more hours." She went back into the kitchen and brought him a glass of milk and a plate of Oreos. "Maybe this will distract you."

He reached over, pulled the side table closer and smirked. "My dunking hand is out of commission, but I'll do my best."

She set the plate within easy reach. Prowling around his apartment, she picked up a framed photo. "This is a nice one of you and Will." She wiggled her eyebrows. "You look pretty spiffy."

Adam chuckled. "I don't think anyone has ever said a Marine in his dress uniform is spiffy."

"I'm sure someone has at some point in time, but a man in uniform always looks good." She dropped her eyes. He guessed she was thinking of John. Melinda hadn't completely dealt with her grief yet. Of that he was sure.

"I'm really sorry about your husband."

Her eyes met his, they were clouded with sorrow. "Me too." She shrugged as if to indicate the pain wasn't raw. "Some days are better than others, I'm not going to lie. Today the hospital was unexpectedly tough." She sat on the edge of the couch.

"You shouldn't have driven me."

With a shake of her head, she said, "I'm glad I did. I had to confront it at some point."

"Did you have support from his family after the accident?"

"John has a brother, Joe, but they had a falling out. He seemed to get into trouble all the time, choosing to live on the wrong side of the law. John tried to help him. When I called to tell him about what had happened, Joe informed me he wasn't coming to the funeral."

With a low whistle Adam said, "That's cold."

"I feel bad for Joe. He'll never have the chance to reconnect with John."

"Did John regret the relationship with his brother?"

Melinda nodded. "Of course, but as a cop he had to take a hard line with Joe. But I can tell you this, if Joe had called John to say he wanted to get clean, my husband would have dropped everything to help him."

"He sounds like a good man."

The corners of Melinda's mouth turned upward. "He was the best. They broke the mold when they made him." She leaned back against the cushions. "We had the best life."

"I'm sorry." He waited half a beat. "But you still have time, to start over. Who knows, you might meet a great guy who wants to have a bunch of kids."

"We've talked about this, Adam. I can't."

Keeping his voice steady, he asked, "Do you think John would want you to spend the rest of your life alone?"

"I have a great life. Wonderful friends. I can travel where I like. I'm financially comfortable."

"If you can find anyone a great match, you should seriously consider finding someone for yourself. At least someone to go to the movies with, or maybe out to dinner occasionally, and what about vacationing to some exotic part of the world? That would be great fun with someone special." Adam wasn't sure why he felt compelled to convince her to date.

She gave a soft chuckle. "Well, a funny thing happened this week. One of my clients called to ask me out. Even after I found him a great match, he asked me to think about it."

Adam felt his jaw clench. "And then what happened?"

"I very politely turned him down and encouraged him to go out on the date. I think they're going to get along very well."

Adam said, "We're friends, right?"

She laughed. "Good friends. But Nick and I are not friends. Besides, I'm sure the last thing you'd think about is hitting on me. I'm not your type at all."

CHAPTER 20

Melinda watched as Adam blanched. She was by his side in two quick steps. "Adam, what's wrong? Are you in pain?"

With a frown, he said, "I'm fine."

"Should I call the hospital to see if you can take your pain meds early?"

"No. It's not my hand that's giving me a problem." He brought his eyes up to meet hers. "I'm shocked that you'd think we're not compatible."

"What?" She sat down, dumbfounded.

"Wait, that didn't come out right." He seemed to fumble for what he wanted to say. "Over the last few weeks, we've become close. If there wasn't some sort of chemistry or connection, we wouldn't have any kind of a relationship."

Stunned, she asked, "Are you asking me out?" Her heart thudded in her chest.

"All I'm saying is you're an amazing woman. If I had met you before asking you to be my matchmaker, I would have asked for your number."

Stuttering she said, "I-I don't know what to say." She began to arrange items on the top of his coffee table.

"Melinda. Relax." He gave her a reassuring smile. "No need to get all flustered."

"I'm not." She was mildly annoyed he could read her so well. "You haven't eaten your snack yet."

He picked up the milk and downed it in one long gulp. He grinned. "How's that?"

Hearing a car door close, she crossed to the window that overlooked the driveway. "Stacey's home. I'm going to run down and see if she'll run me to my place. I can bring back dinner and have my car for later."

"When you tell her what happened, please assure her I'm fine. She tends to worry about me."

"I won't be gone long." She placed his cell phone within easy reaching distance. "If you need something call."

"When will you be back?"

"About an hour, if not before." She watched him closely, looking for signs of distress. "I'm going to put a casserole together at my house and bring it back. It will be better for you than takeout."

"I don't want you to fret over me." His voice was stern.

"I hear that disapproving tone in your voice, mister, and I'll do as I please," she teased.

"If that's the case, can you swing by the store and pick up something for dessert?" He wiggled his eyebrows, causing Mel to laugh. "After the day I've had, I deserve something decadent."

"Is this how you got around your mom as a kid?"

He grinned. "My sister was way better at getting what she wanted compared to me."

"Good to know." She picked up her handbag and looked at him. "Are you sure you're going to be all right?"

"Melinda, I've sustained injuries worse than this and I'm still standing."

Her eyebrow arched. "Really, I sense a story lurking."

"Nothing to tell here." He teased, "Just don't come back

without something sweet."

"Sir, yes, sir." She gave him a mock salute, which caused him to laugh. "I'm outta here."

She closed the door behind her and heard the television click on. Stacey was opening her back door. Melinda called out to her. "Stacey!"

Turning, she looked up the stairs. Surprise was apparent on her face. "Melinda, what are you doing here?"

"Adam was working at my place and had a little disagreement with a saw. I took him to the ER and they stitched him up. But I was wondering, any chance you could give me a lift home?"

"Is Adam okay?" Stacey placed a foot on the bottom rung of the stairs. "I need to check on him."

Melinda walked down a few steps. "Adam told me to tell you he's fine and not to worry."

She looked up at the closed door and hesitated. "Are you sure?"

Melinda made a cross sign over her heart. "Trust me, I wouldn't steer you wrong."

Stacey stepped back and said, "Why don't you come in for coffee first? You can fill me in on the details."

Melinda descended the stairs. "Thanks for the offer, but I need to get home. I'm going to fix something for dinner for us and bring it back. I want to help Adam out as much as I can until he gets a handle on the pain meds."

"How bad is it?"

"The blade missed the bone, but the gash was long and he bled a lot." With an involuntary shudder, she pushed away the mental flash of the ER.

Stacey reached out a steadying hand. "Are you okay? You're as white as a ghost."

She swallowed hard. "Hospitals and I don't get along."

"Let me get you home and we'll have coffee at your house while you cook."

Melinda allowed Stacey to steer her toward the car. Maybe it was a good thing that she was going to be sitting down; the ground seemed to be very uneven under her feet.

During the short drive to Melinda's house, Stacey asked a lot of questions, most of which Melinda couldn't answer.

"He is so testy," Melinda stated. "Like, I thought he'd be more comfortable taking off his work boots, but when I suggested it he flipped out."

Stacey gave her a sidelong glance. "Maybe his feet smell."

With a snort Melinda said, "After what I saw at the hospital, the last thing that would gross me out would be stinky feet."

"Men are funny creatures." Stacey slowed and turned into Melinda's driveway. As they entered the house, Stacey looked out the back door. "Where's your hose?"

"Why?"

"I'll wash the patio down while you brew the coffee."

Melinda sank onto a bar stool and laid her head on the cool counter top. She mumbled, "I forgot about the blood."

"I'll get it taken care of."

Melinda lifted her head. "The hose is hanging on the side of the garage."

Stacey gave her a sympathetic look before she hurried outside, leaving Melinda to collect herself. Her hands started to shake and then her whole body followed suit. She wrapped her arms around herself and held on. This too would pass. It always did.

She closed her eyes and concentrated on taking slow, deep, cleansing breaths. She focused on breathing in through her nose and out of her mouth. Counting to herself would help her get a handle on the panic attack. It had been a long time since she had one.

She lost track of time. Forgetting that she wasn't alone, she was surprised to hear, "Melinda?" She felt Stacey gently shake her. "Talk to me."

Slowly unfolding her arms, she stretched them over her head as if she was limbering up to exercise. "I'm fine."

"I'm not buying it." Stacey pulled up the stool and sat quietly, for what seemed like forever to Melinda.

Her voice cracked. "I hate the smell of the hospital."

"And…" Stacey prodded. Melinda started to get up, but Stacey placed a hand on her arm. "Everyone needs a shoulder to lean on."

Melinda hung her head. "Today, being in the ER, was a razor-sharp reminder of the day John died." She blinked away the tears that threatened to blur her vision.

"I'm sorry."

"I told Adam. Everything," she stated with simplicity.

"I'm sure he was sympathetic. He is a good man, one of the best."

Melinda exhaled softly. "He was sweet. Despite being in extreme pain and unsure if he was going to lose part of his finger, he was more concerned when I passed out than for himself."

"I didn't know you fainted."

Melinda felt a flush of embarrassment. "I think the stress of the entire situation overwhelmed me. Before I could stop myself, everything went black and I was down for the count. If I had been a boxer, I would have lost the bout."

"Interesting analogy." Stacey gave her a half smile. "You're one tough cookie."

"Ha. You wouldn't say that if you could have seen a nurse help me up off the floor. He brought me some water while Adam was waiting to be wheeled to X-ray."

"I've known Adam for a long time, and I'm sure he didn't give a thought to his situation. His concern would have been for you."

Melinda looked at Stacey. "You do like him, and not just because he's Will's best friend."

"Adam has become my dear friend too."

Deciding to divert the subject from the emergency room, she said, "I found a match for him."

Stacey said, "I know." She smiled. "We drove by the lookout to make sure that he didn't need a reason to escape."

"I had no idea people still did that." Her smile grew. "What did you think of her?"

"We only saw her from a distance, but she was very pretty." Stacey grinned. "You may have just let your Cupid's arrow find a new target."

"I wouldn't liken me to Cupid." Melinda cocked her head and then the corners of her lips twitched. "Well, maybe I could add that to my website and business cards. Cupid's Matchmaker."

"It has a nice ring to it." Stacey nodded. "Now, how about I help you whip up something delicious for dinner?"

"I'd like that." Melinda opened the refrigerator and studied the contents. "I've got nothing suitable to cook. I told Adam I was going to throw together some kind of casserole but all I have are eggs. I could make a frittata."

Stacey picked up her handbag and keys. "I've got a stew in the crockpot and more than enough for four."

"Are you sure? If you provide dinner, I'll swing by and pick up some bread and dessert."

Stacey held up her phone. "I'll text Will and let him know the plan. He can take the crockpot up to Adam's and we'll meet him there."

"I'm going to call Adam and make sure he doesn't need anything else. Then I'll meet you at his place."

Stacey threw her arms around Melinda and hugged her tight. "Tomorrow is going to be a better day. That's a promise."

Melinda held Stacey and nodded. The lump in her throat made it difficult to talk. She finally said, "Thanks."

Stacey stepped back and gave her a smile. "See you in a bit."

Melinda waited until Stacey closed the door and then called

Adam. He answered on the second ring. "Hello." He sounded groggy.

"Adam, its Mel. Are you doing okay?"

"The pain pill kicked in and I'm feeling pretty darn good."

"Are you still in the recliner?" she asked. *I need to get my butt in gear and get back there. He sounds really out of it.*

With a chuckle he said, "Yup, with Skye on my shoulder."

"Do you need anything besides dessert?"

"Any chance you could pick up some sweet tea? I have a hankering."

Melinda smiled into the phone. "Not a problem. Oh, I hope it's okay—Stacey and Will are going to have dinner with us. Stacey had the crockpot going."

"Cool, the more the merrier." She heard Adam yawn.

"I should be there in about thirty minutes."

"Drive carefully and just walk in when you get here." His voice was fading.

"Adam, take a snooze and I'll be there before you know it."

He chuckled. "Okey dokey. I'll be waiting for you."

CHAPTER 21

Melinda and Stacey walked into the living room to rejoin the guys after going for a short walk around the neighborhood. "Adam, I'm going home, but do you need anything else before I do?"

He gave her a slightly goofy smile. She thought it must be from the painkillers.

"No." His shoulders dropped. "I'm going to see if I can convince Will to hang out and watch the game for a while and then call it a night."

She felt a strange sense of responsibility toward him. Was it because he'd injured himself at her place? It was something she wasn't going to dwell on, as the situation could have been far worse. "I'll just check on Skye."

"No need, she's tucked between the side of the chair and my leg. I think she's keeping warm." He dislodged the sleeping kitten and set her in his lap. She began to purr softly. He said, "Thanks for everything today."

"It was the least I could do."

"Changing the subject," Will said as he propped his sneaker clad feet up on the coffee table, "have you guys heard about Molly and Tim's wedding?"

"No, what's going on? Adam and I were going to catch the ferry over together and basically be each other's plus one." Melinda frowned. "Are you going to feel like going after today?"

"Of course. This will be healed by then and besides, you're going to drive and I'll be the co-pilot." Adam yawned.

She laughed and rose to her feet. "I thought you were going to drive, but we can talk about this later."

"If you two are done making plans," Will joked, "they had to postpone—the wedding venue is booked solid. They were hoping for a cancellation but, well, Molly is very disappointed."

"That stinks." Adam said.

The women looked at each other. Stacey said, "I'll give her a call tomorrow."

"Let me know if I can help." Melinda picked up her bag. "You're tired. I'm going to take off, but I can stop over tomorrow to help out if you need something."

"Nah. Will can be my slave for the next few days." He inched forward and plucked Skye from his lap, setting her on the arm of his chair. "I'll walk you out."

Melinda gave him a gentle shove backward. "You'll do no such thing." She looked at Will. "I'll call you tomorrow to see how our patient is doing."

Stacey said, "I'll go down with you. The guys want to watch the game and I'm not a huge fan of baseball."

"Good night, Adam." Melinda's fingers grazed his shoulder. "If you need something, remember, I'm just a phone call away."

"Thanks, Mel." He looked up at her. "For everything."

~

After the door closed behind the ladies, Adam let out a groan and slumped back in the chair. He had wanted to tell Melinda he appreciated her trust in sharing with him the pain of losing her husband. In addition to the fact that she'd sucked it up and gone with him to the hospital. What kind of woman did that? Walked bravely into the one place that held the most sorrow, and then stayed by his side despite the memories that couldn't be ignored. Mel was an amazingly strong woman.

"So what was up with that comment?" Will asked. "I know you, and there was way more subtext there."

Adam gave a one-shoulder shrug. "Mel shared some very personal details of her past with me today and it was extremely painful for her."

Will raised an eyebrow. "And did you share *your* past with Melinda?"

He noticed the strong emphasis on the word *your*. With a sharp look, Adam said, "No."

"Why not?"

"I was caught up in what she told me. I didn't want to add to her burden by sharing something small by comparison."

"Dude, what you endured was far from minor. When the IED exploded and tore the unit apart, you lost good people under your command, not to mention your injuries. That is a lot for any man to deal with. Even a tough guy like you."

"I don't like to talk about it." Adam could barely croak out the words. The helplessness that had engulfed him after the accident caused him shame. He hadn't protected his team. That's what a good leader was supposed to do. Protect his team at all costs.

Will slammed his fist on the couch. "I get it. I was there too. I know what it was like, seeing your friends, your brothers and sisters come home in a box."

A shadowy memory flashed through his mind. "You don't understand. This was different. I was hurt and...I couldn't help anyone. I was weak, defenseless. I needed people to come to my aid." His voice rose as he continued. "That's not how it's supposed to be. My job was to take care of my people and I couldn't."

Adam heaved himself up from the chair. Holding his arm close to his body, he walked to the front window and looked out over the quiet street. His voice was low. "I understand Mel so much better now. Why she holds herself back. In some ways, we're a lot alike."

"She's your friend. I get that. Stacey and I love Melinda. And you're like a brother to me."

"What if Mel reacts like Anita did? Sees me as less than a man?" He stared into the growing darkness. "I don't want her to pity me or see a look of disgust on her face."

"If you think that's Melinda, then you have no idea what makes that woman tick. She is compassionate and caring and is nonjudgmental."

Adam tapped his chest. "I know that in here." Then he tapped his forehead. "But not here."

"She's not Anita."

With a slow shake of his head, Adam looked at Will. He could hear the bitterness in his voice. "You didn't see Anita in the hospital. You have no idea what it felt like to have someone who you loved look at you. Her eyes cold and empty. She stared at where my leg should have been. Her look of revulsion is something I'll never forget."

"Maybe she wasn't prepared to handle the gravity of the situation. Most significant others react exactly the same way. We've seen it time and time again."

Pressing fingers to his forehead Adam said, "Are you making excuses for her?"

Will blanched. "Absolutely not. I'm trying to find a way to tell you to be honest with Mel. So that if your relationship with her grows…" He let his voice trail off, "Anita was never right for you and that's why she's your past."

"I know what you're trying to do, but for tonight just let it go!"

Will studied Adam before saying, "Yeah. But don't wait too long before you tell Melinda. You can trust her."

Adam picked up the remote and turned on the television. "Are you staying to watch the game with me?"

"Yeah. You heard my bride, she has no interest in baseball."

Adam chuckled. "Is this why you wanted me to live over the garage, so you'd have me around for sports?"

With a grin Will said, "Well, you found me out."

"Since you're staying, we're going to need snack foods. Can't watch a game without them. But before you do that, can you help me? I need to get into sweatpants. It's going to be tough with one hand."

"I wondered why you were still wearing boots. You didn't want to take the chance Melinda would see your foot." With a shake of his head Will joked, "Let's get this over with. After being in work shoes all day, your feet are going to be ripe."

He chuckled. "That's the real reason. I didn't want Melinda to faint twice in one day." Adam stuck his foot out and jiggled it. "That special honor is just for you."

∽

Melinda sat in bed, too keyed up to sleep. She looked through the photo album she kept in her nightstand. After John died, her mother had put this together for her, condensing all the special moments they had shared into this one book. She had other photos packed away, but this one was always at the ready to provide comfort when she was missing John. And tonight, the loss was acute.

She ran her fingers over the embossed cover and turned to the first page. It was a picture of John and her at their engagement party. The young people looking at the camera wore bright smiles; their eyes were full of the promise of wonderful things to come. She turned the page. It was their wedding picture. *He was so handsome.*

Page after page, memories filled her heart with joy. She had been truly blessed to have loved John. Despite their short marriage, she wouldn't have traded it for a single thing. Her only regret was that they'd never had a baby. If they had, at least she would have a part of him with her today.

She turned to the last page. It was the final picture of the two of them at the shore about a month before he died. No tears fell, just the overwhelming sense of loneliness engulfed her. She closed the album and set it aside.

With a flick of the knob, she turned off the bedside table lamp and lay back on the mound of pillows. Her eyes were wide open, sleep eluding her. She could hear the minutes click slowly on the grandfather clock in the hallway. It struck midnight and then one. She flipped back the covers and got out of bed, prowling through the shadows in the house.

Warm milk would help. She pulled a carton from the refrigerator and put a mug into the microwave. After it was warm, she stirred cocoa powder in and then shuffled back to her room, climbing under the covers. The warm cocoa soothed the edges of her jangled nerves, but it was going to be a long night.

Images of John filled her thoughts. She sipped the soothing beverage and snuggled into her mountain of down pillows and pale green comforter. With eyes growing heavy the sounds of the night lulled her to sleep.

Melinda lingered over her morning coffee. She had a perfect view out the back door to where Adam stood on the patio. What was he doing at her house so early? Her heart quickened. A slow, easy smile danced on his oh so kissable lips. When he turned and looked at her his eyes were like rich dark chocolate. He lifted his hand, extending it to her as if he was beckoning for her to join him.

She was inexplicably drawn to him. She longed to be in his arms. She seemed to glide out the door and down the steps. His fingers curled towards him, propelling her forward without words. She placed her small hand in his. Warmth radiated up her arm, heating her skin. His eyes seemed to drink in every inch of her face. He cupped her cheek and let his fingers guide her lips towards his.

Melinda could almost taste the sweet smell of chocolate that clung to him. She held her breath, waiting anxiously for the moment when his lips would caress hers. A warm sensation crept up her midsection.

Forced to open her eyes, she sat straight up. She was in bed alone with what was left of her cocoa pooling on the bedcovers and soaking her pajamas. Confused, she looked around. The patio and Adam had vanished.

Setting the mug on the bedside table, she eased out of bed and dashed into the adjoining bath to get something to sop up the mess. Mumbling under her breath about the stupidity of spilling cocoa, she blotted the liquid as best she could, turning her pretty white towels a dull brown.

"Great, just great." She tossed the towel into the tub. Then she shed her silky nightgown and wrapped her terry robe around her. Hands on hips, she decided she was not going to be sleeping in that bed for the rest of the night. Without turning on any additional lights, she padded barefoot across the hall, the deep plush carpet drowned out the annoyance in her walk.

What was she doing dreaming of Adam Bell? He was a client and a friend. She shouldn't be imagining what it would be like to have his fingers trail along the curve of her cheek as if relishing the feel of her skin. And what was her dream-self doing, actually yearning for his touch?

She pulled back the covers of her guest bed and slipped in between the cool jersey sheets. She lay back and closed her eyes, but she couldn't shake the image of Adam's seductive smile. She flipped over and readjusted the blankets. Closing her eyes, Melinda forced her mind to go blank. Dear heaven, she needed some sleep.

~

*I*t had been three days since Melinda had seen Adam. They'd talked on the phone and texted a bit, but each time she volunteered to stop by, he said he was resting. Was he dealing with some PTSD? The injury to his hand may have triggered something.

Finally, having been stalled long enough, she decided to take the bull by the horns. She finished packing a cooler with fresh fruit, vegetables and salads. After loading everything in the car, she sent a quick text: *Stopping by, don't plan on staying but you'll have provisions.*

She turned her phone off so she couldn't receive his usual no thanks text.

After making the short drive to his place, she walked up the stairs. With a sharp knock on the door, she heard, "Hold on a minute."

She called out, "Are you decent?"

A chuckle answered her. "Not quite."

She could hear a few cuss words, a thump and something crash.

"Adam, let me in." The doorknob didn't turn. "Unlock the door or I'm going to call Will."

"I'm okay, I just knocked over the side table. Give me one more minute."

She pulled her phone out just as the door opened. Adam had a three-day growth on his chin. At first glance she saw the apartment was a mess, which was surprising given his tendency toward neat and tidy. His face lit up when he saw her. His brown eyes twinkled with merriment as he noticed the cooler over one arm and she balanced her phone and handbag in her other hand. He held out his good hand to take the cooler. "You're a persistent lady, aren't you?"

Melinda stepped into the apartment, dropped a bag on the sofa and immediately walked over to the table, righting it and picking up the shards of coffee-coated glass.

"I'll get that," Adam said, coming up behind her.

"It'll be quicker if I do it." She gestured to the kitchen. "You can unload the cooler and I'll take it with me."

With a soft laugh, he did as she asked. She heard him give a low whistle. "I'm not starving or anything." He poked his head out of the kitchen. "But everything looks great."

"That's good." She entered the kitchen and walked to a long cupboard. "Is the broom in there?"

"I'll get it for you."

She found it cute as the flush covered his cheeks. "Tell you what, you can make us coffee and I'll finish cleaning up, and then I need to get back to my office."

"Working today?" He filled the coffeepot with fresh water and measured out the beans to grind.

Melinda took the container from him and nodded appreciatively at the label. "Grinding beans? You've got fancy coffee."

"My sister got me hooked on it when I retired from the Corps."

"Remind me to thank your sister, if I ever meet her."

"By any chance did you tuck anything sweet in that other bag?" He pointed to the one she had set on the sofa.

"You're incorrigible, but yes. I brought muffins—banana nut, which I believe is your favorite." She gave him a saucy grin.

With mild surprise he beamed. "A woman who takes note of the little things. Nice." Turning the coffee on to brew he said, "One of these days I'm taking you out for coffee."

She started to mildly protest and Adam laughed. "Mel, it's just coffee."

She wiggled her eyebrows. "In my line of work lots of things can happen with 'it's just coffee'."

CHAPTER 22

Adam left his doctor appointment feeling pretty pumped. He was going back to work. Taking a week to let the cut heal without pulling at the stitches had been the right thing to do, but he was bored out of his mind. There were only so many crossword puzzles he could do and daytime television didn't interest him.

After stopping at the drugstore for latex gloves to protect his hand, he drove straight to Melinda's house. When he arrived, there was a car in the driveway, so he headed for the backyard.

After setting the sawhorses in place, he remembered Mel had said his tools were in the garage. He debated between knocking on the door to see if she could open the garage or just sit and wait until she was done. He wasn't all that anxious to interrupt her, so he flopped into a chair, stuck his legs out in front of him and soaked up the afternoon rays. There was a nip in the air—fall was on its way too quickly, as far as he was concerned.

He felt his leg being nudged and quickly sat up straight. Melinda was staring at him as she tried to hold back a smile. "Adam, what are you doing here?"

"The doc said I could go back to work, so here I am."

Melinda teased. "Snoozing in my yard constitutes as work now?"

He had never met anyone who was as good at bantering with him as Mel. "In my defense, I got here and realized all my tools were locked in your garage. I knew you were with a client, so I was just going to wait until you finished." With a sheepish grin he said, "I must have nodded off."

She crossed her arms over her stomach. "Maybe this is a sign you should give yourself another day?"

He sprang up. "I don't think so." He put his hands together like he was praying. "Please, if you would be so kind as to let me into your garage I can get busy."

"Sit back down and keep me company. I've been in the office all day and could use some fresh air and vitamin D."

He sat down with a smirk. "You're the boss."

She gave him an annoyed looked before saying, "The doctor said you're healed?'

"He did." Adam was done talking about his medical issues. "How's business?"

"Brisk. If I didn't know better, I would swear it was spring."

"I don't understand. What's special about spring?" he asked.

"People come out of hibernation and all thoughts turn to love, especially after Valentine's Day."

He cocked his head. "I had no idea."

She kicked off her sandals and wiggled her bright pink toes. "Statistics show most people are anxious for warm weather and new adventures. Hence higher numbers of first dates in the spring, and most break-ups happen before the holidays to avoid that awkwardness of taking someone home to meet the family. You get through the holidays solo, cocoon for the winter months and say *hello* in spring again." She tilted her head back and closed her eyes. "So, statistically speaking, I should be slowing down as we're sliding into fall and winter."

He liked listening to her talk about business, with a touch of sass. "Does that mean if you meet someone now it won't last?"

Without looking at him she said, "Not at all. It typically takes one to two years to know if someone will really fit into your life."

"Well, that's good. I wouldn't want to be setting myself up to fail."

"Adam," she chuckled, "you're a great catch." She dropped her head and leveled her gaze at him. "Have you talked to Beth?"

"No. With this happening"— he held up his hand — "I haven't felt much like putting the effort into dating."

"Maybe you should say something to her. She's probably wondering if you fell off the end of the earth. Or you decided you didn't want to go out again."

Adam heard a subtle reproach in Mel's voice. "You're right. I'll call her tonight. What about you and that guy, the client you said hit on you? Have you heard if things went well with his match?"

Her eyebrow arched. "Actually, I heard from Nick and Gretchen. Things are going well for them."

Mildly curious he asked, "He didn't ask you out again?"

"No, I was pretty firm." Melinda stood up. "I have to get back into the office and finish up some computer work. Before I do, I'll help you haul out whatever tools you need."

Adam's gazed slid up and down. "I don't think so. Pale pink top and white pants. You'll be wearing grease and grime from head to toe."

"I'm washable," she said pointedly.

"All you need to do is unlock the door and we can both get back to work."

Melinda paused. "You're kind of bossy you know?"

He gave a hearty laugh. "Military training. Lots of practice at both giving and receiving them." He pointed to her back door. "Now, if you would so kindly open the door, I can get back to work."

She stormed toward the house, but over her shoulder she laughed, "Catch you later."

As soon as she went inside Adam began taking measurements. Concentrating on the tape he didn't notice Will had come around the corner of Melinda's garage. "Adam." Will held up his tool belt. "Thought I'd lend you a hand." He snickered. "No pun intended."

Adam frowned. "That's a bad joke."

"What do you have left to do?" Will glanced at the structure and gave a low, appreciative whistle. "When Stacey sees this, I'm in trouble. She's going to want one in our backyard."

Adam gave him a sidelong look and chuckled. "That can be arranged. For a price."

Casually Will said, "Have you seen Melinda today?"

"Why?"

Will hitched the belt into place and said, "No reason."

"I need to get this decorative trim ripped down."

"So that's how you sliced your finger."

"Yeah."

Will stretched out the tape and said, "How wide does this need to be?"

Adam handed him a piece of paper with the measurements. "Let's get the tools from the garage and you can handle the saw."

They worked together cutting the long lengths of board and laying them to one side.

Adam stuck a pencil behind his ear. "There's another ladder in my truck if you want to grab it."

Will said, "It's none of my business, but..."

Adam gave him one of his stern Major looks. "Then maybe you shouldn't say anything."

Will's face lit up with humor. "Do you like Melinda?"

Thinking fast he said, "Of course, I do. She's a great lady and we've become good friends."

"No," Will said slowly, "heart-pounding like."

Sharper than he intended, Adam said, "Of course not."

With a nod of his head Will grinned. "Just as I thought."

Adam's temper spiked. "I have no idea what you mean."

"I'll get that ladder." Will started to walk away. Over his shoulder he said, "Talk to her, bro."

Adam looked at the house. One thing Will had right—Adam did need to share a few more details about his last tour. But maybe not a full disclosure. Not yet.

~

Melinda heard a tentative knock on her back door as she chopped vegetables for a salad. She peered around the corner and saw Adam standing on the step. "Come on in."

Adam opened up the screen door. "Hey, Mel. I'm done for today and the trim is finished. I think it looks pretty good."

"Give me a minute and you can show me." She dumped the shredded carrots in the bowl. "Did I hear Will earlier?"

"Yeah. He thought I could use an extra hand."

She nodded thoughtfully. "I would have helped."

"You're the client. I couldn't have you on a ladder holding up boards." His voice had a sharp edge to it.

She studied his face. Something seemed to be on his mind. "Is everything okay?"

"Yeah. I want to finish this job."

She wondered if she'd shared too much about John and made things awkward with Adam.

"Any chance you can take a break and we can talk?"

Melinda paused. "Let me just cut up this broccoli and onion, and then we can sit out back and have a beer or glass of wine."

"I'll get them, if that's okay."

"Help yourself. There are frosted mugs in the freezer, and would you grab a beer for me too?"

Adam opened the freezer drawer and pulled out the frosted mugs and then took two bottles of pale ale from the fridge. He slowly poured the beer into the mugs.

Teasing, she said, "You're really concentrating on those glasses."

"Well, I want to keep it from overflowing onto the counter. That would be a waste of good beer."

Melinda slid the bowl of chopped vegetables into the refrigerator and picked up a mug. "I'm all set. Let's go out back and talk. You can tell me whatever it is that's distracting you."

Adam's head snapped up. "What makes you say that?"

"You're quiet and distant today, and usually you're smiling or teasing me." Melinda pushed open the door and held it for Adam.

He didn't say anything until they were both settled. Seeming to stall, he took a long drink of his beer. He set the mug down. "I've been doing a lot of thinking since you told me about John."

Melinda averted her eyes. She knew it had been way too much information to share.

He laid a hand on the arm of her chair. "I'm humbled by your strength."

She felt tears prick her eyes, but she blinked them away. "From the hospital to the day after the funeral, every day was horrific. I'm not sure how I made it through."

"I would guess between the support of your family and John's brothers in blue, you took it one day at a time."

"His squad members were amazing. Even after the funeral and right up until I moved. They were there for every rough day. Donating his clothes, sorting and packing his fitness gear for the local Y. You know, weights, golf clubs, stuff like that."

Adam leaned forward in his chair. "You were lucky to have them."

"I know. When life-changing events occur, not everyone has people to support them. Sometimes you just need a friend willing to be in the same room while you process whatever emotions your feeling, never pushing, just offering support."

"Exactly." He wrung his hands. "Which is what I wanted to talk to you about. I'd like to tell you why I broke it off with my ex, Anita."

CHAPTER 23

Adam swallowed hard. "Where to begin." He looked across the yard. This was going to be tough. He had decided not to tell her about his leg. It would be too much to dump on her at once. Who was he kidding? It was too much for him. What if she felt sorry for him? He couldn't bear to see the pity in her eyes.

Melinda watched him. Patiently waiting. She wasn't at all like Anita.

"I'll do my best to skip the gory details."

Softly she said, "I'm a good listener." She scooted her chair closer.

"I went into the service with a plan. I'd retire sometime around forty. I had been in for about five years when I met Anita. In the beginning she didn't seem to mind that I was gone for six months or more at a time. She lived close to where I was stationed in San Diego and we stayed in touch when I was deployed, but when I was stateside we spent all our time together. Hiking, biking, climbing, surfing, you name it. We did it all. She loved going full throttle, all the time. We traveled extensively. All good times."

"You loved her."

"I did." He took a sip of his beer. "I was going to ask her to marry me."

Melinda's eyes grew wide but she remained quiet.

Adam's voice dropped. "Nothing can prepare you for when you're shipped to the sandbox." Mel's eyes drew together, confused. "That's how the military personnel deployed with me referred to the desert. It's like a never-ending sandbox. Only in the war zone instead of ants and bugs crawling around, the bastards sink IEDs into roadways."

He kept his voice steady. "In the military you train, train and train some more. We're willing to fight for our country. You can never fully be prepared for what the enemy is going to do. As an officer my primary job is to always protect my men. I will take whatever comes our way as long as they're okay I was good. It's our mentality and it's difficult to explain that connection of brotherhood."

Adam felt his gut tighten. He pushed himself to keep talking. "We were on a routine patrol. My men and I were driving behind the lead vehicle. They hit an IED. They died instantly. Three men and one woman. Good Marines. Gone." His voice cracked. "Before I could register what happened to the Humvee in front of us, we hit another IED."

He dropped his head into his hands. He felt Mel come to his side and slide her arms around him. She held him close. This small act comforted him.

He choked on the next few sentences. Gulping to take in oxygen. He felt as if there was a vise constricting the air from his lungs. Beads of sweat covered his forehead. His heart began to pound. He forced himself to keep going. "My driver and I were injured in the next blast. I never felt such pain. I could see him screaming. I was temporarily deaf. His arm was gone." He shuddered. "After that, time stopped. Everything seemed to happen in ultra-slow motion. I have no idea how long it took until we were airlifted out. I had several surgeries to put me back together and a pretty bad concussion." He paused. Mel didn't ask any questions. She waited for him to continue. "A lot of lives changed that day. Mine included."

Melinda smoothed away the beads of sweat that popped up on his forehead, and wrapped him in her arms.

"Anita came to see me in the hospital. At first, she was compassionate and understanding. Losing my people was unbearable. For those of us who survived, our injuries were severe. She said she understood and would stand by me." He shook his head slowly from side to side. "When she came to see me in the rehab facility, the reality that I was different changed things between us. Not for me, but I could see the look in her eyes. In an instant it changed her. I took early retirement, I went back to a small town near Parris Island. I rented a house and Anita moved in with me. I wanted to believe everything was going to work out. But that was the beginning of the end."

"You don't have to talk about it anymore. I get the idea. It was easier for her when you were gone for long stretches of time."

"No. While I was healing and going through physical therapy, she knew I was dealing with my physical injuries. But the PTSD, that was worse. I kept blaming myself. What could I have done differently to keep my men safe?"

"Adam. That is normal. Especially as an officer it is part of your training." She moved to her chair and grasped his hands with hers. She tilted his chin up to meet her eyes. The simple gesture almost pushed him over the emotional edge as the memories engulfed him.

"Anita couldn't deal with the reality that I had changed. I shut down. I guess she thought we could just start a new life and enjoy my retirement." With a snort he said, "Unplanned retirement."

"How did you end up in Connecticut?"

"Anita and I had a disagreement. She wanted things the way they used to be, me to be the way I used to be. I wasn't that easygoing guy anymore. She moved back to California and I moved here."

"I'm sure Will was thrilled to have you close by."

"He was. Is." Adam finally looked Mel directly in the eye. "I know I have a hard time connecting with people. I'm much warier when I meet someone new."

"Which is why dating is challenging for you." It wasn't a question, but a statement.

"What if the way I changed, because I hold myself responsible for the deaths of my team, will affect any future relationship? Look at what it did with Anita."

"I don't know what she felt or why. You must know it's not uncommon for a spouse or loved one to have a harder time dealing with a veteran when they return home from a war zone whether they wear their injuries on the inside or externally. I do know we all change as a result of events in our lives. I know I'm different." She rested her hand over his hammering heart. "You need to be who you are today. Let go of the pain you feel she caused. The right woman will love you, scars and all."

Her tender smile cracked the icy band that encased his heart. She was right. Someday he would find love. He took her hand from his chest and gently kissed the top of it.

That was when he knew Will was dead on. He was falling in love with Melinda.

He let go of her hand. Melinda didn't seem to notice it was abrupt. He picked up his mug and gulped down the lukewarm beer. "Thank you for listening."

In a quiet voice she said, "I'm always here for you, Adam."

He knew she meant it. "You're very sweet."

They sat quietly in the waning light, listening to the peepers, each lost in their own thoughts. When darkness had fallen he broke the silence. "I'm quite the mess, aren't I?"

"You're not. I wish you had told me about this before I started working to find you a match. It would have helped me."

He couldn't help but flash her a big grin. "Are you saying if I had shown you my warts, we might have skipped Susan?"

She held her hands up in mock defense. "I can't be held responsible for someone who deliberately evades the truth."

"No sweat. I've forgiven you." He watched her cheeks flush an attractive shade of pink.

"If I had something to throw at you, I would." She laughed.

"Any interest in staying for dinner?"

"Thanks, but I'm going to head home. I told Will I'd swing by. He says Stacey is going to want a pergola in their backyard. Seems you're a trendsetter."

She beamed. "That's good for you, more clients."

He nodded. "I hadn't thought of it in that context. Would you mind if I took a few pictures? I put together an idea book for when I meet with new customers."

"Of course. Take as many as you want."

Adam tilted his mug back and drained the remnants of his beer. "I appreciate the beer and the talk."

"If you can keep a secret, I'll tell you something I haven't told anyone since I moved to Chester."

His eyes grew wide and he said, "Of course."

"Before starting the matchmaking business, I was a therapist. Listening is kind of my gig." Mel held a finger to her lips and smiled.

Adam looked at her and said, "I can see how you'd be a great therapist. Why did you stop?"

"I'd rather help people find love, and my background helps." She cautioned, "I wouldn't want word getting around, though. Some people might get turned off thinking they were talking to a shrink instead of a simple matchmaker."

"Are you Dr. Phillips?"

With a shake of her head, she said, "Phillips is my married name, I was Dr. Melinda Grayson."

Slack-jawed, he asked, "Didn't you have some night time radio show?"

Her eyes popped. "How would you know about that?"

"I used to listen to a lot of talk radio when I was in the hospital. You were good. Why did you stop?" What he didn't say was she helped him through some very dark, very lonely nights.

"I needed a change. I left all that behind when I moved here."

"That's a shame. A lot of people would call in just to tell you how your advice helped them. I know listening to you helped me. You were kind of a big deal at the rehab facility."

"I'm glad. After the accident, I didn't have anything to give. I needed to heal myself first."

Adam nodded in understanding. "It's like in an airplane. The attendant always instructs you to put your oxygen mask on first and then help others."

"I guess that does apply to this situation." Melinda stood up and took his glass. "Please keep my secret."

Adam stood next to Mel. "You know, I could help you set up a studio and you could do it from the privacy of your home. Nobody would have to ever know and you could help people again."

"Adam."

He could hear the warning in her voice. He had tread on ground best left alone. "Sorry, Mel."

She laid a hand on his arm. "I appreciate the offer, but I am very happy being a matchmaker." She crossed the patio and looked back over her shoulder. "Take your pictures and come in before you leave. I have a check for you."

Melinda disappeared inside the house leaving Adam alone. Should he have gone further and told her the extent of his injuries?

∼

*M*elinda closed the door behind her and sagged against the frame. She was shaken to the core. Angry at a woman she had never met, Anita.

Adam had served his country with honor and because of that suffered terrible injuries, endured emotional trauma, and he blamed himself for the loss of his people. She had worked with a few police officers after a particularly bad altercation and understood how someone in Adam's position would have felt. It was unfathomable to Melinda that Anita didn't support him better during his recovery. Not that she would ever tell Adam, but he was better off without Anita in his life. He was a good man and deserved so much better and she was going to make sure he found that woman.

The back door banged and Adam strolled in. "I got a couple of pictures to show Stacey. Will's going to have an impatient woman on his hands until we get it done."

Melinda grinned. "You know, I was thinking—I could host a barbeque and invite people over. You might get a few more clients."

"Or, if you really wanted to throw a party, just have one." He winked. "After all, from what I've heard from Stacey, your parties are legendary."

"Then it's settled. And if you happen to get any new clients as a result, you can take me to dinner as a thank you."

"It's a date." Color rushed to Adam's cheeks. "I didn't mean date."

"Relax. I know it's just dinner." She tore a piece of paper from her checkbook. "If that's not right, just let me know."

He glanced at it and frowned. "You overpaid me by ten percent."

Her eyes were bright. "It's a tip for helping me to fulfill a dream."

"You're too much, Dr. Melinda Grayson Phillips."

She wagged a finger at him. "Don't use my full name. You promised."

He gave a solemn salute. "Won't happen again, ma'am."

With a laugh Melinda steered him toward a barstool. "And you're staying for dinner and I won't take no for an answer."

CHAPTER 24

The party at Melinda's was in full swing when Adam arrived. He knew it was going to be a good time when he saw all the cars lining the street and he had to park at the very end. He could hear the music from the backyard and noticed the vibrant red and orange colors just beginning to emerge on the large maple trees lining the street. There was nothing like early fall in New England. He marveled at how quickly the summer had flown by.

He walked in the front door and through the kitchen. Smiling to himself, he set a bouquet of pink asters on the counter before he joined the party. He wondered if he'd be around when she saw them. He was sure Mel would like them.

His gaze roamed over the backyard. She had strung white twinkle lights on the beams of the pergola and hung lanterns, more likely for bugs than light. Stacey and Will were sitting with Molly and Tim next to the fire pit as it crackled and shot sparks in the air. He spotted Melinda nearby. She looked fantastic in snug-fitting jeans, a deep pink turtleneck sweater and loafers. She was carrying a platter of what he guessed were appetizers across the lawn to a group of people.

Before intercepting Mel, he grabbed a beer, said hello to some friends and walked over to where she was standing. Softly he said in her ear, "Hey, great party," and then took the tray out of her hands.

She turned quickly and his lips grazed her mouth. Without missing a beat, her face lit up. "About time you arrived." She pointed to a couple admiring his handiwork. "Sara and Marcia asked who my carpenter was." She took the tray back. "Go talk to them. Sounds like they might have some work for you." She gave him a nudge and murmured, "Remember our deal. I'm counting on a nice dinner and I don't plan on eating that day."

Her laughter followed him as he went over to introduce himself.

∼

What was that? He sort-of kissed me. Choosing to ignore the momentary awkwardness Melinda kept one eye on Adam and the other on the food table. It must have been purely by accident. If she hadn't turned quickly and if he hadn't been trying to be funny it would never have occurred. There was one thing she just couldn't let happen, and that was for anyone to be less than half full when they went home. She even had to-go containers ready for her guests to take home leftovers.

"Melinda, over here," Molly called and waved to her.

She strolled across the grass. Holding the tray out to Tim, he took a slice of the Stromboli and said, "You're spoiling us, Melinda. We were just saying we should have all our parties' right here."

"Tim, stop." She hoped she wasn't about to blush. She enjoyed being the hostess. It was much easier than being a guest —she had a reason to stay busy and it helped her avoid any personal conversations.

Molly looped arms with Tim. "We have good and bad news."

Melinda looked at Stacey. "Do we want to talk bad news today?"

"Well, there is a very happy conclusion, so here goes." Molly's face glowed. "You know I wanted to get married on Block Island and have a Christmas-themed wedding, but when the venue we wanted wasn't available on short notice, we had to postpone."

"Were you able to get your date for next year?"

"Funny you should ask, Melinda. We made some calls and by a fluke"—her voice went up several decibels—"someone cancelled at a mansion in Newport!" She squeezed Tim's hand so tight that Melinda thought he would lose feeling. "We're getting married at Rosecliff!" She bounced on her toes. "Can you believe it? We're all going to spend a weekend in Newport and have a beautiful Christmas-themed wedding."

Melinda wrapped her arms around Molly and Tim. "That's unbelievable," she said. "You're going to be a beautiful bride."

Adam hurried over. "What's going on? Molly, are you crying?"

"Happy tears, Adam. We've moved the wedding to Newport."

Adam clapped Tim on the back and grinned. "Wow, that is quite a change."

"It is, but I've always said I was doing this one time, and we're going to make it an unforgettable weekend." He kissed Molly's forehead. "It's still going to be small, around seventy-five people. When we saw pictures of the mansion decorated for Christmas and that heart-shaped staircase, I had to agree with Molly. It is the best place for us to start our married life."

Adam looked around the group. "Guess that means we need to make plans."

Melinda said, "We'd all better make hotel reservations. Don't keep us in suspense, what's the new date?"

"It's the second Friday in December. Not too close to Thanksgiving or Christmas. And since we're not on an island we don't need to worry about the weather and we can have my Christmas-themed wedding after all." Molly beamed. "This way our anniversary won't be too close to either holiday."

"And the people we want at the wedding should be able to come." Tim smiled at Melinda and Adam and Will and Stacey. "You'll be there, right?"

Melinda said, "I wouldn't miss it for the world."

Adam nodded. "You can count on me."

Molly looked at Tim and then said, "One last thing. It's an evening wedding, so the wedding will be black tie. The ladies will wear gowns and the men tuxedos."

For the first time Will interjected. "Monkey suits?"

Adam laughed. "It won't kill you, and I seem to recall your bride exclaiming you looked very handsome in yours."

"Easy for you to say—you didn't wear one that day."

"I wore a suit."

Melinda jumped in. "Stacey, let's go shopping for dresses together."

"Sounds like fun." She poked Will. "You and Adam can go to the tux shop."

Will groaned. Molly jutted her lower lip out, pretending to pout. "Will, for me?"

"Not to worry. You can count on me and my brother from another mother." Will pointed to Adam. "You. Me. Tuxedos."

"Speaking of dates," Stacey said, "how was yours with Beth last night?"

"So, you finally called her?" Melinda said quietly. "Good for you."

"Was this a Melinda match?" Tim asked.

"It was." Adam kept his eyes on Mel. "We had a nice time. We were going to see that biopic about the rock band. But the lines were long, so instead we went to dinner."

Tim looked around the small group gathered around the fire. "Maybe we'll hear wedding bells again."

Adam held up his hand. "Let's not get carried away. It was our second date."

Molly grinned. "Tim can give you pointers on engagement rings."

Melinda felt her heart drop and noticed Adam's face flush red. "Adam, any chance you can help me for a minute. Inside?"

"Sure." He fell into step next to her. "Thanks."

"I can see they weren't going to give up on you. At least until you're standing at the alter with a bride."

"I'm not in any rush. I only want to get married once." He opened the door for her and stepped to one side. "What do you need help with?"

"Nothing." She flashed him a grin. "However, we'll need to do something to save face."

"I'm good at dishes."

"Oh, Adam." Melinda's eyes grew bright and she sighed. "Did you bring me flowers?"

"Why do you think it was me?" He gave her a lopsided smile.

"I seem to recall one of our first conversations was about my love of flowers." She leaned in and kissed his cheek. "This was very thoughtful." She couldn't help but notice his aftershave. Musky and very male.

"It was no big deal." He turned to the sink and filled it with steaming water and soap bubbles. He began to scrub a few pots and, after rinsing them, set them aside to drain.

Melinda watched and smiled. She remembered another guy doing the exact same thing when they had friends over, flowers and dish duty. In some ways Adam reminded her of John but in so many more they were very different men.

"Mel?"

"What? I'm sorry. I was lost in thought."

"I could tell. Looked like a nice memory." He dried his hands. "I've finished up these dishes. Are there more?"

"Not right now." She looked around. "Can you grab a couple of bottles of wine and we'll go back out?"

"Right." He slipped a corkscrew in his back pocket. "No sense in opening them now."

"Thinking on your feet."

"Are you sure you're doing okay?"

Melinda could see the concern on his face. "I was just remembering something about John." She laid a hand on his arm. "It was a nice memory."

"I wish I had met him," Adam said with sincerity.

"You would have been good friends." She picked up a stack of clear plastic cups. "Ready?"

~

Melinda finished the last of the dishes after the party ended. She went to lock the front door and was surprised to find it secured. "Adam."

The house was quiet as she wandered around, double-checking the windows and doors. The more time she spent with Adam and her friends, the more she discovered the silence could become oppressive. Was she wrong to decide she was done with love? Could she give her heart to another man? Would that be betraying John's memory?

She fired up her laptop and sent an email to Stacey, asking when she wanted to go dress shopping. She shut it down and, at a loss, decided to call Adam.

No. That was too weird. Besides, he was planning a third date with Beth. She had to wonder, since the wedding wasn't for two months...would he rather go with her? She dialed him before she could change her mind again.

Adam answered on the first ring. "Hi, Mel. Is everything okay?"

"I was thinking about Molly and Tim's wedding. If you want

to change our plans so you can bring a plus one, I'll understand."

"Do you want to go alone?"

She couldn't gauge his reaction by the tone in his deep, rich voice. "No, I'd love to go with you, it would be fun. I just didn't want you to feel obligated since we made our plans before you and Beth..." Her voice drifted off.

"I'm glad you called. I was concerned you'd think we needed to change our plans. How about I stop over tomorrow and we can check out local hotels and get one booked? I'll drive if you like—we can take the truck. It's very comfortable."

Melinda's heart fluttered. "We'll take my car, and I'll do some research and see if I can find a couple of hotel options."

"Tim mentioned it's less than a two-hour drive."

"Good." Melinda hesitated. "Well, I guess that's it for tonight." She couldn't find a reason to keep the conversation going.

"I'm glad that's settled."

"Adam, if you do change your mind, I'd understand."

"I won't and you can't either. We're going to this extravaganza together." He chuckled. "Just curious. Do you know how to fix a bow tie?"

She laughed. "I do."

CHAPTER 25

Melinda had dashed through the shower after spending the morning puttering around the yard getting everything ready for winter. She was a grimy mess and hardly fit to spend time with Adam and make plans for the wedding weekend.

She heard a knock on the front door. "I'll be right out," she called through the open bedroom door. She grabbed the tube of mascara and coated her lashes, added a swish of blush and ran lip gloss over her lips. She was ready.

She pulled open the door and discovered Nick standing on her doorstep, holding a bouquet of flowers. Taken aback she said, "Nick."

"Melinda." He handed her the brightly colored mix. "I only have a minute. Gretchen is waiting for me in the car."

Adam's truck pulled into the driveway. Conversation stalled as he strode purposefully up the walk.

"Hey, Mel." He looked at the other man.

"Adam." She gave him a tight smile. "This is Nick."

Adam stepped around Nick and slipped his arm possessively around her waist. He kissed her cheek. "How can we help you?" Melinda held her smile in check.

"I'm here to thank Melinda. She's been working with me. I wanted to express my appreciation." He looked at Melinda and grinned. "Gretchen is amazing."

She accepted the flowers. "These weren't necessary, but thank you. They're lovely."

"It's a small token of my, or I should say, *our* appreciation."

Gretchen got out of the car and strolled up the walk. She gave Melinda a slow smile. "Thank you, Melinda." She slipped her arm through Nick's.

"I'm thrilled for both of you."

Nick held out his hand and shook hers. "Have a good night."

The couple walked hand in hand back to his car.

Adam stepped away and smirked. "Sorry about that."

"It's nice to know you've got my back." They walked inside and she closed the door behind them.

Adam trailed behind Melinda as she walked into the living room. She set the flowers on a side table. "I remember you telling me about one of your clients coming on to you. When I saw Nick, I figured he was the guy and I was hoping he wasn't putting pressure on you to go out."

"I'll have to admit, I had the same thought." She eased down to the sofa. "Please have a seat."

Adam sat next to her and said, "You smell nice. Like lily of the valley."

She hit a key on her laptop and it came to life. "I spent the afternoon in the garden and wanted to get cleaned up before you got here." She waved her hand from head to toe. "This was as far as I got."

"You look great."

"Apparently you need to have your eyes checked." She smirked and pointed to the screen. "I found three options for a hotel." She turned it around so Adam could see too. "I like them all, full of old-world charm."

He studied the screen. "Do you have a favorite?"

"Oh no." She laughed. "I'm not saying a word until you rank them."

"I prefer an inn over a chain hotel."

Her eyebrow shot up. "Really?"

He clicked on the Captain's Inn and scrolled. "What about this one? It's not far from the mansions and within walking distance to downtown. Maybe we could walk around and have lunch while we're there."

"That sounds like fun." She turned the laptop back around. Clicking keys, she pulled up the reservation link. "We'll go down on Thursday and back on Saturday?"

"Let's come home on Sunday. We can make it a long weekend."

"I've never been to Newport, have you?"

Adam said, "No. But there must be a lot of stuff to do there." He inched closer to her. They were thigh to thigh. "Let's take a look." His eyes twinkled. "This will be my first vacation in a long time."

Melinda gave him a sidelong glance, ignoring the tingling sensation zipping through her blood. "Then we'd better make the most of it."

~

With reservations confirmed and a plan for activities, which included a winery tour and a few other mansions after the wedding, Melinda set the laptop aside. "I'll let Stacey know where we're going to stay. Maybe they'll want to stay at the same inn."

Adam gave her a half hug. "That would be fun."

She smoothed back her hair and asked, "Do you want to talk about your date with Beth?" Her heart felt like a weight in her chest.

"She's nice," he began, "high energy and always seems to be on the go."

Melinda picked at a thread on the cushion next to her. "I got the distinct impression no grass was going to grow under her feet."

"There is something to be said for sitting and relaxing. Like walking on the beach, holding hands with a pretty girl." He smiled, "Or kicking back on the patio. If you're rushing around all the time, you miss stuff."

Melinda's cheeks grew pink. "You do," she said slowly.

"I love being outside, but I also enjoy movies and concerts. Which are not high on Beth's list of things to do."

"Do you think you should go out again, maybe take in a movie or concert? What if she does enjoy them but it's not her first thought of a fun date night?"

"That's a good idea. I *have* enjoyed her company." Adam flashed Melinda a grin. "I'll ask if she'd like to go listen to a band."

"An excellent idea."

Melinda moved to get up from the couch when Adam decided to ask, "I might be beating a dead horse, but what about you? Have you thought about dipping your toe into the dating world?"

"No." She chewed on her bottom lip. "I was flattered when Nick flirted with me, but he wasn't my type."

"I wasn't necessarily referring to him." He regarded her carefully before asking his next question. "Don't get mad but I want to ask you again, do you think John would have wanted you to spend the rest of your life alone?"

He saw her grief flash across her face. "I don't think that is a fair question. It wasn't like John and I had a reason to discuss his death."

"Mel, of course you didn't. I'm sure the last thing either of you thought about was what would happen if one of you died. But you must have had some type of conversation about what if. After all, he was a cop in a city. He had to face danger every day."

She thrust out her chin. "He was a good police officer."

He could see the challenge in her eyes and said quietly, "I have no doubt, but there is an inherent risk as a cop."

"We did talk about the future once. We set up life insurance policies and wrote our wills."

"That sounds like you made plans." He noticed her eyes filled with sadness. A depth he had never seen in them before.

Her voice quavered. "Can we change the subject?"

"So how about those Sox?"

She gave him a quizzical look. "What socks?"

Adam chuckled. "The baseball team? You know, out of Boston?"

"Oh, right."

"You're not a fan?"

"I wasn't prepared for you to switch our conversation to baseball." She gave him a smile. "Have you ever been to Fenway?"

"No. It's on my list."

"Your list? You have to go. All that history, the Big Green Monster. It is something to experience."

"You've been?"

"Heck yeah. I love baseball." She leaned forward. "Tell me more about your list."

Adam's interest was piqued. He wondered why he hadn't known this about Mel. They could have gone to a game. "One of my life goals is to visit all thirty stadiums."

Her eyes grew wide. "Now that's an interesting goal! How many have you been to?"

"So far, nine, including the one in Toronto."

"That leaves twenty-two. What's your plan for hitting them all?"

"I need a plan?" He gave a snort.

Completely serious, she opened the laptop. "Let's make one."

"I was kind of hoping to have someone to go with me."

"I'll go with you." Even before the words were out, she

wondered how that must sound. She decided to overlook her stupid comment. She tilted her head up and looked at him in dismay. "Why didn't you mention this when we were filling out your questionnaire?"

"I didn't think of it?"

Melinda leaned back against the cushions and gave an exasperated sigh. "Adam, really. The more information you give me, the easier it is to match you with the right woman. Is there anything else you've neglected to tell me?"

He waited for a moment and then said, "I can't tell if you're teasing or serious."

"This is my business and I take it very serious." She gave him a smile to soften her words.

Adam said, "I'm sorry. It just seems things that I think aren't that big of a deal are relevant to this whole dating thing."

"Hold on a minute." Melinda rose from the sofa and crossed the front hall into her office. He saw a light glow after he heard a click.

Curiosity got the better of him. Adam followed her. "What's going on?"

She held up a manila folder. "I wanted to look at your file."

With a snort he asked, "Why?"

She held up a finger. "Patience." She scanned the first couple of pages and nodded. "Just as I thought, Beth can't stand baseball or football or basketball either."

He leaned against the doorjamb. "That puts a wrinkle in dating her. I'd like my lady to want to go to an occasional game with me."

Were they now thinking of excuses for Adam to *not* date Beth?

"We need to go over your questionnaire again. I have an idea that there are some key pieces of information missing."

He crossed his arms over his chest. "Maybe I'm a lost cause."

"No one is." She dropped the file on the desk.

"I'm glad one of us thinks so."

"Huh?"

"We've circled back to my original question."

Her brow wrinkled. "I don't know what you mean?"

"No one is a lost cause so maybe you should make your magic work on you." He dropped his arms to his sides. "I happen to think you're amazing. You're beautiful. You should be enjoying life and have someone to share it with. You should be looking at some of those questionnaires for yourself." He couldn't believe he had strung so many words together.

Melinda flicked off the light and said, "First of all, that would be unethical, and you forget, I have a date for Molly and Tim's wedding. I believe that counts for something."

"Now I'm confused." Was she about to say they had a real date, not just each other's plus one?

"You." She grinned and poked him playfully in the chest. "You're my date for the wedding."

Adam felt his heart thud deep in his chest. If only. "That is not the same thing and you know it."

"But I speak the truth." Melinda flashed him a flirtatious smile. "And we're going to have a great time."

CHAPTER 26

"Bridal shower or a Jack and Jill?" Stacey sat in Melinda's kitchen with a blank pad in front of her. She was tapping the closed end of the pen on it. "What do you think the happy couple would like better?"

"Did you ask Molly?" Melinda set the teapot on the counter and poured them each a cup.

"She said she trusts me and whatever I decide is fine." Stacey sipped her tea. "To be honest, I think working with the wedding planner in Newport is overwhelming her and they're just too busy to make any additional decisions."

"I'm sure the wedding is going to be stunning. I've looked online at other weddings held in the mansion, and what a setting." Melinda sighed and fanned herself. With a smile she said, "So romantic, and a Christmas theme will put it over the top."

Stacey brightened. "I think we should do a girls-only party. She deserves to be pampered. We could keep it small and intimate, go to the spa, and then we can meet up with the guys and enjoy a nice dinner. Molly is wound up like a top and this would be just the thing."

"That does sound nice. When should we do it?" Melinda

grabbed the calendar from the wall and slid it across the counter to Stacey. "With the wedding in early December, we're just about out of weekends, especially with Thanksgiving right around the corner."

Chewing her lip, Stacey pointed to the Saturday before the holiday. "Do you think we'll be able to book the spa and restaurant on short notice?"

Melinda hurried out of the room and yelled over her shoulder, "Only one way to find out. Let me look up the number and we'll make a few calls."

"I'll work on the guest list." Stacey replied.

She came back into the kitchen with her computer. "Did you figure out how many girls?"

"There are two, including me, in the wedding party. Molly gave me the guest list." She looked at Melinda. "I think if we invite the girls who are local, we'd have ten."

"Nice size group." Melinda clicked a few keys. "Here we go, the Blue Door. It has a five-star rating." She scrolled down the page. "There is a four-hour package that includes a massage, mani and pedi, shampoo, blow dry and then makeup session. We could spend the afternoon there, then go to dinner at Vera's. I'll request the private dining room."

"That sounds great. We could have the guys meet us for drinks and dinner. Pamper the bride and share our stunning beauty with the men afterward."

Melinda laughed. "Sounds like a plan. I'll call the spa and you call the restaurant. Book it for twenty. Are you sure we don't need to check with Molly?"

Stacey smiled. "She loves surprises, and I happen to know Tim said whatever we planned he'd make sure it worked." She picked up her cell.

Busy with their own tasks, they quickly wrapped up their respective phone calls. Melinda set her phone aside. "I'll create the invitations and then when we get paper we can print them here, and get them out tomorrow."

"While you do that, I'll run down to the office supply store and get fancy paper and envelopes." Stacey set her empty teacup aside and stood up. "I'll pick up sandwiches for lunch while I'm out."

"Sounds good." Melinda stretched her arms over her head working a kink out of her lower back. She really could use a massage. Too many hours in front of her computer was killing her back. "Stacey, has Adam mentioned anything about Beth to you?"

With a slow shake of her head, Stacey said, "Not to me. I know he and Will talk a lot, pretty much about everything. It's been like that since I started dating Will."

Melinda frowned. "I don't think it's going well."

"Why do you think that?" Stacey sat back down. "Has Adam said something to you?"

"He was telling me she's high energy and doesn't want to slow down and enjoy some of the quieter things in life, like a ball game, dinner, movies and concerts." She twirled a lock of hair around her finger, her brain working in overdrive. "I thought he was a big outdoors kind of guy."

Slowly, Stacey said, "Well, he is, but after he got out of the service he was different."

"Different how?" Melinda's curiosity was piqued.

Stacey seemed to measure her words carefully. "He's less talkative than he was."

"I'm not trying to pry, but I seem to be striking out in the love connection process. I've never had two poor choices in a row with one client."

"Melinda, you're being too hard on yourself. Beth and Adam had fun, but there just seems to be a lack of chemistry. That is something you can't calculate with a questionnaire. You can match two people on paper, but that doesn't necessarily translate into what you like to call a love connection."

"I know you're right, but I really want to find him someone wonderful." Melinda shrugged. "He's a special man."

"I have faith in you and I'm sure he'll fall in love before long." Stacey grabbed her handbag from the back of the chair. "I'll be back soon." She pointed to Melinda's laptop. "And you need to get creative."

Melinda tapped the middle of her forehead and smiled. "I've got it all right here."

Stacey laughed as she walked toward the front door. "Then get cracking."

Melinda returned to the task at hand and jotted down the address of the spa and the date and time. She typed out the information to print later. Clicking a few keys, she pulled up Adam's questionnaire. After scrolling down the page, she sat back, even more confused. Based on Beth and Adam's personal compatibility and this document, they should be a decent match. "Was there something I missed? Or what is Adam holding back?"

A sharp rap on the back door distracted her. She looked around the corner and on the other side of the glass was Adam, grinning from ear to ear. She waved him inside.

He pulled open the door. "Hey, Mel."

"Hey yourself." Adam stepped into the kitchen. Melinda closed the door behind him. "I thought you and Will were working on Stacey's pergola."

"We were. Are. But I needed to see you."

"Why?" She leaned against the counter, trying to look casual.

"Beth agreed to go to the Stones cover band at Geer Musical Hall. And I have to thank you for pushing me to try again."

"That sounds like a lot of fun. The Stones are great." She couldn't help but notice the excitement didn't reach his eyes.

He cocked his head. "I told myself to give it one more date before I make a final decision."

"Adam?"

"Mel?" His voice was light and teasing.

"Am I pushing you too hard to date Beth?"

"No, not at all. I haven't dated for a while. I forgot it's tough, putting yourself out there."

"That's just it, dating shouldn't be hard. It should be exciting, nerve wracking, and most of all, something you look forward to. You shouldn't have to convince yourself to keep seeing someone."

Adam's brow furrowed. "I thought you'd be happy. She agreed to do something I enjoy." Irritated and frustrated, he spun around and started to stalk out the back door. He stopped and turned to look at her. "Mel, I'm confused. Are you trying to discourage me from going out with her again?"

Her stomach clenched. *Is that what I'm doing?* "Not at all. I want you to be happy."

"Would you be honest if I was going about this all wrong?"

She was at a loss for words. She finally said, "Of course I would. You're doing all the right things. Be patient and see if you feel differently after Friday night."

"So…I'm going out with Beth." His voice was lacking enthusiasm.

Her heart felt heavy in her chest. She felt like a fraud. She wished she was going with him on Friday. What was wrong with her? The next words came out in a rush. "You'll have a good time."

"All right then." A look of confusion slipped across his face.

"Be sure to let me know how it goes." Melinda forced herself to smile.

"I'll talk to you on Saturday. Let's get together for breakfast. My treat."

"Sounds fun." Melinda knew she spoke the truth. She was already looking forward to seeing Adam again. She quickly told herself it was nothing more than to hear about his date.

He crossed the room and gave her a peck on the cheek. "I'll swing by and pick you up around eight?"

"Sure." She nodded and watched as the door banged closed behind him. She reached up and touched her cheek. What the heck was happening? She never had another client take her to breakfast or kiss her.

Flustered, she went back and tapped on the computer keys while she waited for Stacey to return.

~

*A*dam pulled into the sandwich shop's parking lot. He turned off the ignition and sat there. What was it about Mel that had him wanting to tell her what happened to him; how he felt lost when he had to retire and of course the part of himself that was ripped away.

He hit the steering wheel with his fist and swore softly to himself. Mel wasn't Anita. When she learned the truth, she would understand why he hadn't said anything.

He turned the rearview mirror so he could look at his face. Talking to his reflection, he said, "Is this why you're not connecting to Beth? You don't want her to know about your extra hardware? Or is it really because of Mel?"

He didn't have answers to his questions. Since Anita had walked away from him, Adam had protected his heart from feeling an emotional connection with any woman. Will understood as much as anyone could who hadn't lived through it, and Stacey was a sweetheart. They kept his secret.

A sharp rap on the window broke his train of thought. Stacey was smiling at him. He pushed the button and the window slid down. "Adam, what are you doing here?"

"I stopped to pick up lunch for me and Will."

Stacey held up a bag. "Great minds think alike. I'm on my way back to Melinda's."

"Really? I was just over there and she didn't say anything about you."

Stacey cocked her head. "What were you doing there?"

"I wanted to tell her I have another date with Beth."

Stacey looked at him but didn't speak.

"We're going to listen to music and have a bite to eat." Silence from Stacey urged him to keep talking. "And if that goes well, we'll go out again."

She was still silent. "Aren't you going to say something?" he asked.

She lifted a shoulder. "I'm going to be honest with you."

"I wouldn't expect anything less."

"When you met Beth, what was your first thought?"

Adam was confused. "I'm not sure what you're asking."

"Did you think she was smart, pretty, interesting? You know, what did you think?"

He dropped his head. "I wondered how I'd ever keep up with her. Based on her profile and just her personality, she's like the Energizer bunny."

"But did she catch your attention?"

"Well, no."

"When was the last time you felt that way, totally captivated and like you never wanted the conversation or the moment to end?"

He slumped against the seat cushion. Without answering Stacey, he thought, *Every time I'm with Mel.*

CHAPTER 27

Stacey beamed at him while Adam groaned, "What have I done, broken the cardinal rule of working with a matchmaker?"

"My work here is done." She smirked and tossed her hair. "I'm going back to Melinda's. Tell Will I'll be home later." She poked Adam in the arm. "Don't be hard on yourself, you two are perfect for each other."

"Except that she has zero interest in dating me or anyone else."

Stacey grinned. "You've fallen in love with a woman you haven't even dated. Give it time." She patted his arm. "She's a great person."

He nodded. "I know. She's the best."

"Adam…" He could hear the cautionary tone in her voice. "You have to tell her the truth about your injury before she finds out. It's best for you and her."

"We've known each other for a few months. Do you think I should have told her already?"

"As part of the matchmaking process, yes."

"You know I don't like to talk about it." He lifted his head. "I don't want her to treat me differently."

"Trust her." Before Stacey walked away, she paused. "You should have asked Mel to the concert. Not Beth." Without another word, she got in her car and drove away.

He pushed open his truck door and stepped out. He had a date with Beth on Friday and he was going to keep his distance from Melinda until Saturday. That would give him time to figure out what he really wanted.

"Damn it." In a few weeks he and Mel would be spending the weekend together at a wedding. How the hell was he going to hide his growing feelings from her? Or did he have to hide them? He wondered if it was time to throw caution to the wind and go after the woman he really wanted to be with.

∼

Adam took a deep breath before he knocked on Beth's door. He didn't want to hurt her feelings, but once he had made the decision to cancel their date, he needed to do it in person.

Knock, knock.

It opened before his arm returned to his side. "Hi, Adam, it's nice to see you." Beth stepped away from the door and turned to walk down the hallway. "Come on in."

Adam closed the door behind him. He couldn't help but notice she wasn't very tidy. She had sporting gear strewn around the hallway and a few dirty dishes on the side table. Unconsciously he compared it to Melinda's home and stopped himself.

He entered the small kitchen. Beth smiled brightly. "Can I get you a cup of coffee or perhaps a beer?"

"No, thanks. I can't stay long."

She wiped off the counter with a rag. "I've heard the band we're going to hear on Friday is really good."

"That's what I wanted to talk to you about."

"Oh?" Beth stopped what she was doing and leaned against the counter.

"I'm sorry, but I don't think we should go out again."

Her facial expression never changed. "May I ask why?"

He shifted uncomfortably from foot to foot. "I don't see a relationship developing between us. I didn't think it was fair to you to go out again once I made this decision."

A look of relief washed over Beth's face. "Thank heavens one of us had the courage to be honest."

Relief flooded him. "You felt the same way?"

A smile broke out across Beth's face. "I did. But you are such a good guy I kept telling myself to give it one more date, just to be sure something didn't spark."

"So you're not upset?"

She came around the counter and gave him a friendly hug. "Not in the least." She took a step back. "Is there someone you are interested in?"

"Am I that transparent?"

"Not at all. She's a lucky girl."

"Thanks, Beth. I appreciate you saying that."

"Good luck."

She walked him to the door, and Adam stopped on the threshold. "I hope Mel can help you find someone."

She gave him a knowing look. "Mel, huh?" He wasn't sure how to respond. With a laugh Beth said, "Don't look so shocked. You just saying her name speaks volumes."

He stepped onto the front walkway. "I have no idea what you mean."

"It's written all over your face. She is an amazing person and she's lucky too. Good luck Adam."

"See you later." Adam slowly walked down the path to his truck. All he had to do now was ask Mel to go out with him on Friday night.

Adam drove from Beth's to Mel's and then parked in her driveway. He sat there for over ten minutes. He couldn't procrastinate any longer. Before he had a chance to give it another thought, the front door opened and Melinda ran lightly down the front steps, the late afternoon sun glinting off her copper-colored curls.

She smiled at him. "Hey. Twice in one day."

He got out of the truck. "I hope I didn't catch you at a bad time?"

"Not at all. I just finished in the office and thought I saw your truck out here. Want to come in?"

"Yeah." Silently he admonished himself. He was going to have to do better than this. He caught the line of conversation Mel was on…

"Stacey and I have planned a wonderful bridal shower for Molly. The guys are invited to meet us for dinner. Do you want to join us too?"

Adam pulled open the front door and Mel stepped inside. "Sounds like a fun time." He wondered what she would wear to a nice dinner, he was sure she would look amazing. He grinned.

"Come on in the kitchen. I was just going to have a glass of wine. Interested?"

He couldn't take his eyes off her face. She seemed to sparkle.

"Sure." Another clever one-word answer. If Mel noticed, she didn't seem to take exception.

He waited while she poured two glasses of red wine and said, "It's cool out back—let's sit in the living room."

He followed as she strolled inside, clicking on a few lights as she walked. She settled on one end of the deep cushioned sofa while Adam sat at the other end.

"So, what brings you by?" She took a sip of wine and set her glass on the maple coffee table.

He shifted in his seat and set his glass down. "I came to a decision today."

"Do tell." Her smile gave him courage.

"I stopped by Beth's and cancelled our date for Friday night."

Melinda pulled at the fringe on a decorative pillow. "I'm not sure I understand. Earlier you said you were going to give it one more shot."

He inched forward on the cushion. "I had to be honest with myself, and with Beth."

Slowly she said, "Of course, but…?"

He took her hand. "Mel, I wanted to ask you to go see the cover band with me."

With a nervous laugh she said, "Adam, you hired me to be your matchmaker."

"Well, I'm firing you," he stated with simplicity. "You only need one when you have no idea where to look for someone to spend time with."

She pulled her hand away and got up. Going to stand in front of the fireplace, she looked at the cold, empty hearth. "I don't date."

He got up and went to her side. "Then don't call it a date. Just say you'll spend time with me and have fun. We don't need to label it, we can just enjoy time together."

"I wouldn't want to lead you on." She glanced his way. "It wouldn't be fair to you."

He lightly touched her arm and turned her to face him. She looked into his eyes. Hers filled with a mixture of fear and maybe a little hope. "Let me worry about me. You're the woman I'd like to spend time with."

Mel remained silent.

"Agree to have dinner with me and we'll see the band." He gave her a big grin. "It's just dinner."

A tentative smile tugged at the corners of her mouth. "We can go Dutch."

He cocked his head. He had no intention of letting that happen, but that was something he wouldn't get into now. He was raised in the old-fashioned way—the man paid for dinner.

"It sounds like we have plans for Friday night." He stopped short of saying the word date.

Her face lit up. "I guess we do."

"Great, I'll pick you up at six forty-five."

She nodded and smiled. "Is the place dressy?"

He let his gaze slide over her. "No, it's casual, so anything you choose will be perfect." He picked up his glass. "I need to get going, but I'll see you Friday."

"Sounds like we'll have a lot of fun." She took the glass from his hand and her fingers grazed his. He felt the warmth flow from her into him. This was exactly the right decision for both of them, and he would give her time to come to that same conclusion.

She walked him to the door. He could feel her watching him as he sauntered down the steps. She called after him, "Adam, I really am looking forward to Friday night."

He turned to look at her, thrilled to see her eyes light up. "Me too, Mel."

～

Friday night finally arrived and Adam picked her up exactly on time. She looked amazing in snug-fitting jeans, dark boots, a white top and suede jacket and long dangling earrings. He drove listening to Mel talk about her garden and other safe topics.

The restaurant came into sight. "Here we are."

Mel unbuckled herself and opened the door, not waiting for Adam. "I've never been here before." She looked around. "Looks like it's going to be busy tonight."

"Not to worry, we have a reservation. The acoustics are excellent." Adam locked the truck and walked next to her. There was definitely a sizzle of electricity between them. He opened the door and they stepped into a buzz of activity.

While they waited for a table, Mel looked around. "This place is really hopping tonight. I'm not surprised, a Stones cover band would be popular."

Before Adam could answer, they were shown to a table halfway into the room and off to one side. It had a good view of the stage, but they'd still be able to hear each other talk. Well, at least before the band started to play. It was as if the host knew they were on a date and was allowing them the opportunity to get to know each other.

After ordering cocktails, Mel perused the menu. "Do you have a favorite here?"

"The steak is always tender. I've also had a few nightly specials. I think you can't go wrong no matter what you order."

The drinks were delivered and they placed their order. The silence that settled over the table made Adam wonder what he should say next. Small talk was not his strong point.

With a nervous laugh, she said, "So this is what it's like"—she did air quotes—"spending time together? It's been a while for me."

He groaned. "Mel, let's just be ourselves. It's just like any other time we've hung out."

He could see her visibly relax. Placing a hand on his arm, she said, "Agreed."

~

Melinda took a slow, deep breath. It did little to quiet her racing heart. Now that she and Adam agreed to treat the evening like any other time they had gotten together, she needed to relax. She stole a peek at him as she pretended to unfold her napkin over her lap. She had a hard time believing she had agreed to have dinner with him tonight. Not that she wasn't excited. After all, it had taken her over an hour to decide what to wear. She smiled to herself. If he only knew.

"So, I wonder how many people will come to hear the band." A nice safe topic, the band.

He took a quick look around as his eyes met hers. "I'll bet it will be standing room only. I'm glad we came for dinner. We have great seats."

The way he held her gaze did nothing to slow her heart rate.

A man hadn't looked at her like this since John. She broke the connection and looked at the stage. Could he sense her apprehension?

"Mel?" His voice was low as he touched her hand very lightly. "Are you okay?"

She nodded but couldn't look him in the eye. She looked at his mouth. Her gaze slid up. She didn't want to stare at his mouth, wondering what it would feel like if his lips touched hers.

With a shake of her head, she willed herself to look into his eyes. "I'm fine. It's just that this is the first time I've gone on a date in a very long time." She leaned in closer. "Am I doing it right?"

He chuckled. "This from the matchmaker." He leaned in too and let his finger trace the line of her cheek to her chin. "You're perfect."

A long-forgotten sensation slipped over her. "You're very sweet."

With nerves on edge she picked up her glass and took a sip, breaking the moment. For now.

~

Mel stretched out on her bedcovers still dressed in her jeans and blouse, her boots were kicked off the moment she came into the door. What a night. Adam had been a total gentleman and let her set the pace of their date.

She squealed. She had been on a date! It felt good. Well, who was she trying to kid, it felt great! Tomorrow he was picking her up and they were having breakfast. There was something about his past he wanted to talk to her about. How was she going to fall asleep?

She replayed so many moments of the evening. The way his eyes grew big when she opened the door was the first of many moments where she felt an old familiar zing of excitement.

CHAPTER 28

Adam and Mel got out of the truck at the diner. She slipped her arm through his as they strolled to the door. He gave her a nervous smile.

"If you're not ready to talk about the past, we don't have to."

"I want to." He opened the door and let her go in first.

Melinda seemed to give him the opportunity to take the lead. She busied herself with fixing her coffee and made small talk about what they would order. After the waitress set a full carafe on the table, she slipped away.

He took a sip of coffee and in a clear, steady voice said, "Some of this may be repetitious, but I want to be clear, I'm a Marine. I'm not former. I'm retired."

"I think I understand." Mel nodded, encouraging him. "Go on."

"I would still serve if I could, but something happened on my last tour that changed my plans for the future."

"It was your third tour, going to the desert?"

Melinda's voice was gentle. Adam could tell he had her undivided attention. "It was."

Their breakfast was delivered and Adam began to eat

without tasting. Melinda picked up her fork and cut into the soft-boiled egg.

He knew starting from the beginning was the only way he was going to get through this. "When people talk about the war, most times they have no idea what it is really like. What you see on the news wouldn't prepare anyone for the harsh reality. The sand gets everywhere. I dreamed of grass and trees."

He toyed with his toast, gathering his thoughts. "Strong bonds are formed. You depend on your buddies' eyes and ears and they on you. I was lucky the first two times. I saw first-hand what happened when one of our Humvees hit an IED, how it ended up twisted and distorted, just a hunk of metal. The seats where men and women sat were mere shells of what had been. Intel was critical in keeping us safe. Sadly, there were times our worst nightmares became our reality." He knew his comments were stilted, but it was difficult explaining this to Mel.

"I can't imagine living that way. Especially going back two more times." She shuddered.

Adam pushed his eggs around.

"What was deployment like?" Her eyes searched his face. But he held his emotions in check.

"It's not easy. Sharing it with men and women who trained alongside you, they become your family. I would have taken a bullet for anyone in my unit."

Melinda's mouth fell open.

"You rely on each other to get back to base in the same condition as you left."

Adam paused and refilled their coffee mugs. "We talked about this before." He took a sip. It burned like acid in his stomach. He added a splash of cream. "My last tour began the same as the first two. I should have been on a desk in camp, but I wanted to be with my team. It was supposed to be a routine patrol." He faltered and dropped his head. "They died instantly. Four Marines, gone." The ache behind his eyes gained in intensity. "Then it was our turn."

Almost in a whisper Mel asked, "Adam?"

"I was medevac'd out." He stopped short of telling her he lost his leg. Once again, he didn't want to tell her he got off easy when his men hadn't. That was the burden he carried with him every day of his life and he would until he drew his last breath. Slowly he lifted his head. "I've battled with depression, panic attacks and nightmares. I relive that day over and over again." His voice cracked, thick with unshed tears. "It's my fault those soldiers died."

Mel laid her hand on his. "What could you have done differently?"

With a heavy heart, he looked into her eyes. "I've asked myself that question a million times." It felt good to talk to her about this. It was cathartic, an unburdening of his soul.

"Have you come up with an answer?" Her tone was so gentle it soothed the ache deep inside of him.

"Not yet."

"And counseling?"

He dropped his gaze. "Yeah. I was lucky. When I was in the hospital, the doctors and nurses understood what I was going through. I resisted at first, but thank God they persisted. They never gave up on me."

"Do you still talk to someone?" Mel clung tight to his hand.

"I do, and I have Will. He encourages me to talk about what happened."

"I'm sorry you had to go through such a horrific trauma."

He reminded himself he still hadn't told her the full story. "Mel, I need to tell you..."

"I understand. You don't need to explain anything more."

He leaned back in his chair, stopping short. Maybe it was cowardly, but she had just given him an out.

"We all have scars." Melinda took his other hand. "Is this why you had a hard time to date? You weren't ready to share your pain?"

"I guess. After my ex broke it off, something inside of me died. Until I met you."

She seemed unsure how to respond, so he decided to lighten the mood. With a small smile he said, "What a way to start the day, with all this heavy stuff."

Her pretty sea-green eyes locked onto his face. "You can always talk to me, about anything. I care about you."

He squeezed her hand. For now, that sounded really nice. Given time, he'd hope to see this relationship develop into more, much more. "I care about you too." He thought to himself, *that was an understatement.*

She pulled out her wallet. "Breakfast is my treat. You can get it next time."

He started to protest, but she gave him a stern look, one he had seen when she set her mind to something and there was no changing it. "Besides you paid for dinner."

"I'll leave the tip and there will definitely be a next time. After all, we're going to Newport in a few weeks."

Melinda flashed him a grin. "I wonder if they make lobster eggs benedict?"

"That sounds expensive," he teased.

"But I can guarantee you, I'm worth every penny." With a laugh she signed her name to the slip the waitress had handed her.

Adam dropped a few bills on the table while Mel slipped into her jacket. He followed her out of the small diner. His next stop would be to talk to Will. Maybe he knew of a way to find the courage to tell her the rest of his truth.

~

Stacey was sitting at Melinda's breakfast bar nursing a glass of wine, filling goody bags for the ladies attending the spa day. She and Melinda were going over the last of the details for Molly's bridal shower.

"Has Adam talked to you about his last deployment?"

With a one-shoulder shrug Melinda said, "Some. I think he held back more of the horrific details. As I listened to him give me the condensed version, my heart broke for him and for all military people. How do they deal with that day after day?"

"Will did two tours and for the most part he doesn't talk about it. I respect his privacy. He and Adam have times when they talk for hours about friends they lost and the innocence left behind when these men and women come home."

"Was Will injured?"

"Nothing like what Adam endured."

Melinda paused and looked up from the note she was writing. "What do you mean?"

Stammering, Stacey said, "You know, the PTSD."

Melinda wanted—no, needed—to know the truth. "Stacey? Is there more to hear?"

"It's not my story to tell. Talk to Adam."

She shook her head. Her intuition was in overdrive after all the patients she had counseled she knew there was something he was holding close to the vest. He had the opportunity to tell her all that had happened. Melinda knew what PTSD felt like. John's death changed her. The depression that had engulfed her in the months that followed was a dark, oppressive cloud.

"Melinda?" She heard the concern in Stacey's voice.

"Sorry. I got distracted."

"Please don't be upset with me. Adam is Will's best friend, more like a brother, and I love him like family."

"He is a good man." Melinda smiled, hoping to reassure her friend. "It's not a secret, but he and Beth have decided they're not going to continue to date."

Stacey tucked small splits of wine into the cloth bags on the counter. "I saw that coming. She didn't ring any bells for him."

Melinda felt a smidge guilty for taking Stacey down this path, but she was curious about why Beth hadn't been a good match and why Adam was attracted to her. "Really? They both love the outdoorsy stuff. But she hates sports so I guess I'm not completely surprised."

"That is just one side of Adam. His friends mean the world to him."

"I know. When I met him at the wedding, I could see how much everyone there liked him. He just fit, if you know what I mean. Although I did get the impression he loved spending time outdoors, and with his job I just figured he'd want someone who was as active as he seemed to be."

"He's like all of us," Stacey laughed. "Some days it's tough getting out of bed. I feel like an old lady."

"I know. If I spend the day gardening, I get stiff. That's when I tell myself if I were a couch potato, it would be even worse."

Stacey added bars of gourmet chocolate to the bags. "Have you heard from Molly?"

"We talked last night. She is very excited for the spa and then meeting her fiancé and the guys for a night of dinner and dancing."

Surprise flitted across Stacey's face. "Dancing? Did we get a band or something?"

Melinda smiled. "Relax. I checked with the restaurant, and in the dining room we've reserved they have a small dance floor. I've arranged to have romantic music play, so she and Tim can dance to their hearts' content."

"You think of all the details."

Melinda held up a small notebook and waved it in midair. "If I were to ever lose this, I'd be sunk. My planner keeps me ultra-organized."

"You don't use your phone?"

Melinda laughed. "I need to physically write it down. That's the only way to make sure everything gets done."

"Maybe I should try that too. Will says I'd lose my head if it wasn't attached."

"Stacey, you guys really are happy, aren't you?"

She beamed and a glow of happiness filled her eyes. "You

helped me find the love of my life. Sometimes I feel like you were given a gift from the goddess of love. I've never met anyone who has such a knack for matchmaking." She added small tubes of hand lotion to the bags.

Melinda couldn't help but laugh. "This is the very first time I've ever been compared to a goddess."

"Well, I could compare you to Cupid." Stacey folded down the tops of the bags.

"It sounds like being compared to the goddess is quite a lot to live up to." She laughed. "I wonder if I can add that to my website, as a testimonial from a satisfied client."

Stacey grinned. "Of course you can, anything I can do to help support your business. After all, you should share your gift with the world."

CHAPTER 29

The spa day bridal shower was a smashing success. Molly was radiant and seemed to float on air as they entered the restaurant. The guys should be waiting for them. Melinda was looking forward to seeing Adam. It had been a week since they had seen each other. She had been busy with the shower details and clients and Adam was working a job north of town. She checked the mirror in the entrance and wiped a smudge of lipstick from her lower lip.

Standing inside the dining room, she watched as the couples paired up. A stab of sadness momentarily washed over her. John would have liked this wonderful group of people who had become her close friends. He would have especially liked Adam. Both men had that quiet strength people instinctively recognized. It was comforting that in a few ways they were a lot alike.

There he was. She pressed her hand to her midsection to quiet the flash of nerves. Her eyes never left his as he made his way to her side. He looked dashing in his dark slacks, gray herringbone jacket and light blue shirt, which was open at the throat. The way he carried himself Adam looked every inch of a military man, even without the uniform.

"Mel." He took her hand in his. It was warm and firm. "You

look stunning." He pulled her close and kissed her cheek. "And smell even better."

She felt the flush creep up her cheeks as she glanced down at her deep forest green dress. It was simply tailored as she didn't want to stand out. The hairstylist had curled her already wavy hair and piled it on top of her head. After her facial, she felt as if her face glowed. The cosmetologist had done an excellent job with her makeup as she didn't look made-up. She had contoured blush to follow the angle of her high cheekbones, and although her makeup was subtle, her eyes shimmered with a touch of gold on the lid and a swish of purple under her lower lashes.

Pleased he seemed to think she was attractive, she said, "You're looking pretty snazzy yourself."

"Can I buy you a drink?" He tugged her hand and steered her farther into the room.

She looked around. "Everything looks perfect. Just as I had hoped."

Adam glanced at the room. "You and Stacey out did yourselves."

Melinda could feel a flush warm her cheeks. "Molly and Tim deserve a special night before their big day."

"You've played a big part in their happiness." He gave her a quizzical look. "How many couples do you think have walked down an aisle because of you?"

"You're giving me too much credit. But, if I was keeping track," with a laugh she said, "and I do, I'd say at least twenty-one couples, give or take." She knew she was beaming. She was very proud of what she had accomplished since starting *It's Just Coffee*.

"That's forty-two satisfied clients."

"Look at you, doing math on the fly." She bumped his shoulder. It wasn't the first time she noticed he was tall and solid.

"Smart aleck." He chuckled. "For the record, I'm a whiz at trivia games too."

"I'll keep that in mind if I'm looking for a partner." She

paused and felt her face grow warm. If Adam noticed the quip, he didn't say anything. "For games."

They stepped up to the bar and Adam ordered her a glass of red wine. She raised an eyebrow as he did. "Would you prefer something else?" he asked.

"No. I just didn't realize you were paying attention to my preferred beverage choice."

"Of course I do." He leaned in toward her. "It's a bad habit, watching over the people in my life."

Feeling suddenly nervous, she looked down. What would it be like to have Adam aware of more than just her wine preference?

He grinned. "We've been through a lot since we met, don't you think?"

She looked up at him through her lashes. "A building project, a trip to the ER, adoption of the four-legged kind." She stopped short of adding in dating. "Speaking of which, how is the fur baby?"

"Skye is growing like a weed. She's discovered sleeping at the foot of my bed means she can stretch out or curl up at will."

"I see the smile on your face. You've fallen under her spell."

"I never thought I was much of a cat person, but Skye is a lot of fun to have around." Adam put his hand on the small of her back and ushered her to the table. "I snuck in before and saved us seats."

The room was set in four tables of six with an additional two tables, one with an assortment of appetizers and the other set with coffee service. "Stacey thought having a plated meal would be elegant, and I have to agree it was the right choice."

"Do you know everyone here?" Adam asked her.

"Well, I've been introduced to everyone a few times and I know the ladies much better after today. There is something about bonding over manicures."

Adam snorted. "I can imagine. Do you mull over color selections, making sure toes and fingers match?"

"Stop teasing me." Again, she could feel her cheeks grow warm. "You're a brat."

"Oh wait, looks like the bride and groom to-be are taking their places." Adam pointed to the next table over. "I hope it's okay that we're sitting with Will and Stacey."

"Of course. They're a great couple."

"Stacey's super sweet. Will came to life when he met her."

"What do you mean?" Melinda looked up at Adam.

"He spent time with me when I was in the hospital recovering. I think it brought back some of what he had been through before he got out of the Corps. I kept telling him to go home and that I'd be fine, but he insisted on staying."

"He's a good friend." Melinda wanted to bring Adam back from wherever he seemed to be going. "Look." She pointed to a tray. "They just set out stuffed mushrooms. Would you like a couple?"

"Oh, that sounds good. I'll get them for us."

Melinda watched him walk across the room. For a moment she thought he was limping. Maybe it had to do with the burden he carried from his final tour. The weight of the world on his shoulders. She made a mental note to ask Stacey if Will had any residual effects from his tour. If he did, she could recommend someone. Being haunted by the horrors of a war had to be difficult. She knew better than most that sad memories lingered and reared their ugly head when least expected.

Adam came back to the table and pulled out her chair. He set down the small plate with several options for appetizers. "I wasn't sure what else you might want."

"Thank you." She patted the cushion next to her. "Have a seat."

Adam eased down and gave her a tight smile. "Sorry. I needed a breather."

Gently she asked, "Do you want to talk about it?"

"Not tonight. We're here to celebrate our friends." The music changed to Elvis Presley singing how he can't help falling in love. Adam held out a hand. "Dance with me?"

"Didn't you want to sit?"

"Not when the King is singing." He wiggled his fingers. "Please?"

It's been a long time," Melinda stated. "I might step on your toes."

"I'm tough."

Melinda took his hand and in one fluid motion stood as he pulled back her chair. Not letting go, he escorted her to the dance floor. It was just the two of them. He slid one arm around her waist and with the other held her hand in his. She felt delicate in his arms. It had been a long, long time since she danced like this. Felt like this.

He pulled her closer and inwardly she sighed. This was nice, very nice. She swayed to the melody, the lyrics casting a spell over her. As the song ended, she dropped her head to his shoulder, unwilling to look into Adam's eyes. That was a song for lovers.

"Thank you, Mel." His voice was low and husky. Just for her ears he said, "You're an excellent dancer." He relaxed his arms and she stepped back.

"It was nice to dance again, and you've got some smooth moves too."

He looked down at her and tilted her chin up. He gazed into her eyes. His voice smooth, he said, "No doubt it was my partner."

Her breath caught, was he about to kiss her? Her pulse quickened and her blood warmed in her veins. She realized she *wanted* Adam to kiss her.

Adam cleared his throat. "We dance well together." He guided her back to the table. His manners were impeccable as he held her chair again.

What just happened? Melinda was confused. She sat down and murmured, "Thank you."

Salads were being served, which left little time for anything more than casual conversation. After he pulled in his chair, Adam's thigh rested against hers, hidden from view under the tablecloth. Melinda didn't make a move away from him. She glanced his way and caught his eye. His brow quirked as if asking if she was okay. Slowly she winked and returned to her salad. It was as if they shared a secret or communicated as a couple would.

Molly's parents were sitting at their table, and Melinda was happy to answer questions about *It's Just Coffee*. Molly's mom, Clair, was fascinated with the entire process.

"Back when I was young, you met a man, fell in love and got married. Nowadays, it is much more complicated. By the time I was Molly's age, I had two young children."

Melinda understood where she was coming from. "It's not that easy anymore. People are waiting longer and then do all they can to find the right partner."

Clair patted Melinda's hand. "Dear, I'm very pleased with Tim. You did a wonderful job as their matchmaker."

"Thank you. I always say I get the credit, but it's really my clients who do the hard work by opening their hearts to the possibility of love. It is intimidating to allow yourself to be vulnerable to another."

Stacey interjected, "She successfully matched me and Will too."

Taking the opportunity to shift the focus from her business, Melinda said to no one in particular, "Have you been to Newport before, or will this be your first time?" Her eyes scanned the table.

Will said, "I've been, but never to the mansions, so it'll be a first for me." His eyes caught Stacey's. "For us."

Molly's dad, Mark, said, "My wife has dragged me through every mansion that is open for the Christmas season. She just loves the decorations."

Clair snorted. "Mark, that's rich. If I recall, it was *your* suggestion that Molly contact the historical society to see how to secure Rose Mansion for the wedding."

He beamed. "Guilty as charged. However, you have to admit this will be the perfect setting for our little girl and Tim. Imagine starting your married life at one of the most romantic places on the East Coast."

Adam took this moment to jump into the conversation. "I'm looking forward to the shindig. Mel and I are going together. We're going to check out the local winery, wander through the shops and who knows what else." He winked at Mel. "And, we have finding the best eggs benedict with lobster on the list too."

Stacey glanced at Will, who in turn looked at Mel. She held up her hands and grinned. Unwilling to share her budding relationship with Adam, she said, "We struck a deal. I'm driving and he has to buy breakfast." Anxious to avoid additional questions she stood and lifted her glass. "To Molly and Tim. May your wedding be filled with lots of wonderful memories with friends."

The evening passed with more dancing and toasts. When the party began to break up Melinda remembered she had left her car at home. "Stacey, can I catch a ride with you and Will?"

"Of course." She caught Will's attention and pointed to Melinda. He gave a nod and he and Adam came over.

Adam said, "Mel, I can take you home."

"I don't want you to have to go out of your way."

He chuckled. "You seem to forget I live above their garage, so we're all going the same direction."

Feeling a little foolish, she laughed. "I'd love a ride. Thank you."

"Will, let's get the girls' coats."

They moved to the coatroom and Stacey tugged on Melinda's arm. She hip-bumped Melinda. "Are you going to ask him in for a nightcap?"

"It's just a ride home, don't make more of it than it is. After all, I'm sure he's tired. It's been a busy day for everyone."

Melinda's eyes never left Adam. She had an involuntary shiver of nerves. Should she ask him in?

"A cup of decaf would be a nice gesture." Stacey grazed her hand. "And maybe a little goodnight kiss?"

Oh yes, a kiss would be the best way to end this night. Melinda sighed.

Stacey pulled her into a quick hug. She whispered in Mel's ear, "Have fun."

Adam walked toward her with her coat open ready for her to slip into. "Ready to go, Mel?"

She tucked her hand into the crook of his arm. "Yes. I'm ready."

∾

The short drive to Mel's seemed to be over in a flash. Adam pulled into her driveway and put the truck in park. Should he turn it off?

"I'll walk you to the door." He opened his door, and Mel asked, "Would you like to stay for a cup of decaf or tea?"

He swallowed a laugh. He wasn't a tea drinker. "Decaf would be great."

He hopped out of the truck and hurried around before Mel could get out. He pulled open the door and held out his hand. She took it and slipped from the seat into his arms. He held her close and looked down into her eyes. He hadn't kissed her the last time he held her this close. He wasn't going to let the opportunity slip by him again.

He dipped his head and tentatively brushed her lips with his. Mel took a step deeper in his arms, and that was all the encouragement he needed. He took his time kissing her until she was breathless. It was pure heaven.

CHAPTER 30

Heaven. Kissing Adam had seemed so right. She traced her fingers across her lips and relived the sweet memory of standing in her driveway, getting lost in his kiss.

The ringing phone cut short her daydream. "Hello?"

"Hi, sweetie. It's Mom."

Melinda smiled into the phone. Her mom always announced herself when she called. "I'm all packed and ready to see you and Dad tomorrow, just in time to go to the market and get all the fixings for Turkey Day."

"That's why I'm calling." Mom coughed. "Dad and I have both come down with a nasty flu bug and we don't want you to come out and get exposed to it too."

"But Mom, I could help out." Mel sank down on a stool. She had always had Thanksgiving with her parents.

"We'll have some of our special dishes at Christmas instead." Mom coughed again. "Of course, we'll cover your plane ticket."

"That's not necessary, Mom. Are you sure you don't want me to come out?"

"We've made up our mind. And once we get over this bug, we'll make new plans. Okay?"

She knew she wasn't going to change her mom's mind. Reluctantly she agreed and promised to call the next day to check in on them.

Melinda hung up the phone, dejected. She wasn't going to see her family for Thanksgiving. Feeling sorry for herself, she grabbed a pint of chocolate ice cream and a spoon; this was dinner.

After inhaling the first half, she sighed. *Why can't I make a special meal for myself? Maybe I can invite Adam over, unless he's going to see his family. Why don't I ask him?* She heaved herself off the couch and put the pint back in the freezer. Checking the time, she realized the grocery store didn't close for a few more hours. Making a snap decision, she grabbed her car keys and coat. She was off.

After walking into the brightly lit store, Christmas music playing in the background, she pushed a small cart. Menu planning on the spur of the moment was sure to mean she'd forget a critical ingredient.

She rounded a corner and Stacey was in the baking aisle. Embarrassed, with her cart overfull of all the traditional holiday meal ingredients, she tried to spin her cart around before she was seen, but it was too late.

"Melinda." Stacey smiled. "I thought you were catching a flight to California to see your mom and dad."

With a shrug she said, "That was the plan. Mom called a little while ago and said not to come. She and Dad have a bad case of the flu and don't want me to get it."

"I'm sorry to hear that." Stacey brightened. "Does that mean you can join us? It's going to be an eclectic group. Will's parents, Molly and Tim, along with her parents, and Adam. This year my mom and dad are going to my uncle's in Vermont."

Melinda gripped the cart handle. This was exactly what she had been afraid of, being an extra wheel. "I don't want to intrude on your family celebration."

Stacey protested, "You *are* family, Melinda." She grinned. "Say you'll come."

"Well…" She hesitated. It wasn't that she wouldn't enjoy herself, but she didn't want anyone feeling sorry for her.

Stacey continued, "I won't take no for an answer."

She relented. "Only if I can bring something."

"Dessert. What's your specialty?" Stacey pointed to the shelves. "I'm a hopeless baker. I was going to resort to the bakery."

"Heavens," Melinda joked. "I can make a pumpkin cheesecake and maybe an apple pie?"

"Oh, both of those sound delicious." A gleam came into Stacey's eye. "Are you going to use that cookie crust for the apple pie like you served at your party?"

With a chuckle Melinda said, "If that's what you'd like, of course I can."

Stacey rubbed her hands together with anticipation. "My mouth is watering already."

"Based on how you cook I don't think anyone will have room for dessert."

Stacey's cheeks went light pink. "This is my first time hosting Thanksgiving. I'm a little nervous."

"If you need anything, you just let me know."

"Thanks, Mel. Dinner's at two. See you Thursday."

Stacey hurried off straining to steer her overfull shopping cart.

Melinda smiled to herself, "Now, she's calling me Mel. Adam must be rubbing off on people."

She picked up the ingredients she needed for baking the cake and pie and glanced at her cart. Then she headed back toward the meat counter. No reason to buy the turkey now.

THE MATCHMAKER AND THE MARINE

*R*ock music drifted down Melinda's driveway. Adam smiled the minute he started up the walkway amidst a few flakes of snow. He gave a loud knock on the door and waited. No response. He peeked in through the side windowpane and saw lights on, but he didn't hear or see Mel coming to the door. He held up his hand to knock again and changed his mind. She had her music up loud and probably couldn't hear him. Stepping carefully off the slick steps, he wondered if she had ice melt. If not, he'd pick some up for her. He wandered around the garage and to the back door. He knocked again, and this time he saw Mel pop her face around the wall and wave.

"Come in!" she yelled.

The knob turned and Adam frowned. She shouldn't have her door unlocked.

"Hey." He raised his voice above the strains of Aerosmith. "I can hear your music from the street."

She had flour everywhere, including on her face and in her hair.

"What are you making, besides a mess?" He couldn't help but tease her.

With a quick retort she said, "Apple pie. And if you're not nicer to me, you won't be getting any tomorrow." Putting her hands on her hips, she asked, "And just how may I help you today?"

"Stacey mentioned you were coming to dinner, and since you weren't packing for your trip I thought I'd drop by and hang out. If that's okay? Or should I have called first?" He dropped a kiss on her cheek and withdrew a single daisy from inside his jacket. "For you."

"You don't ever need to call first." Melinda wiped her hand on her apron and gave him a warm smile as she accepted the flower. "This is very sweet."

With a shrug, he dropped his butt on the only empty barstool at the high-top counter. "I swung by the store for my contribution, rolls, and saw some flowers. This one had your name on it." He looked around. With a grin he teased, "Your kitchen isn't its normal tidy."

She laughed. "When I cook, I tend to spread out. I like everything within easy reach."

She pointed to the stool next to him. He pulled back to discover a bowl of apples. "Apples on a barstool? That's an interesting place to store them."

Melinda was patting a circular piece of dough on the flour-covered counter. After dusting her rolling pin, she said, "Maybe instead of sitting there poking fun at the genius of my baking strategy, you could wash your hands and peel them."

"What if I don't know how?" he said with a grin.

Exasperated she said, "Adam, you took men into battle. Surely you can use a knife to peel off the skin, cut it into thin slices and then take out a few seeds."

"Is that all there is to it?" He smirked and tossed his coat over the table. Crossing to the sink, he washed his hands. "For the record, I've peeled an apple or two before."

"Good." She laughed. She pointed to a drawer. "You'll find a knife in there."

He pulled open the drawer. "You sure do love kitchen gadgets."

She shrugged and smiled. "It's a weakness." Before Adam could sit down again, Melinda pointed to the drainer. "You can use that metal bowl for the peels."

He gave her a mock salute and with a chuckle said, "Ma'am, yes, ma'am."

She shot him a look that he thought held just the right amount of sass. Which of course made him want to take her in his arms and kiss her. But he vowed to take this budding relationship at a pace he felt she was comfortable with.

"Speaking of calling me Mel, do you know you have Stacey saying it too?"

He pretended to look horrified and clutched his chest. "No, you can't be serious."

She flicked a handful of flour in his direction. "Now you're just being a jerk. I wanted to maintain a more professional image by using my full name."

His tone softened. "But Mel, well, it suits you. It's sweet, fun and easygoing. Melinda is so formal."

She raised an eyebrow and gave him an injured look. "Are you saying I'm uptight and rigid?"

"No, not at all. I can see Dr. Melinda Grayson or Melinda Phillips on your business cards, but when you're with friends, you should loosen up. They're both sides of the real you."

Melinda fell silent. Under her breath she said, "I don't want anyone to think I take my matchmaker responsibility frivolously."

"All anyone has to do is meet you and they'll know right away you are one of the most caring and kind individuals they'll ever meet." He picked up an apple and cut it in half. "At least that is how I felt when I met you at Will's wedding."

"We barely talked. How could you have made a snap judgment?"

"I've learned over the years to trust my instincts. Seldom am I wrong."

She gave him a look. Whatever retort she had was left unsaid. "Thank you. That means a lot to me."

Adam peeled apples and Melinda finished rolling out the crust. When she looked over the bowl was full of thin, neatly sliced apples. "Ready to help with the next step?" she asked.

"Are you sure you trust me?" he teased, and silently hoped she knew he'd protect her from anything.

"I'm impressed with your slicing skill." Focusing on the task at hand she said, "Toss in half a stick of butter in the pan. Mix in the apples and spices and simmer over medium heat. We just want the flavors to combine and the apples to begin to soften."

"Ya know, if this pie is good, I'm taking the credit."

Snorting Melinda said, "Will anyone believe you?"

With a playful snap of the towel in her direction, he said, "No. But I can try."

She pointed back to the pan. "All right, chef, keep the apples moving. You don't want them to burn."

He started to salute her again and she laughed. "Oh, stop. You're going to injure your arm if you keep that up."

∼

From the corner of her eye, she kept close watch on what Adam was doing. She marveled at his attentiveness. This was nice. Spending time together, even just making a couple of desserts. Mel was starting to realize she had been wrong, thinking she could live the rest of her life alone. He made her contemplate a different kind of future.

With a shake of her head, she stopped letting her brain go down that path. "Since you've got the handle on the pie, I'm going to start the cheesecake."

His head swiveled almost off his neck. "Did you really say cheesecake?"

"I did."

"A plain one with fruit toppings?"

"No. Pumpkin." She gave him a sidelong glance. Her heart skipped a beat. "Since I don't have those ingredients, I'll make you a deal."

"I'm listening," he drawled and leaned in attentively.

"I'll make the pumpkin for Thanksgiving, and for Christmas I'll make a plain cheesecake with fruit toppings. It will be your gift."

"On one condition." He leaned against the counter and his smile looked slightly wicked in a playful sort of way. Her insides melted. This playful banter was... nice.

She asked. "I'm afraid to hear, but what's your condition?"

"That you spend part of the holiday with me and we have

dinner together." He held up his hand. "I know family stuff has to come first but"—he had a serious undertone to his voice—"this would mean a lot to me, Melinda."

Taken aback by hearing him say her given name, she answered, "Of course I want to have dinner with you."

CHAPTER 31

Melinda had been thinking about what she was about to do for weeks. Getting to know Adam and spending time with him made her think and feel things. Emotions she thought she had buried with her sweet husband resurfaced. It wasn't exactly like it had been with John, but she was happy and living life again. She adjusted the clasp on her pearl necklace and smoothed her hand over the soft deep blue dress. In the mirror she looked at her left hand, her wedding ring. Slowly she slipped the thin gold band from her finger.

She opened the lid on the intricately carved jewelry box sitting on the top of her dresser. It had been a wedding gift from John. There it was, John's wedding band, nestled in the velvet lining. Exhaling slowly, she placed her matching ring next to his and took one last lingering look before closing it.

She rested her hand on the carved wood. "It's time for me to move on, my love."

THE MATCHMAKER AND THE MARINE

Toot. Toot. Melinda glanced up toward Adam's apartment door and wondered who was taking care of Skye while they were gone. She saw Adam wave as he came out and pulled the door closed.

She slid the window down and called out, "What the heck are you doing, pokey?" Maybe the lighthearted approach would calm the butterflies in her stomach.

They had plenty of time to get to Newport before the wedding fun began. But who knew what traffic was going to be like on a Thursday during the holiday season?

Adam came down the steps carrying a black leather satchel and a garment bag slung over his shoulder. She popped the trunk and waited for him to stow his stuff. After a minute, he opened the passenger door.

"Good morning." He beamed as he buckled up. "I'm ready to hit the open road."

She backed out of the driveway and gave him a grin. "Are you buying coffee?"

His laughter warmed her heart. "Sure."

Cruising down his street she asked, "Who's taking care of your fur baby while you're gone?"

"Actually, Beth is going to stop in and check on her tomorrow and then on Saturday too."

"Really?"

"I didn't know who else to ask since all our friends will be in Newport." He gave her a quick glance. She liked the sound of that, *all our friends.*

She flashed him a wide smile. "It sounds like the perfect solution." She slowed and turned into the café parking lot. "Thank goodness, coffee."

He unbuckled his seat belt. "I'll be right back." Before he got out of the car he asked, "Anything sweet?"

"Surprise me."

Melinda watched as Adam walked into the café. "I wonder

why he's limping. He must have injured it pretty badly when he got hurt." She tuned the radio to a country station, good background music, and then plugged her cell phone in to charge. After that she tapped in the driving directions on the navigation system. When the door opened, the smell of cinnamon and sugar made her mouth water.

Taking the bag from Adam, she opened it up and peeked inside. "Muffins?" She pretended to roll her eyes back.

"Not just any muffins, they're coffeecake."

Grinning she said, "To go with our coffee." She held out her hand to take a cup. She set it in the holder between the seats. "Driver gets the front holder." She teased.

Adam laughed. "Mel, do you have rules for road trips?"

She cocked her head and smiled. "I'd like to think of them more as guidelines."

"Good to know."

She loved the easy banter with him. It definitely made her nerves settle down. She tapped the screen on the dashboard and said, "I've programmed in the shortest route, unless you'd prefer to take secondary roads."

"I like the idea of getting there so we can explore. We might not have much free time once we meet up with everyone later tonight."

Melinda backed out and pulled into the light traffic. "Next stop, Newport."

Adam broke off a piece of muffin and handed it to her. "Try this."

She popped it in her mouth and mumbled, "This is really good," after she took a tiny sip of her coffee. "Hey, I noticed you were limping when you got out of the car. Anything serious?"

The look he gave her was unreadable. "Nah, I just turned funny and my knee is bothering me, but nothing to worry about."

Melinda wasn't sure if she believed him, but since he didn't want to talk about it, she said, "Good. I intend to spend some serious time on the dance floor with you."

"Sounds like a plan."

She could feel his gaze linger on her as she maneuvered through the small downtown with ease. It was a short distance before they picked up the highway. After she merged, she noticed Adam had become very quiet. "Everything okay over there?"

Adam looked at her and smiled. "I was just wondering how much time we'll have before dinner tonight."

"GPS puts us there around two." She gave him a quick look. "Do you want to do something specific?"

"I wanted to tour the car museum, or how would you feel about a drive near the ocean?"

"Before we check into the inn or after?"

"Let's check in and get settled. Then we can go for a drive and meet everyone at the Brick Alley Pub for cocktails and dinner."

She gave him a bright smile. "That sounds like a good idea."

∼

*A*dam watched the scenery slip by as Mel's fingers tapped on the steering wheel in time to the music on the radio. What the hell had he been thinking? His knee was killing him. It was a good thing they were driving around Ocean Boulevard. There was no way an afternoon of walking would have hidden his discomfort.

Inwardly he groaned. Tripping over a duffel bag and twisting his knee was stupid enough, but then add in the macho guy act walking into the diner for coffee, which had caused even more pain.

He glanced at Mel. Did she suspect something? Was it too late to tell her the truth, here and now? Or would she think his omission a lie?

If he wasn't with Mel, he'd massage his stump, but that was not an option right now. He shifted his position, hoping to alleviate some of his discomfort.

"Do you need an aspirin or something?" She handed him her bag. "There's some in the inside pocket."

"Why?"

"You're fidgeting. I'm guessing your leg hurts more than you're willing to let on." She gave him a sympathetic look.

Her voice was so kind he had to wonder how she would feel if she knew the truth. *Would she pretend it doesn't matter when I know it does? Or maybe Mel really wouldn't care. She isn't a judgmental person.*

"Earth to Adam."

"Sorry. I was lost in thought."

She laughed. "I could tell. I was asking you for another piece of muffin. You're holding onto that bag with a vise grip."

He looked down and saw the top of the paper was crumpled in his hand. "Oops." Folding back the top of the bag, he offered it to her and then changed his mind and set it on the console. "Help yourself."

"Adam, are you sure you're okay? You're strangely quiet."

He could hear the concern in her voice and forced himself to grin. "I was wondering how we can fit everything in before Sunday—the winery, the fort, the cliff walk. You know, all the high spots." He wondered had he packed enough aspirin to do all of those things.

"Whatever we don't finish on Saturday, we have Sunday. We can head home later in the afternoon. We're on our own schedule. Well, other than the nuptials."

"I need to stop worrying about trying to control everything." He looked over his sunglasses. "Let's make a pact that we'll do our best to do it all."

Mel's laughter bubbled up. "You're incorrigible. And yes, we will do our best."

He pretended to wipe his brow. "What a relief." Deciding to

stop worrying about everything, he turned up the radio and began to sing off key to a popular country song. Singing always put a smile on his face and in his heart. He glanced at Mel, who was mouthing the words.

"I can't hear you..." he said in a sing-song voice.

She belted out the next line, and to his astonishment she sang like a professional.

"Oh, we are so finding a karaoke contest and entering." He beamed. "We'll enter you and I'm your moral support."

"Oh no. I don't sing without backup." She flicked her hair and grinned. "After all, the greats always have eye candy on stage with them"—she ran her eyes over him—"and you qualify."

He puffed up his chest a bit and laughed. "Glad you noticed."

*M*elinda peered through the windshield as they parked in the small lot. She looked at Adam. "Can you believe this place? It's like a mini Victorian mansion."

Adam pushed open the door. "I can't wait to see inside. Do you think it's haunted?"

Melinda scoffed at the idea. "Do you believe in ghosts?"

He grinned. "No more than any other average guy. But just look at those tiny windows in the attic. And the widow's walk."

She did a one-eighty. "I can't see the ocean."

"Most of the houses between this one and the sea were likely built afterward." He turned back to look at the house. "This grand of a house was built for someone of wealth. Like a sea captain."

"That would make sense." She grabbed her bags from the trunk, and after Adam took his out, she closed it and locked the car. "I can't wait to see our rooms. Do you think we can go out on the widow's walk?"

"Probably not. Hopefully we'll have a great view from our rooms." Adam held the front door open. "After you."

She swept through the door and stopped mid-step. Her mouth formed an O. He was sure she was transfixed by the beauty of the foyer and side parlor. The deep rich mahogany wood gleamed in the sunlight. Maroon velvet cushions graced the antique side chair and small sofa. The old polished floors were covered with oriental rugs that seemed to be old but well maintained.

"It's gorgeous," she breathed. There was a small bell on the desk and she tapped it. She grinned at Adam.

A woman's voice drifted down the staircase. "No need to whisper."

Melinda looked up and smiled.

They watched as a woman descended the stairs. She appeared to be in her late sixties based on the crinkles around her eyes and the subtle gray strands in her hair.

Melinda said, "It's just so beautiful in here and old, it makes me want to talk in hushed tones."

Adam teased, "You'll have to excuse her. Before we came in, she was speculating if the inn would be haunted."

"Adam," Melinda admonished. She smiled at the innkeeper. "Don't listen to him, he was the one thinking about ghosts."

The woman's eyes twinkled with mischief. "You never know. But welcome—I'm Diana and I own this little slice of heaven. It's been in my family for generations."

"Did you grow up here?" Melinda asked.

"I did." She stepped behind the desk. "Are you checking in?"

"Yes," Adam set down his bag and reached for his wallet. "Adam Bell and this is Melinda Phillips. We're here through Sunday."

Diana consulted a large, old-fashioned leather bound book. "Here you are."

Melinda dug into her bag and pulled out her credit card. "You're old school."

Diana smiled. "We have the online system, but I think this adds to the ambience. When our guests check in, they see we still have the same kind of book that has been here since my grandparents were the innkeepers."

Adam handed her his credit card. "Oh wait, that's my military ID."

She handed it back to him. "My daughter was in the Army."

Melinda noticed the slight downturn of her mouth. She lightly touched Adam's sleeve and swept her eyes toward Diana.

He said, "You must be very proud of her."

"We are. Were."

In that instant, Melinda knew they had lost their daughter.

Very softly Adam said, "I'm sorry for your loss."

"Thank you." Her smile was bright but didn't reach her eyes. "I've put you in adjoining rooms. You can keep the door locked or not, your preference."

He signed the slip and then Melinda did the same as she felt herself blush. "Thank you," she stammered.

Adam picked up his bag. Quick to lighten the mood, he said, "Come on, toots, let's find our rooms so we can take a drive before dinner."

Diana handed them keys. "Rooms Twelve and Fourteen. At the top of the stairs, take a left. Your rooms overlook the harbor."

"Thank you, Diana." Melinda nudged Adam. "I get the room with the best view."

She laughed quietly. "They have the same view, so you won't need to fight over one or the other."

Melinda smiled at her before walking up the grand stairwell ahead of Adam. She could hear by his steps he was still favoring one leg. Teasing him she said, "Are you going to make it, Hopalong Cassidy?"

She noticed a flash of pain in his eyes before he said, "Just waiting on you, slowpoke."

With that, Melinda gave a laugh and ran up the last two steps. "Come on, I want to get outside and smell the sea air."

Good-naturedly he grumbled, "Can we at least get a snack for the road?"

Melinda patted her shoulder bag. "I'm way ahead of you. I have granola bars right here and bottled water in the car. No need to waste time."

"Lady, I'm going to need to teach you about being away and relaxing." He shook his head as he took the last step toward Room Fourteen. "And if for any reason you don't like your view, we can switch."

"Ya know, you're a pretty sweet guy." Melinda pushed open the door and stopped in her tracks.

Adam stepped over the threshold and stood beside her. The sweeping view through the triple windows was nothing less than spectacular. Boats were gently dancing on the waves and the sun glistening off the surface of the ocean were sparks of light. Mel crossed to the window and opened it halfway. She leaned forward, her nose almost touching the screen, and inhaled deeply.

"Adam, no need to switch. It's perfect."

CHAPTER 32

Melinda woke feeling refreshed. She stretched her arms overhead and got out of bed. Pulling on her bath robe, she tapped lightly on the connecting door to Adam's room.

"Good morning," she called out, "are you awake?"

The door opened and Adam was standing there, bare chested and wearing loose-fitting sweatpants and sneakers. His face wore the scruff of a one-day beard and damn it looked good on him. "Good morning, beautiful. You look well rested."

"I slept great, and you?"

"Me too." He glanced over his shoulder at the bedside clock. "How much time do you need to get ready? We'll have to be at the mansion by ten to help the bride and groom get things organized for the big event."

"I think we're really providing moral support." He flashed her a smile. "But give me thirty minutes. That should give us plenty of time for breakfast." He leaned against the doorjamb. "Dress warm. The weatherman was calling for freezing rain and sleet."

She gave him thumbs-up and closed the door. She waited to hear if he would flip the lock between them, but it was quiet.

Adam propped himself up against the door with his hand. Thank heavens he'd strapped his leg on before she knocked. There was no way he could have moved quickly and appear calm and cool. He gave a soft chuckle. It would be nice if Mel thought she was the reason he was a little off kilter.

Lying in bed last night, he had decided when they got home he was going to tell her about his leg and the rest of what had happened to him after the IED explosion. He owed it to her, but he also owed it to himself to find the courage to let her into his life and bare all his scars.

Once he was ready Adam tapped on the door from the hallway. He didn't want Mel to feel like she didn't have enough privacy by always using the connector door.

When she opened it, she was dressed in a cream turtleneck sweater, a long red vest and black leggings with knee-high boots. Not that he was noticing the particulars, he chided himself.

"Ready?" he said.

"I'm starving. Do you think Diana has something downstairs?"

"I'm sure she does, but if not, I'll bet there is a good place to eat nearby." Adam moved to one side and Mel fell in step next to him.

"Do you think we'll have time to tour Rosecliff after we are done with the rehearsal?"

They strolled down the wide staircase. Mel's heel caught on a tread. She began to pitch forward, but Adam reached out and grabbed her arm to steady her.

Her eyes were wide. His heart quickened. "Are you okay?"

"Yeah. Thanks. It would stink to take a tumble down the stairs." Her voice had a slight quiver to it.

She smiled at him and he exhaled with relief. "You'll need to be careful tonight in your heels." He drank in the sight of her heart-shaped face. "I assume you're wearing high heels?" To his ears the words sounded brusque.

She winked at him. "Ladies typically do wear them when we get all gussied up." She glanced down. "How is your leg feeling today? Any pain?"

"None. Just a temporary thing."

He could see the concern appear in her eyes. "Does it have anything to do with your injury from your last tour?"

He wanted to deny it, but since he had come to the decision to tell her everything, he simply said, "Yes."

Melinda opened her mouth and then closed it. Adam wasn't going to push her to talk to him. There would be time for lots of questions when they got home on Sunday night. Not Monday or Tuesday, but Sunday. "I'll tell you about it sometime soon."

She nodded and perked up when she saw Diana come out of the dining room.

"Good morning, Diana. By chance is there any sort of breakfast or coffee?" Melinda put a real emphasis on coffee.

Diana gestured to an archway off to the left. "Right through there. Help yourself, and if you need more coffee, just let me know. I'll be at the desk."

As they crossed the front entrance into the dining room Adam could feel Diana watching him. Did she see his gait wasn't as smooth as it should be? If she lost a daughter, he guessed it had something to do with the war. He glanced over his shoulder as Diana averted her eyes.

Melinda headed for the buffet that held several covered platters. She picked up the lid on the first one, flipped a look at Adam and said, "Bacon and sausage." She opened the next one and it was filled with an assortment of warm muffins. The next, a pan with fried potatoes and the last dish was eggs. "They look like they just came off the stove."

Adam handed her a plate and she made short work of filling it. "This was more than I expected."

He filled another plate to the edges while Melinda meandered to a table by the window and sat down. There was a daisy in a bud vase on the table. He could hear her say, "This is just lovely."

Adam brought a carafe of coffee with him and poured her a cup before sitting down. "This is just what we need to start our day." He looked around and reached for a ketchup bottle from the table behind them. He grinned. "Sorry, ketchup is a must in my book."

"Of course, the potatoes." Melinda took the bottle from him.

Adam waited until she was done and then took it back. "No, for the eggs."

Melinda wrinkled her nose. "Really?"

"I got used to it when I was in basic." He handed her the bottle. "Try it."

She held up her hand and shook her head. "No, thank you."

He laughed and scooped up a forkful. "Your loss."

Breakfast with Mel was a treat. Conversation was easy. They talked about the wedding and what other fun things they might want to do. She expressed an interest in going to the tennis museum.

"Really, that's on your to-do list?" Adam asked.

"Where else can you find one, and so close to home?" She drained her coffee. "Do you think Diana has to-go cups? The coffee is delicious."

As if right on cue, Diana sailed into the dining room. "How was breakfast?"

"Not what we expected," Adam said. "This exceeded my"— he smiled at Mel — "*our* expectations."

With an elbow resting on the table, Melinda propped her chin in her hand. "Is there any chance you have to-go cups so we can take coffee with us? We have a busy morning at Rosecliff helping our friends get ready for their wedding. Your coffee is just what we'll need for the extra push of energy."

"I do. But you won't be able to take anything in with you. The rules are pretty strict." She crossed the room and opened a cabinet door. She pulled out two heavy paper cups and lids and walked back to the table. "Will these work for you?"

Adam took them from her. "Thank you." He teased, "Mel will be a happy camper."

She protested, "Come on you thought it was a good idea too." Melinda stacked their plates and looked around. "Where can I put these?"

"Leave them on the table and I'll take care of them. You two should run along. Take Ocean Boulevard—it's the best route to the mansion. It is breathtaking in the morning." Diana winked. "One might even say romantic." Before Melinda could blush again, Diana said, "Have a fun day. Will you be back before the wedding?"

"We will." Adam was already looking forward to seeing Mel in her dress and high heels.

Mel looked around. "Oh shoot, I forgot my handbag upstairs." She pushed back from the table and said, "I'll be right back."

Diana lingered in the dining room while Adam fixed their coffees. Uncertain what she might say, he thanked her again for the cups and wandered into the lobby. He wanted to sit down; his knee was beginning to throb. It was going to be a long day with a lot of standing. Maybe he should sit and wait for Mel.

Just as he did, she dashed down the stairs and deftly avoided the one stair that she had trouble with earlier. "See, I remembered." She jingled the keys. "Did you think I was going to take forever?"

He looked into her eyes. They were more blue today than green. "Not at all." Thinking fast he said, "I wanted to sit in a genuine antique chair from an old ship." *Jeez, that sounds lame, even to me.* He got up and followed Mel to the front door.

She looked over her shoulder. "I hope we have time to stop at that pretty park we saw near the ocean. You know, the one before the fort?"

"A good spot to enjoy our coffee." Adam followed her

outside. The air was crisp and cool and the sky was a brilliant shade of blue. He took a deep breath. "There is something invigorating about this air, don't you think?"

Mel stopped and dropped her head back, face toward the sun. She inhaled deeply. A grin spread across her face. "You are right. It is." She gave him a sly look. "What?"

"I've never seen you so carefree." He swallowed and said, "You're very pretty."

A flush rose in her cheeks. "Adam, stop."

"I didn't mean to embarrass you. But I wanted to tell you."

"Once again, I'm at a loss for words. It seems to happen from time to time when I'm with you." She clicked the button on the key fob and the car locks clicked. "There's an ocean waiting to be looked at."

Adam got into the car. Will had been right. The chemistry between them was undeniable. After Sunday, he hoped she would still want to spend time with him. He looked at her out of the corner of his eye in the driver's seat. She was the only woman for him.

"Hey, you." She poked him in the arm. "Are you seeing the birds bobbing in the water? How does that cold not bother them? The wind is whipping and there they go, plunging their heads in the frigid water to get a snack."

He listened as she rattled off two more questions without giving him a chance to answer the first one. He wanted to say something profound, but all he could think to say was, "Mel, it's how life works. They just keep doing what they know."

"Life does march forward, doesn't it?" She flashed him a grin. "This is the best time I've had in ages. You're a pretty good travel partner."

"You make a good partner too." He reached over and took her hand from the steering wheel in his. He joked, "Even if we need to get you an insulated mug for our next road trip."

CHAPTER 33

Melinda and Adam entered the grand hall at Rosecliff. She felt her mouth drop open. She was speechless.

"Mel." Adam grabbed her hand and chuckled. "Are you okay?"

She nodded and in slow motion turned a three-sixty, lost in the moment. She crossed to the heart-shaped staircase, walked up four wide marble stairs and ran her hand over the ornate banister.

In a reverent voice she said, "Molly is going to walk down these stairs tonight."

"That's her plan." He smiled as he walked up the stairs to stand next to her. "This is stunning."

"They sure did get lucky with this place."

A hum of voices caught Melinda's attention. "That must be the happy couple." She skipped down the stairs and looked back in time to see Adam wince.

"Your knee is still bothering you." She stated it as a fact, not a question.

He shook his head. "You don't miss a trick."

She lightly ran back up the steps and gave him her hand.

"You kept me from tumbling down the stairs earlier—the least I can do is be here for you."

He took her hand and their fingers interlaced. She looked down and saw how well they fit together. His long fingers were warm and he held hers with just the right amount of pressure. She gave his hand a squeeze.

He gave her a wink. "This is going to be quite a day."

She couldn't help but wonder what he might be thinking.

She noticed Molly and Tim were waiting near an archway. Molly called to them, "Hi, guys! Isn't this the most amazing place you've ever seen?" She gazed at Tim. "And tonight, I'm marrying the love of my life."

Tim tenderly kissed her lips and murmured something that Melinda was sure was sweet.

Adam clapped him on his back. "You guys are having the wedding of the year."

Tim grinned. "No one is going to top this, especially since there's only a couple of weeks left."

Adam chuckled. "Timing is everything."

Melinda turned to Molly and asked, "What do you need me to do?"

"Come see the table settings. They're stunning and the flowers are spectacular." She seemed to float on air. "The holiday season is the perfect time to get married. Built-in decorations that just need a tweak or two, and there you go." Molly pointed to the candelabras that flanked either side of a table for two. "Can you picture them lit? We'll dine in a romantic glow."

"Molly, I don't think the candlelight can add a thing. You're glowing now." Melinda gave her a one-armed hug. "What does your bouquet look like?"

She gushed, "White roses, with holly and ivy, tied with red satin ribbon entwined with white lace that matches my dress."

"That is going to be beautiful."

"Melinda, come with me a minute, I want to be serious." She pulled out two chairs and Melinda sat down. Molly faced her and said, "The best thing that has ever happened to me is because of you. If Stacey and Will hadn't signed up for *It's Just Coffee*, they wouldn't have met. That was the beginning of so many couples meeting, including Tim and me."

Melinda clasped her hand. "I was doing what you hired me to do."

"Yes, you were, but will you do something else for me?"

"If I can."

She glanced in Adam's direction. "I'm not sure what happened to your husband, but I have eyes. I see how Adam looks at you. He cares for you."

"Molly, I don't think we should be talking about me—today is your special day." She didn't want to tell Molly she had strong feelings for Adam. She just wasn't sure what to do about them.

Molly's eyes grew wide. "This is exactly the right time. You helped me find love. All I'm suggesting is that you give Adam a real chance. Take a long look at him. You might just find what you help so many others find, true happiness." She clasped Melinda's hand. "Please think about it."

Melinda was at a loss for words. She nodded. "I will."

Molly pulled her into a hug. "Let's go find the guys and see if we can round up Stacey and Will. We have things to do."

"We'd better get busy. I think Stacey and Will are going back to the inn to get changed when we leave," Melinda said.

"Oh, you could have gotten ready here. There are plenty of rooms." Molly giggled like a schoolgirl. "This place is huge."

"Don't worry, we'll be back in plenty of time." Melinda gave her a quick hug. "Besides I want to come up the driveway and walk through the doors, sort of pretending we're in the gilded age of high society."

Molly laughed. "Then by all means make an entrance."

"Hey, I just thought of something—isn't it bad luck for the groom to see the bride before *the big moment*?"

"Only if I'm wearing my wedding dress. Trust me, there is no way Tim is going to see me in that until the clock strikes six."

$\sim$

*A*dam stood at the bottom of the stairs, mesmerized as Melinda glided down the staircase. She had carefully arranged her hair on top of her head, and long, sparkly pearl earrings gently swayed from her ears. A strand of pearls with a teardrop gem graced her throat. Her dark green dress moved as if it was made of silk and hugged to her curves in all the right places. Around her shoulders she wore a black stole. She walked carefully on high-heels, and as she approached the stair with the troublesome edge, Adam took a step toward her.

He held out his hand. "You look gorgeous." He leaned in and kissed her cheek. "You smell great too."

She smiled and ran her gaze from the tips of his shoes to his eyes. "You're not so bad yourself."

He held tight to her hand as she finished descending the stairs. "I've heard all men look good in formalwear."

She cocked her head. "Some more than others." They reached the bottom of the stairs and she held out the car keys. "Would you care to drive?"

Without taking them, he opened up the front door. Parked in the driveway a driver stood next to a town car. The driver opened the door when he saw them.

"I thought we'd catch a ride tonight."

She squeezed his hand. "Oh. Adam, how sweet."

"It's nothing." Adam held up the hem of her dress as she got into the car so it wouldn't get wet and closed her door. He adjusted his tie, taking a minute to settle his nerves. Looking at Mel made him want to skip the wedding and have a romantic night for two. He then went around to the other side and got in. The car was warm and the back seat felt intimate. Mel sank into the plush cushions.

"Too bad we don't have a longer trip. I could get used to this."

As they drove down Main Street, Christmas lights were

sparkling, entwined around old-fashioned lampposts. Wreaths with large red bows dotted many doorways, and they even saw a group of carolers dressed in turn-of-the-century costumes in King Park.

She leaned forward and slid the window down. "We're taking Ocean Boulevard."

He grinned. "I knew the direct route wouldn't be near as much fun as going this way. We have plenty of time."

Mel took his hand and Adam felt her warmth spread through him. He wished these moments would never end. He was surprised at himself, all these tender thoughts for his matchmaker, the woman who was going to help him find love and maybe even lifelong happiness. He suspected he'd found it in her. Life certainly had its twists and turns.

The car slowed as they turned down the street lined with mansions. She gave a slight shiver due to the cold air that wafted into the car as they made their way, slowly down the street. It allowed her time to drink in the sights. Her eyes were bright as she closed the window and looked at Adam. "I wonder how Molly is feeling right this moment."

"I'll bet the bride and groom are a bundle of nerves." Adam pointed. "Look. Rosecliff."

Lights spilled across the snow-covered lawn. The mansion dressed in her holiday best. Shimmering, welcoming Adam and Melinda.

Their car stopped and the driver opened Adam's door first. "Give me a minute to get around to your door."

Melinda touched his arm. "I will."

Standing next to the curb, Adam held out his hand. "Shall we?"

She put hers in his and looked into his eyes. His heart flipped. She had so much more than just physical beauty. She radiated elegance, charm and warmth.

"You're being very formal."

He swept his free arm toward the grandeur behind them. "I do believe it's the setting. It must be rubbing off on me."

They climbed the few stairs and the front door swung open. A woman was waiting for them in the main entrance and offered to take their coats. Melinda slipped her stole off. Her cheeks were pink. Adam wondered if it was the cold outside or the opulence indoors. He, for one, certainly had the distinct impression they had stepped back into another era.

Adam tucked Mel's hand into the crook of his arm. "Let's find a seat where we can see everything."

"I'm sure they're all excellent." Mel's voice was hushed. "Do you want to sit on the bride or groom's side?"

"You choose." He smiled down at her.

She pointed to two chairs close to the center on the right. They proceeded to sit down. Soft music emanated from the string quartet. She whispered, "I didn't realize so many people were coming." She scanned the room. "There must be at least seventy-five chairs."

"Will said when everyone heard the location, they had very few people decline."

Melinda turned around. The minister had taken his spot on the bottom of the heart-shaped staircase. Next Tim came down the aisle with Will by his side. They were smiling and shaking hands and greeting everyone as they walked.

Adam leaned over. "He doesn't look nervous at all."

"I'm not surprised. They're ready for this next step," Melinda whispered back.

The music changed and the quartet began to play "A Thousand Years." Adam sang the words to himself: he felt as if he had loved Melinda for a thousand years…

He glanced at the bride but then watched Mel watching Molly. Her apparent joy at their happiness filled his heart.

Tim took a step toward his bride and stretched out his hand to her. They walked to the minister together. Adam slipped his arm around Mel and held her close. He was proud that her skill brought two wonderful people to this place and time.

She leaned into him and turned her face to his. "Look at Molly and Tim. That is true love."

He tenderly kissed her lips.

CHAPTER 34

The ceremony had been perfect. Melinda and Adam ate, drank and danced their way through the reception. The music had been chosen specifically for people in love. Each song, whether fast or slow, was romantic. She didn't want the night to end.

They had wandered out onto the terrace and he wrapped his arms around her as they watched the moon glisten over the ocean. He kissed the top of her head drinking in her subtle floral perfume. She shivered. "Are you ready to go?"

She stifled a yawn. "I guess so, but it's been a day to remember."

Adam held the glass door open and they stepped into the grand ballroom. They made their away across the dance floor toward the coatroom. Melinda leaned into him. She was happy. "I've never been to a more romantic wedding."

"You seemed to have a great time."

She sighed and looked into his eyes. "I did, and you?"

"I most definitely did." His attention was diverted. "Let's go look at the Christmas tree one last time."

For the wedding Molly had a rose-covered arbor set up as the segue into the drawing room, where an enormous evergreen had been decorated. As the couple walked under it, Adam took her hand and stopped her. He pointed up.

"Mistletoe." His voice was husky.

"So it is." Melinda's heart fluttered.

"We shouldn't let it go to waste."

Solemnly she said, "No, that would be a sin."

Adam tilted her face toward his. He lowered his lips until they were a hairsbreadth apart. "Tonight was incredible." She felt his mouth graze hers.

She stepped into his arms and pulled him into the kiss. Her insides sighed. It was as if the trickle of longing she had been holding back cracked. She wanted more of Adam. She kissed him again as he gathered her in the circle of his arms. For how long they stood in the embrace, Melinda wasn't sure. It felt right.

A loud crash tore them apart.

Melinda swung around and saw one of the wait-staff pick up a small silver tray and then disappear through a swinging door.

"Where were we?" Adam said.

With her heart hammering in her chest, common sense took hold of Melinda. Reluctantly she said, "We were getting our coats. The car is waiting."

If Adam was disappointed, it didn't show on his handsome face, although his deep brown eyes held a hint of amusement mixed with desire.

After the attendant handed them their coats, Adam took Melinda's stole and wrapped it around her shoulders. He slipped into his after tipping the young woman.

Melinda and Adam strolled hand in hand out the front door. The air had turned sharply colder than when they'd arrived. The light mist that had been falling made the steps slick.

Melinda tightened her arm on his. As she was about to say *be careful*, Adam began to fall. She tried to hold on, but he landed heavily on the ground and his pant leg ripped.

Melinda looked around for help. Their driver hurried over as Will came rushing out the door. Skidding on the stairs, he called,

"Are you okay, bud?" He reached down and slipped his hands under Adam's arms to help him up.

It was then that Adam groaned. "Wait. My leg."

Melinda knelt down heedless of the slush she was kneeling in. "Do you think it's broken?"

"No, it came out of the socket."

"I'll call an ambulance." Melinda opened her bag to get her cell.

Will said, "Melinda, it's okay. Don't call."

Confused, she looked at Will and then Adam. "If he needs to go to the hospital, an ambulance is best."

Will helped Adam to one foot. She heard a snap. Will supported him as they hobbled to the car.

She demanded, "What is going on here?"

"Mel." Adam's face was ashen. "This isn't how I planned to tell you." He swallowed hard. "I have a prosthetic leg."

"Huh? What are you talking about?" Melinda looked at Will. "Did he hit his head?"

Under his breath Will said, "You should have told her."

Adam searched her face with his eyes. "I lost it. From the IED."

All the air in Melinda's lungs seemed to evaporate. She croaked, "What?"

Adam was sitting in the passenger seat of the car. He looked at her and pleaded, "Can we talk about this at the hotel?"

At a loss for words she nodded. Will said, "I'm going to get Stacey and we'll meet you two there. Adam will need help getting up the stairs."

Adam heaved himself to a standing position. He hobbled to the back door, using the car for support. He half fell inside and looked at Melinda. "Come with me."

She looked at Will. Softly she said, "I'll ride with Adam."

The ride back to the inn was silent and the air filled with tension. Adam stared out the window. Melinda had a thousand questions, but she didn't want to ask them, at least not yet. The most important one of all was—why hadn't he told her? After the past weeks of them seeing each other and growing closer, it mystified her why he hadn't.

Melinda turned her head to stare out into the inky darkness. She thought they were friends. No, that wasn't true. She thought they were more than friends on the path to something potentially significant between them. She had shared the single most painful and life-altering event in her life with Adam, and yet he had held back from her.

She noticed the streetlights cast flickering shadows across his face. His mouth was set in a grim line. Was he in pain, embarrassed or mad?

All too soon the town car stopped in front of the inn. The driver opened Melinda's door first and helped her from the back seat. She walked around and stood on the bottom step. Adam pushed his door open. His eyes locked with hers.

He pulled himself upright. Melinda stepped toward him and held out her hand. "Let me help you up the stairs."

Adam seemed to hesitate before taking her hand. "You're cold."

Without answering she said, "Let's get inside."

One stair at a time, Melinda held Adam steady. He was concentrating on each step. "Your leg hurts, doesn't it?"

He let go of his breath. "Yeah."

The driver ran up the steps and held open the door. Melinda said, "Thank you."

She paused to dig in her purse for a tip and he said, "It's all set, miss."

Adam cocked his head. "I planned ahead."

They entered the semi-darkened entrance. There was a Victorian lamp glowing on the desk and a similar one on the mahogany credenza. An overhead light illuminated the stairwell.

"Do you want to sit or just head upstairs?"

"Will should be pulling in. He can help me get to my room."

He pointed to the dimly lit drawing room. "Would you mind helping me get to the chair?"

Melinda slipped her arm around his waist and turned toward the archway. "Ready?"

Just help him get comfortable and then you can escape. Will knows what to do.

She flicked the dimmer switch and the room was bathed in light. There was a loveseat a few steps away. "Over there?" She gestured to it.

Adam took a hop. "I'm fine."

She threw up her hands, her anger bubbling beneath the surface. "A second ago you wanted my help, now you want to hop?"

He forced a smile. "What can I say, I'm a complicated guy."

"That's an understatement." She guided Adam to the sofa and stuck a cushion behind him. "Can I get you anything else?"

"No, thank you."

"I'm going up to bed." She turned, feeling the weight of sadness envelope her. Without looking at him she said softly, "Good night, Adam."

"Night, Melinda."

~

Adam watched Mel leave the room. He had a sinking feeling she was walking out of his life permanently. How could he make this up to her? Will would know what to do. He leaned his head back and closed his eyes.

Mel's lips touching his under the mistletoe had been a magical moment. The emotions that rolled over him were intense. He had never experienced something so sweet and tender, and that had him longing for more, much more.

He could feel someone watching him. His eyes opened. For a split second he prayed Mel had come back.

"Will."

Will's tie was draped around his neck and the top of the shirt buttons were undone. He looked around. "Where's Melinda?"

"She went upstairs."

Will held up two glasses partially filled with amber liquid. "Scotch?"

Adam knew what this meant. Will only pulled out the strong stuff when it was time for a serious conversation. "Have a seat."

Handing Adam one glass, Will sat down and stretched out his legs in front of him. Casually he said, "It's nice here."

Adam absentmindedly swirled the liquid in the glass. "Mel found it online."

"Stacey was thrilled when Melinda said you were staying here. That's why she wanted to as well."

"Sorry we haven't spent much time with you."

"No big deal. We were hoping the two of you would get bitten by the bug."

Adam cocked a brow. "What are you talking about?"

"Stacey calls it the love bug. She happens to think you and Melinda are the perfect couple."

"An hour ago, I thought we might have a chance." Adam took a deep drink. He winced. "I hate scotch."

"It's good for you. It has a way of clearing the fog out of your brain."

Adam snorted. "Only you would say something so ridiculous."

Will balanced his glass on the arm of the chair. "What happened an hour ago?"

"We kissed under the mistletoe. It was like I could see the future and Mel was in it."

Will nodded slowly. "I see."

"Is that all you got?" he demanded.

"Not to ask the obvious question, but why didn't you tell her about what happened in Iraq?"

"You know why." Adam downed the rest of the scotch and set his glass aside.

"Remind me." Will pulled a pint bottle from his inner pocket and poured Adam a splash more. "Anita? She was a shallow, self-centered person. But that has nothing to do with Melinda."

Adam slammed his closed fist on the arm of the sofa cushion. "No! Melinda isn't like that. But I didn't..." He groaned. "As we began spending more time together, I discovered she was amazing. Each week that passed, it got harder to tell her the truth. By not telling her in the beginning, it felt like I had been lying by omission." He took a swallow of his drink. It burned as it went down his throat. "I was scared. Would she think I was less of a man?"

Quietly Will asked, "Is that how you see yourself? As somehow less than the man you were before?"

"I don't know anymore." Adam dropped his chin to his chest. "You knew me then and you know me now. Do you think I'm different?"

As he rubbed the back of his neck Will said, "Yes, but that is to be expected. You have always been one of the best men I know and I'm proud to call you my friend—hell, my brother. But man, it's not how I see you, it's how you see you."

"Do you think Mel would see me as damaged?"

"No. I don't. The woman helped you after you sliced open your hand. Brought you dinner and checked in with you daily." Will shook his head. "Man, you sold both of you short. Your lie robbed you of the opportunity to sit and have a conversation like adults."

"I know. I screwed up." Adam's shoulder sagged. "Now I'll never have the chance."

"Yeah. You won't be able to tell her before she finds out. That ship sailed."

Adam toyed with his now empty glass. "She told me about her husband John's accident." He looked at Will. "The day she took me to the emergency room, she had a flashback. It was from the day he died. I can't imagine what that day had been like."

Will's eyes grew wide. "She told you all of this?"

Adam nodded. "Right after I cut my hand."

"And you didn't think that was a golden opportunity for you to share your experience? Are you an idiot?"

"First class, at your service." He saluted Will.

"So, where do you go from here?"

Adam fell silent. It was several long moments before he spoke. "I was hoping you'd help me upstairs. There's something I should have done a while ago."

CHAPTER 35

He knocked on the adjoining door.

"Hold on," she called before she opened it. He stood, dressed in sweatpants and a Marine sweatshirt.

"H-hi," she stuttered. Melinda's cheeks flushed.

An uncomfortable silence was heavy between them for several long unending minutes.

Melinda started to speak and Adam did at the same time. He said, "You first."

"Do you want to come in?"

He nodded and took a step in. "Can we talk?"

"Of course." She flipped back the covers, perched on the edge of the bed and patted the space next to her. "Care to sit down?"

The bed gave under his weight. "I'm sorry." He gestured to his leg. "About this."

She waved her hand and looked down. "I understand, it's hard to find a way to bring it into a conversation."

He bowed his head. "I'd like to tell you what happened, and some of this I've never shared with anyone, not even Will."

She clasped her hand over his. It gave him strength.

"When I got to the hospital, I still had my leg, barely. It was severely damaged and the doctor told me from the very beginning I might lose it, but he would save my life."

He heard her suck in a breath, but she remained silent.

"Those first few days were a haze. I was on a lot of painkillers and I had a concussion. We trained hard for the mission but someone trying to blow you to smithereens isn't exactly something the Marines can train you for, or what comes after you survive, the initial realization that only some of your people were okay."

Quietly, Mel said, "You told me you lost soldiers on this mission."

His eyes sought hers. "There was one man, they'd just had a new baby. He hadn't even held her yet." He could feel the tears threatening to fall. "But each life that was taken had a similar story. People who loved them." He could hear the catch in his voice. "Once I was stable enough to be flown back to the States, I was relieved. My military career was gone and all I wanted was to get home." He dropped his head. "That was after."

Gently she said, "After what?"

"I developed an infection and it was overtaking my body. The doctor said they had to amputate my leg below the knee to save my life."

"Do you think he knew right from the beginning?"

Adam shook his head. "The odds were never in my favor, but I'm confident the doctor did all he could. He had seen so many of these types of injuries and understood that it was a physical challenge, but the emotional impact was just as hard."

Mel's voice quivered when she asked, "Were you alone? When it happened?"

"I was lucky. Will had flown over to be with me. He was my rock. I don't know if I would have made it without his support."

"I'm glad you had him." Tears slipped silently down her cheeks. He wanted to brush them away. But not yet. He needed to get out what he wanted to say.

"After I was stateside, I went to a rehab clinic. I had to learn how to walk again and deal with the PTSD. That's when Anita came back into the picture." His words rushed out. "I had physical therapy every day, along with the shrink I was pretty busy. One day I was in the PT room, walking between the lateral bars. I was pushing myself, determined. When I looked up she was standing in the doorway watching me. I'll never forget that moment, the look of pity she wore. I could tell from her eyes I wasn't the man she wanted any longer."

"Oh Adam," she cried, "I'm sure you misread the situation."

"It doesn't matter. She stayed around for a couple of weeks in South Carolina, but then she made an excuse that she had to get back to the West Coast. After that her phone calls slowed and pretty soon it was a sporadic text or email."

"I thought she just left?"

"That wasn't the whole truth. I didn't want you to know what really happened. I flew out there. I had to know if we still had anything between us." He could hear the bitterness creep into his voice. "She was at our favorite restaurant, one with outdoor seating. I stopped by to pick up dinner for two and that's when I saw her. On a date."

"Did she see you?"

"Yeah, she ran after me, telling me it wasn't what it looked like. I did her a favor and told her I was coming to break up with her in person. She was free to have the life I knew she wanted."

She squeezed his hand tighter. "I'm so sorry. That had to have been agony for you. You should have told me."

He withdrew his hand. "What's done is done."

"That doesn't explain why you kept it a secret from me."

He could tell she really didn't get it. "I couldn't bear to have another woman pity me. Especially not you." His voice dropped.

She visibly shrank. "We all have scars, Adam. Yours happen to be external as well as internal, but you should know by now that we're a lot alike. My scars are hidden from everyone. I didn't share my past with anyone. Until you."

Her voice was filled with sadness and it broke his heart to know that she was right. Out of all the people he had met, she would never have judged him, just as he understood why she closed herself off.

He asked, "We make quite a pair, don't we?"

"How did you expect to have a relationship with me and keep this a secret?"

"Honestly, I didn't think that far ahead and, in my defense, I've wanted to tell you."

She threw up her hands. "That doesn't make a bit of sense. We have spent so much time together over the last few months. There wasn't one time where you couldn't have said, 'Mel, we need to talk about something serious.'"

He stammered, "I-I..."

Mel leaned forward. "Talk to me. I mean, really talk to me. Not what you think I want to hear."

Adam's gut tightened. How could he tell her what he was really feeling inside? The panic. The fear. What the hell, he had nothing to lose. Except her. On the other hand, maybe he would finally be free to let go of the past.

As if sensing his struggle, she said, "Adam, I would never judge you, but we can't move forward unless we are both totally honest with each other. That's how a relationship works, complete and total honesty."

Taking a deep breath, he said, "I don't know if I can really let someone into my life. My identity was entwined with my persona as a Marine. When I had to retire and learn how to live life as a disabled person, I was devastated. There isn't any part of me that remained the same. Before the accident. Career, body, relationships, gone."

"You said there is no such thing as a former Marine."

He laughed, but it sounded hollow even to himself. "You listened."

She gave him a look that made his laughter die. "I'm serious. Your friendship with Will has endured and I'm sure there are others. Look at how you carry yourself every single day. You are a good man, kind, respectful and loyal."

"It's nice you feel that way, Mel, but I'm seriously flawed. There are times when I'm not strong, when I lean on Will, like when I cut my hand. He had to help me get my leg off and on for the first couple of days. I couldn't even do that by myself."

"Good friends are there when another needs help and support."

He shrugged. "I've counted on him more times than I care to admit."

"If the roles were reversed, what would you do?"

"I know all of this but…" His voice trailed off as he noticed her face looked different somehow. Like he was really seeing her for the first time as Dr. Grayson. "This isn't a therapy session." He shot to his feet and began to pace. "I've been on the couch before—this isn't what I wanted our conversation to be about." He pounded his chest. "This is personal."

Mel leaned back and waited. Adam could feel his temper spiking. "Mel, we're supposed to be talking about why I didn't tell you."

"We are."

"No. You're dredging up how I feel about myself."

Firmly she said, "You can't move forward if you're stuck in the past."

He snorted. "That's rich from the woman who won't date because she says she had her one great love. It's like you stopped living when you buried John."

The moment he said those words in anger he instantly regretted them. He sat next to Mel and took her hand. "I am so sorry. I shouldn't have said that. It was insensitive and—"

Mel put her finger against his lips. "And true." She took her hand away and said, "After I told you about the day John died, I've thought about my life. Moving here was a way to put distance between me and the memories that were too hard to face. I never expected to make wonderful friends and feel at home in this small coastal town. John would want me to be happy again. It's taken me a long time to come to terms with the idea that it's okay to even think about dating. It's not betraying his memory or diminishing our life together."

"Does this mean you're ready to move on?" He wanted her to say yes.

"It does." She gave him a tiny smile.

"That's great." He grinned and then his face fell. He went from happiness to sad in a split second. "This is why you're pushing me. I need to be ready too."

"Adam, I care for you, a great deal. I'm still hurt that you didn't feel you could trust me. But I get it. Moving forward, I expect you to be completely honest with me, and that when direct questions are asked, they are answered truthfully."

Adam got up again and walked to the window. He stood there looking out in the dark night. All he could see was the hurt in Mel's eyes. How could he avoid that again if he didn't let his warts show? In a split second he made up his mind.

"Mel, I need to show you something."

Hesitantly she said, "Okay."

Adam's heart thundered in his chest. He was going to be brave and bare all.

He crossed the short distance and stood by the bed. He slid his sweats down below his butt. With a nervous laugh he said, "Hope you like the boxers. I like wacky prints."

Her eyes were locked on his until her gaze slid down. "Cute, I see you've got a thing for fish."

Adam gave her a small smile. "Yeah, I like to fish," He sat down on the edge of the bed.

Mel looked at his thigh. "Does it hurt? After the fall, I mean?"

"The stump is a little swollen, but not a big deal." He proceeded to toss his pants off. "This is how I take Linus off."

"You named it?"

He glanced over at her. "We needed to become friends."

He pushed a button and the limb came off in his hand. He

heard Mel take a deep breath, but he kept going. "This liner has a ratchet on the silicone sock that secures it to the residual limb." He peeled off one heavy sock and then another exposing the faint, pale pink incision that encircled just below the knee. "That's it."

Her fingertips grazed his hand. She intertwined her fingers with his. They sat there for several long moments.

Finally Adam said, "That's all there is to see."

Melinda leaned in and kissed his cheek. Her kisses trailed down his jaw until they found his mouth. She kissed him tenderly and murmured, "You're the bravest man I know."

"You know everything about me, Mel. I have no secrets from you from this moment forward." A single tear slid down her cheek. He wiped it away with his thumb. "Why the tear?'

"I'm humbled by you."

"Mel." His heart thumped in his chest.

"I'm glad you made friends with Linus."

"Me too." He cleared his throat. "What do you say we get some sleep? We can do something fun tomorrow."

"Can I watch you put Linus on?"

He brushed her hair from her forehead and placed another tender kiss on her lips. "I have nothing to hide."

He slipped the two layers of socks over the stump and then the silicone sleeve. It clicked into place. He stood and pulled his sweats up. He held out his hand to Mel and pulled her into his arms, against his chest.

He murmured in her hair, "I've never shown anyone that before, except Will."

She leaned into his chest and sighed. "Thank you."

Not trusting himself to speak, he held her tight. All he wanted to do was get things back to being the fun weekend they had started. He kissed the top of her head and took a deep, soul-soothing breath. "In the morning would you like to see the winery and then have lunch?"

"I would. But maybe we can see where the road takes us."

"I'd like that." Adam picked up his coat from the side chair.

Mel smiled at him. He felt it go straight to his heart like Cupid's arrow. "I think exploring sounds like a lot of fun." She teased, "Unless you're afraid of getting lost."

He chuckled. "We're on an island. On three sides we have ocean and the other direction will lead us home."

"That leaves us much to see."

Adam stood and pulled her into his arms. He lowered his mouth to hers and tender turned to passionate as he kissed her. She slipped her arms around his waist and pulled him closer. He took his time exploring her lips. Savoring the newfound connection they shared. When he pulled away, he smoothed back her tousled hair. "Time for sleep."

She smiled at him. "As much as I've loved talking and sharing, I think some shut eye is what we both need. Today has been a little emotional."

He kissed her good night walked to the adjoining door. "I'll lock the door when I get on the other side."

"You don't need to do that." Mel crossed the room and flipped the lock. "I trust you implicitly."

Adam swallowed the lump that rose in his throat. He blew her a kiss before saying, "Good night, Mel."

CHAPTER 36

It had been a long week since the wedding. Melinda was sitting on the sofa in her office, legs clad in eye-popping orange leggings and a deep brown tunic with sleeves of the same color orange. She was stretched out and her laptop propped open, a steaming cup of coffee within reach. With Christmas right around the corner, she wanted to catch up on work. She planned to take the week between Christmas and New Year's off for some much-needed downtime. She smiled to herself. It would be time to spend with Adam too. After all he had suggested she take the time off and enjoy herself. He didn't have any jobs scheduled, so the timing was perfect.

Under her leg her cell phone vibrated. When she pulled it out she answered quickly, "Hi, Adam."

"Hi, Mel." She smiled when she heard his deep, rich voice say her name and snuggled deeper into the sofa, work forgotten. "I was thinking about you and wanted to give you a call. How are the plans coming for your parents visit?"

"Funny you should ask. I just got off the phone with Mom and their flight was changed due to some weather issues. So instead of arriving tomorrow, they'll be delayed two days."

"I know how much you're looking forward to them coming."

THE MATCHMAKER AND THE MARINE

Melinda picked up her coffee and took a sip. "I can't wait for you to meet them. I told Mom all about you. Well, that I'm dating a very handsome, retired Marine."

"Oh?" She smiled at the happy surprise in Adam's voice. "Did she ask if I was someone special?" he teased.

Mel chuckled. "What do you think? She's a mom."

"How did she react to your news?"

"She said, and I quote, 'That is wonderful, sweetheart. I'm so happy for you. Tell me a little something about him'."

"And you told her I was devastatingly handsome and smart, right?" he quipped.

"I told her you were kind, and warm-hearted, funny too, and that I really care about you." Melinda couldn't help but laugh. "And I told her you have a beautiful smile."

"That's a little mushy, but I'm looking forward to meeting them. Hopefully they'll like me and think I'm good enough for their daughter."

A tapping on her office door interrupted her next comment. "Adam, I need to run someone's at the door."

"All right. I'll see you tonight for dinner."

She loved how the sound of his voice made her all warm inside. "I can't wait. See you later."

She tossed her cell to the sofa and set her coffee down. "Coming," she called out.

The door swung open and a woman who looked vaguely familiar was standing on the bottom step. "Hi," Melinda said.

"Mary." The woman stuck out a slender gloved hand. "We met last summer at a picnic Will and Stacey had on the beach. I work at Will's office."

"Come in out of the cold and snow." Melinda stepped to one side and Mary entered.

She pulled her dark brown leather gloves off and stuffed them into the pockets of her deep purple tailored coat, and then pulled a knitted cap from her head and did the same with it.

"I hope you don't mind an impromptu visit." Her faced

paled. "Unless you're busy, of course, and maybe I could book an appointment."

Melinda stepped around her. "Not at all, have a seat. As you can see, I wasn't planning on clients." She waved her hand over her outfit.

Mary shrugged out of her coat, folded it in half and placed it over the back of the side chair. She wore a dark skirt and lavender sweater set with hose and knee-high black boots. Melinda held her surprise in check. Her long blonde ringlets were now short soft curls around her face, which seemed to enhance her blue eyes. The only two times she had seen Mary, she was dressed like a teenager, but now she looked like a woman dressed for success.

"Please have a seat. Would you like a cup of coffee?"

Mary sat and smoothed her hands over her skirt. Demurely crossing her legs, she smiled at Melinda. "Yes, thank you. Just cream if you have it. If not, black is fine."

Melinda dropped a coffee pod into the machine and hit start. As the coffee brewed she pulled a carton from the tiny dorm-size refrigerator. She wondered if maybe there were two sides to Mary, the office persona and the weekend girl.

The coffeepot gurgled and sputtered. Melinda handed Mary the mug and carton of half and half, then settled into the sofa, shutting her laptop and setting it aside. "So, tell me, how can I help you?"

Mary toyed with the cap of the half and half. Shyly she looked up. "I would like to hire you to help me find a man. A good man." She blew on her coffee before saying, "The last time I saw you I was in a bit of an identity crisis, running around dressing like, well, not like me." She gestured to her outfit. "I'm more comfortable like this, rather than wearing very short dresses."

Gently Melinda asked, "What changed?"

"I had just been dumped by a cheater who said I wasn't

pretty enough for him to stay faithful. He said he went looking because I dressed like a frump bucket."

Anger flared in Melinda, but she kept her voice even. "First off, you must realize his cheating had nothing to do with you. It is so typical that people deflect their responsibility by blaming someone else. And secondly, you're a beautiful woman, inside and out. If your ex couldn't see that, well, then it's a good thing he's your ex."

For the first time Melinda saw Mary's eyes brighten and then she smiled. Her voice was breathless and soft. "Do you really think that's true?"

"Trust me. I can tell you there is an amazing guy out there looking for you."

A gleam came into Mary's eye. "How soon can we get started?"

"I like your attitude. Is now too soon for you?" Melinda stood up to get her notebook and pen. "I'll give you the questionnaire and you can either fill it out here and we'll go over it now, or you can take it home and we can get back together in a few days."

Excited Mary said, "If you have the time, I'll fill it out here. This will be my Christmas present to me."

Mel stepped behind her desk and opened the file cabinet drawer. She withdrew a folder and then handed a set of papers to Mary along with a clipboard and pen. "I'm going to step into the kitchen and you take your time. When you're done, just yell and I'll come in and we'll go over it all."

"Then what happens?" Mary asked.

"I add your information to my database and run a search or two and see who I think might be a fit. Once I have a few matches, I'll email you the information and you can reach out to who you might like." She handed Mary another paper. "These are my tips for first meetings. I suggest a coffee date in a public setting and during the daytime, and never have someone pick you up at home. Not until you meet each other a couple of times. Safety first."

Mary glanced at the paper. "Do you send my information to men too?"

"I do. But it is confidential, so if you pass on someone or he does, you'll never know. I have found it keeps feelings from getting bruised."

"What if someone contacts me and I don't want to go out with them?"

"I would encourage you to just go for coffee. You never know how someone will be in person as opposed to on paper." Melinda gave her what she hoped was an encouraging smile. "I'll leave you to the paperwork."

"Thank you, Melinda. I've heard you're the best." She gushed, "I just know you'll help me find a nice man."

After she chuckled, Melinda said, "I'll try to live up to my reputation."

EPILOGUE

Melinda opened the door and grinned. Adam was standing on the front steps holding a paper bag in one hand and a bottle of wine from the vineyard in Newport in the other.

"Hello, beautiful. Dinner is served." He stepped inside out of the falling snow. The grass was covered with a thick white blanket.

Melinda took the bag and wine and headed toward the kitchen. "I thought we'd eat in the living room. I started a fire."

"Sounds romantic." He called after her, "I forgot something in the truck. Be right back."

Melinda set out plates and glasses on the kitchen counter and wondered what on earth Adam could have forgotten. She heard the front door close and she peeked down the hallway. He carried a pastry box and a bouquet of flowers.

"These are for you." He presented the flowers with a smile and a kiss. "And I brought dessert. We might get snowed in and will need extra sustenance." He pulled her into his arms and kissed her again. "It's going to be a white Christmas."

Melinda laughed. "I'll uncork the wine."

Adam poured and picked up the glasses. "I'll take these into the living room."

She scooped up the lasagna and salad and added slices of crusty bread to their plates. Adam came around the corner and slipped his arms around her waist. "Everything smells and looks delicious."

Melinda noticed a mischievous grin on his face. "What are you up to?"

"You'll see."

Melinda followed him curious to see what was going on. Soft guitar music filled the room, adding to the romantic ambiance. But she didn't see anything different. The room looked exactly the same other than the wine glasses were on the table near the fireplace. She placed the napkins and silverware down and Adam took her hand.

"Come here." He twirled her into his arms and danced with her. She was captivated by his charm. They swayed together for several minutes until the song ended.

Adam stopped and said, "Look up."

Hanging from a red ribbon on the archway was a spray of mistletoe.

"Do you remember the last time we stood under mistletoe?"

"It was the only time," she teased.

He leaned in and kissed her tenderly at first and then deeper until she felt her blood hum.

"Mel, I hope you don't think this is too soon, but it's almost Christmas and I have a wish." He stopped and tilted her chin up so he was looking into her eyes. "At the beginning of the year, I prayed for a miracle. I found one in you." He let his finger trail down the curve of her cheek. She felt herself melt inside. "Now I'd like to make a special wish, that from this day forward you'll only kiss *me* under mistletoe, or anywhere, for that matter."

Melinda stood on her tiptoes and laced her hands around the back of his neck. "I too have a wish, and you just made it come true."

"I love you, Melinda, and I always will."

She looked into his deep brown eyes and sighed, "Oh Adam, I love you."

The End

LOVE TO READ?

CHECK OUT MY OTHER BOOKS.

The Crescent Lake Winery Series 2021

Blends

Breathe

Crush

Blush

Vintage

Bouquet

The MacLellan Sisters Trilogy

Old and New

Borrowed

Blue

It's Just Coffee Series 2020

The Matchmaker and The Marine

The Loudon Series

The Loudon Series Box Set

Between Here and Heaven

Lost and Found

The Journey Home

The Last First Kiss

Ready to Soar

Love in the Looking Glass

Magic in the Rain

A Dickens Romance Series

Holiday Heart Wishes July 2021

Holly Berries and Hockey Pucks November 2021

ABOUT LUCINDA

Thank you for reading *The Matchmaker and The Marine*. I hope you enjoyed the story. If you did, please help other readers find this book:

- This book is lendable. Send it to a friend you think might like it so she can discover me too.
- Help other people find this book by writing a review.
- Sign up for my newsletter at http://www.lucindarace.com.
- Like my Facebook page, https://facebook.com/lucindaraceauthor
- Join Lucinda Heart Racer's Reader Group on Facebook
- Twitter @lucindarace
- Instagram @lucindraceauthor

Lucinda Race is a lifelong fan of romantic fiction. As a girl, she spent hours reading novels and dreaming of one day becoming a writer. As life twisted and turned, she found herself writing nonfiction articles, but still longed to turn to her true passion, romance. Now living her dream, she spends every free moment clicking computer keys and has published ten books.

ABOUT LUCINDA

Lucinda lives with her husband Rick and two little pups, Jasper and Griffin, in the rolling hills of Western Massachusetts. Her writing is contemporary, fresh, and engaging.

The Crystal Lake Winery Series 2021
Blush
Breathe
Crush
Vintage
Bouquet
The MacLellan Sisters
Old and New – June 19, 2019
Borrowed – July 10, 2019
Blue – July 31, 2019
The Loudon Series
Between Here and Heaven – June 2014
Lost and Found – November 2014
The Journey Home – July 2015
The Last First Kiss – November 2015
Ready to Soar – August 2016
Love in the Looking Glass – June 2017
Magic in the Rain – November 2017

Made in the USA
Columbia, SC
01 June 2021